BATTLETECH:
THE BATTLE OF TUKAYYID
A BATTLETECH ANTHOLOGY

EDITED BY JOHN HELFERS

BATTLETECH: THE BATTLE OF TUKAYYID
Edited by John Helfers
Cover art & design by David Kerber

©2020 The Topps Company, Inc. All Rights Reserved. *BattleTech & MechWarrior* are registered trademarks and/or trademarks of The Topps Company, Inc., in the United States and/or other countries. Catalyst Game Labs and the Catalyst Game Labs logo are trademarks of InMediaRes Productions LLC. No part of this work may be reproduced, stored in a retrieval system, or transmitted in any form or by any means, without the prior permission in writing of the Copyright Owner, nor be otherwise circulated in any form other than that in which it is published.

Printed in USA.

Published by Catalyst Game Labs,
an imprint of InMediaRes Productions, LLC
7108 S. Pheasant Ridge Drive • Spokane, WA 99224

CONTENTS

INTRODUCTION

JOHN HELFERS

Tukayyid. Site of the Inner Sphere's last stand against the overwhelming invasion of the Clans. An untested army facing an unstoppable opponent—with the fate of the entire *BattleTech* universe hanging in the balance.

Hang on a moment—am I referring to the battle of Tukayyid, or what it felt like to put this anthology together (with maybe just a slight bit of exaggeration on that last part).

Don't get me wrong—I love my job. Overseeing the creation of new fiction for the *BattleTech* universe is something I *never* thought I'd be doing back in college when I was rolling dice and having my *BattleMaster* do laps on top of a hill between two enemy forces (only about 3 people on the planet will get this reference, but they know who they are). But here I am.

However, that love can be tested a bit by my co-workers, especially when a certain Line Developer comes up with the idea (spurred partially by our massively successful Clan Invasion Kickstarter) to go deep into the Battle of Tukayyid, far beyond what FASA had done in their sourcebook back... well, let's just say it's been a few decades since this seminal campaign last got a sourcebook.

Then came Randall, who never saw a project he thought couldn't be at least twice the original projected length (, but it's true). So, along with blowing up the original Tukayyid sourcebook, he also came up with the idea for this book (which, to be honest, I am kicking myself in hindsight for not thinking of it first), except that we would have all of the stories written and published on the CGL store website first, once per week.

Oh yeah, and I'd need to get the first story commissioned, written, edited, cover art created, and published in less than a month.

Fortunately, just like in *Shadowrun*, I work with great people on both the writing and editing sides of *BattleTech*. A quick conference with my practically-an-assistant (and fantastic managing editor of *Shrapnel*, our new *BattleTech* quarterly magazine) Phil Lee got a project invite out to a bunch of wonderful *BattleTech* authors to solicit pitches. David Allan Kerber, our amazing layout and cover design wizard, created a fantastic set of matching covers for each short story (you can see them all in the e-book version, but we unfortunately couldn't reproduce them in the POD edition). And last, but absolutely not least, all of the writers whose pitches were selected did heroic work turning their drafts in and going through editorial, including the pass by the fact-check team (too many to mention here, I'm afraid, but you know who you are), which deserves a lot of credit for making sure the stories remained true to the new sourcebook material.

And now, as we are poised on the brink of moving forward in the *BattleTech* universe with the IlClan Era, it seems fitting to take one last look at the previous time the Clans were on the brink of winning it all, on an agricultural planet that no one expected would be a proxy for the biggest battle of all time. I'm very pleased to bring you this collected anthology of all nine stories of the Battle of Tukkayid:

"Blake's Own" by Jason Schmetzer: In the opening salvos of the Battle of Tukayyid, ComStar's Fiftieth Division must test its mettle against the ferocious warriors of Clan Smoke Jaguar.

"Two Roads Diverged" by Michael J. Ciaravella: In Dinju Pass, Smoke Jaguar Star Colonel Brandon Howell leads a spoiling attack against a ComStar force waiting to ambush them.

"Shadow of Death" by Randall N. Bills: Torian Nostra is yoked with an unbearable truth he must endure as the Nova Cats fight for their lives at Losiije.

"The Burdens of Honor" by Blaine Lee Pardoe: Adam Cunningham, a Draconis Combine warrior taken as a bondsman by Clan Ghost Bear, is given the chance to prove his honor to his Clan in the battle for the city of Luk.

"Always Moving" by Steven Mohan, Jr.: During their battle in Kozice Valley, Diamond Shark Khan Ian Hawker learns the true meaning of his Clan's motto.

"The Lions of Prezno" by Bryan Young: Jade Falcon Star Colonel Diane Anu's warriors are attacked from all sides, but something about these hit-and-run assaults does not add up.

"The Icarus Lament" by Chris Hussey: Star Captain Avedis, an Ice Hellion adopted into Clan Steel Viper, fights alongside Khan Natalie Breen in the nightmarish slog through Devil's Bath.

"We Do the Impossible" by Joel Steverson: The infamous Natasha Kerensky of Clan Wolf leads her Wolf Spiders in battle against ComStar forces in the battle for the city of Brzo.

"Broken Promises" by Jason Schmetzer: In the fight for Brzo, the battered survivors of ComStar's 50th Division must guard the 222nd Division against the vicious assaults of Clan Wolf.

Featuring both long-time *BattleTech* authors and bright new *ristars*, these stories reveal many different perspectives in this seminal campaign. I hope you enjoy reading them as much as we enjoyed creating them.

—JOHN HELFERS, EXECUTIVE EDITOR
CATALYST GAME LABS
DECEMBER 2020

BLAKE'S OWN

JASON SCHMETZER

TAMO MOUNTAINS
TUKAYYID
FREE RASALHAGUE REPUBLIC
1 MAY 3052

This was not the first holotank Minka Woloczak had ever seen, but it was one of the largest. The Com Guard MechWarrior adept stood near the corner of it, out of the way, noteputer folio clutched against her thigh, tapping the edge against her gray-white battledress. The bustle of the precentor martial's headquarters continued to swirl around her, but she didn't care.

She watched the stars in the holotank and marveled.

The tank was set for a system-wide strategic view, and the sleepy backwater of Tukayyid had more traffic than Minka had ever seen in one place. The jump points, the distant parts of space where interstellar JumpShips congregated to send their fat, armored DropShips to the planets, were usually places where pinpricks floated. JumpShips were rare and treasured.

Tukayyid's jump points, both the zenith and nadir, now blazed like miniature suns with so many JumpShips. Minka had done a staff cycle in logistics; she knew what it meant to move megatons of shipping around the Inner Sphere. This many hulls in one place was a once-in-a-lifetime thing.

Once in a *century.*

A signal bleeped through the HQ's speakers. "DropShips changing orbit," a monotone voice reported. "Transponders are for Clan Smoke Jaguar."

And that was why.

Conscious of the noteputer she held, Minka straightened and looked around for anyone with precentor's tabs and an Epsilon branch patch. A MechWarrior. Her orders had been to deliver the dispatches by hand, safe from interception, but Precentor Ncuthu hadn't told her *who* to deliver them to. No one else in the HQ wore Fiftieth Division tabs. She didn't know anyone.

And the Clans were coming.

Two years ago the Clans, a vicious band of invaders armed with advanced weaponry and genetically-engineered soldiers, had appeared and conquered a good portion of the Inner Sphere. The Successor States, those star-spanning realms that succeeded the ancient Star League, had been impotent against them. And now it was ComStar's turn. It was Minka's turn, hers and every other soldier of the Com Guard—almost all of which were here, on Tukayyid—to face them.

The best of the Com Guard against the best the Clans. A proxy battle for Terra, ComStar's throneworld. The ultimate prize.

ComStar had been founded more than two-and-a-half centuries earlier by Jerome Blake, the sainted visionary who'd foreseen the war-wracked pit the Inner Sphere would become, and had built ComStar to be the light in these dark times. His faith now flowed through the veins of every acolyte, adept, and precentor on-planet, ready to stand against the darkness of the Clans.

Minka felt that in her bones.

"Move," a voice behind her said. She turned and saw a commando, face covered by a combat helmet, standing near her with his submachine gun held in a tactical carry. More commandos stood behind him.

To her left, a massive armored door opened. Movement made her glance over as a tall, older man, back ramrod-straight, with a shock of white hair and an eyepatch, stepped around the corner and into the opened door.

"Blake's blood," she whispered. That was Precentor Martial Focht himself.

She'd just been within two meters of the precentor martial!

"Adept?" Minka looked behind her. A precentor stood waiting, hand outstretched. "You're the courier from the Fiftieth?"

"Yes, ma'am," Minka said.

"The dispatches?"

Minka frowned. "Oh, right." She held the folio out.

"Your precentor called looking for you," the precentor said, not looking at the noteputer. "Best be getting back to your division."

"Yes, ma'am," Minka said. "Peace of Blake, ma'am."

The matronly precentor just smiled. "Go, adept," she said. "You'll miss your DropShip."

Minka went.

DINJU MOUNTAINS
TUKAYYID

When he heard the *thud* behind him, Enrique Miranda just closed his eyes and counted to four. He knew that sound. It was the sound of a 200-kilogram artillery shell hitting the soft soil of Tukayyid. He'd spent his whole career around Long Tom guns. He could tell from the sound that when he turned around the green round would have one copper ring and one cross-hatched yellow-and-black ring painted on it. Cluster rounds just had that little rattle.

Enrique didn't know how many shells he'd heard hit the dirt in his career. It was a lot. And not one of them had exploded and killed him.

Yet.

He opened his eyes.

But this was still a teachable moment. He considered for a moment, then decided *it will be ibn Ibrami.* He turned around and saw that he was right.

Acolyte I Rashid ibn Ibrami stood there, eyes wide as saucers, in his field white battledress, still holding the waldoes for the exoskeleton he wore that let him carry a one-fifth-ton artillery shell by himself.

"You a traitor, son?" Enrique asked.

"S-sir?" the boy warbled.

"I am not a 'sir,'" Enrique said. "I asked if you're a traitor, seeing as you're standing there where you dropped that round right behind me." He glanced down, saw the rings he'd expected. "You know what that is, right?"

"A cluster round."

"So you know it's got fifty-five individual little bombs inside it, not counting the propellant and the bursting charge, each of which was made by the lowest bidder with nothing more than the ever-present will and eye of the Blessed Blake to ensure it was made to spec?"

"Yes, s-sir-*Acolyte* Miranda."

"And you dropped it?"

"I just stumbled a little—" But Enrique cut him off.

"Pick it up," he said softly. "Get it where it belongs. And next time...next time watch where you're going." He turned his back before the boy could answer, instead taking a moment to survey the positions of the six guns in his Level II battery.

Each of the field pieces called Long Toms was sited, arranged west toward the Dinju Pass, with sandbags going up around them. Word was the Clans didn't bother much with counterbattery, so they'd probably be okay. He twisted his head, looking to where the precentor's Cobra VTOL squatted sixty or so meters away. It was just luck that the bird had parked there, but if the Clans did send some fire their way, they'd be glad of the VTOL's antimissile systems.

Enrique looked forward again, past Six Gun, at the broad expanse of the Dinju Pass. Across the pass, the majority of the Fiftieth Division squatted around the base of the Dinju Heights. The bulk of the Fiftieth's parent Fifth Com Guard Army was hidden in the Heights, waiting for the Smoke Jaguars to take the bait.

The word was they expected the Clan—whichever Clan it was—to land nearby and then challenge the visible Fiftieth to a series of duels. That was how the Clans fought. It would buy time for the rest of Fifth Army to come out and crush them. The plan used misdirection to the fullest, one of the precentor martial's prime virtues.

No one—not Enrique, and he was sure not the precentor martial himself—expected the Fiftieth Division to stop a Clan thrust on its own. Some days the whole division felt like it was populated entirely by clones of Rashid ibn Ibrami. Good, honest boys and girls, but kids. And while they were armed to Com Guard standards—which meant better than the regular Inner Sphere, but not quite as good as the Clans—there were standards and then there were *standards*. An elite division would have mobile Long Toms, not the field pieces Enrique commanded.

It was only the few experienced hands in the division, like Enrique himself, that gave it any stiffening. He chuckled, thinking of an expression his old man had often used when he was a kid. Bullets in a bucket of jelly. He finally understood what it meant.

Someone cleared their throat behind him. Enrique turned to find ibn Ibrami standing there, looking up. "Sir..."

"I'm not..." Enrique rolled his eyes. "What?"

"What's that?" The long, gorilla-like arm of the exoskeleton rose to point.

Enrique squinted and looked up, trying to see what the boy saw. His eyes weren't what they used to be...were those meteors? *Oh, Blake's crooked bones!*

"Get the guns up!" he roared, turning away from the boy and racing for his position near Two Gun. He didn't even look to see if the boy moved; he'd either trained him to do his job right or he hadn't, and now wasn't the time for caring. To his credit, the boy had been the first to see the threat.

Enemy BattleMechs were falling from the sky in custom ablative drop pods.

He had to be in the fire direction pit near Two Gun when they landed.

Right on top of the division.

"Drop in progress!" a voice screamed in Minka Woloczak's neurohelmet. She frowned, looking behind her at the DropShip still steaming cool on the rough field. Her suborbital hop from Tamo had been a lot for a courier, but it could hardly be a drop. She guided her *Exterminator* toward the makeshift gate. She had to get back to her unit before the Clans dropped.

"Case Black!" the voice called. "I say again, Case Black!"

Minka swallowed, then angled her sensors up.

Then she saw them.

She slammed the throttle forward, angling away from the gate. Instead she charged right through the light chain-link fence as the 65-ton 'Mech accelerated up to its full speed.

The drop hadn't been her. It was the Clans.

If the platoon of infantry guarding the makeshift landing field cared, they didn't show it. They were sprinting toward the DropShip. Minka heard the whining roar of its engines spooling back up so it could escape through her *Exterminator*'s ferroglass viewports. For a moment she considered turning and trying to join them.

Based on what she'd heard at the precentor martial's bunker, it was probably the Smoke Jaguars coming down. Of all of the Clans, they had the reputation as the fiercest.

Her *Exterminator* steadied down into its fastest gait. There was no chance she'd make it to her Two's position, but she had to try.

A BattleMech was a ten-meter-tall humanoid war machine, armed and armored to destroy a city block in seconds if another 'Mech didn't stop it. They'd remained the preferred method of warfare since their introduction centuries ago. The decrepit machines of the Successor States were often much-repaired and patched salvaged machines, some of them scores or hundreds of years old. Her own *Exterminator* had been built for the Star League's Royal regiments hundreds of years ago, and lovingly maintained against need by ComStar technicians.

That need would be served today.

Minka looked into her heads-up display again, looking for the estimated time the incoming 'Mechs would touch down. BattleMechs could be dropped from orbit like outsized paratroopers, as these had.

She only had minutes.

Around her, the rear echelon of the Fiftieth Division was swarming to life as the alarm spread. Case Black was the go-to-hell plan; that meant Division thought the incoming 'Mechs were coming down right on top of them. The carefully-rehearsed plans were out the window.

"Blake protect us," Minka prayed.

An explosion tore the ground in front of her as one of the 'Mechs coming down fired downward.

The HUD's time estimate had been wrong.

Enrique listened to the fire mission request again, holding one hand against his helmet to ensure a good seal. The tiny speaker turned the voice tinny, but the numbers were clear.

"Negative, Iota Four Seven," he said for the fourth time. "Grid coordinates incorrect. Fire mission denied." He ripped his helmet off and slammed it down on the small table in front of him.

Across the table, Acolyte II Lynn Flores frowned. "Bad news?"

"Idiot doesn't seem to realize grid coordinates need more than four digits," he said. He stood, looking over the lip of the pit, then sat back down. He swiped a map open on his noteputer, tapped a few locations, and then hit the send pad to send the fire mission date to the guns' automatic fire directors. "I think he means here and here," he told Flores. "Calculate the follow-on salvos, would you? Five rounds per gun, standard HE. I think they'll go this way."

Handing Flores the noteputer, he stood, grabbing his helmet, to take a look around. The whine of Two Gun's electric motors told him the fire mission had been accepted by the battery's fire control computers. The long barrel of the gun twisted right and up in elevation; the target grid wasn't anything like the Long Tom's maximum range.

The Clans were dropping that close.

Enrique looked at each gun in turn, noting the angle of the barrels. They all aligned...except...

Grimacing, he slammed the hated helmet back down on his head. The yammering voice of the idiot 'Mech officer who couldn't read a map was still going, but he toggled a different channel. "Four Gun."

"Gun up, Acolyte!" came the immediate reply.

"Look at the other guns, Phuc," Enrique said, very calmly. He stood still, watching the misaligned barrel of Four Gun. A head popped up above the sandbag line; Com Guard helmets had enough lip that he could see the head turn one way and back, before disappearing.

"Good battery, Acolyte!" Acolyte I Phuc said. "We're going to give those Clanners what for, hey?"

"We sure are, Phuc," Enrique said. "Now look at your gun's barrel."

"Yes, Aco—" The transmission cut out. Enrique waited.

"Fire director set to receive," he muttered, reciting one of the steps of the Long Tom's manual of arms. The step Phuc's gun crew had clearly missed. His right index finger tapped against his leg. It was the only sign of the white-hot rage burning through him.

He wasn't angry at Phuc, not really. The kid, like ibn Ibrami, was green as grass. They all were. Instead, Enrique was angry at himself. It had been his job to get these kids ready for war, and he'd failed. It didn't matter that he'd done all he could. Not even Blake and all his saints could have done more.

It was still Enrique Miranda's job to get them ready for today.

And he'd clearly failed.

Four Gun's barrel lurched into motion, aligning with the rest of the battery. Static rasped in Enrique's helmet. "Four Gun up," Acolyte Phuc said, again, his voice more subdued.

"Very good," Enrique said, and cut the channel. He pried the helmet off again, this time looking across the field, toward the pass.

The first Clan 'Mechs were already down. He saw more than heard the battle, but the low-frequency rumble of heavy weapons fire in the distance was already starting to become noticeable, like a distant storm on the ocean.

Enrique chewed his lower lip, watching the movement of the 'Mechs. His mind, with the unasked-for precision of long years of practice, superimposed the grid coordinates over what he saw, and he watched, his mind computing time of flight and guessing where the enemy might go. Just because he wasn't a high and mighty MechWarrior didn't mean he didn't know how they fought.

Clapping the helmet back on his head, he stepped back and jumped down into the FD pit. He took the noteputer back from Flores, noted her additions, and grunted a quick "nice work," to her before keying his helmet.

"Battery, battery fire, five rounds, HE quick!"

The warning given, he stabbed the *execute* button on the noteputer.

As one, the six guns of the battery exploded, twenty-meter licks of flame erupting from their barrels. The autoloaders started chucking immediately, before even Enrique was done feeling his internal organs ripple against his ribs from the compression wave.

On the noteputer, a counter started counting down. He dialed a different frequency, waited, and then stabbed the transmit button.

"All Iota elements! Splash in five seconds, 30 rounds HE!"

"—30 rounds HE!" Minka heard. Her mouth went dry.

She couldn't remember who Iota was—a division was a big place, and her own Kappa was too far away—and she didn't hear any grid coordinates for where the artillery was aimed. All she knew was five tons of high explosive were going to start falling out of the sky in a few seconds.

The *Exterminator* rocked from an impact. At first Minka thought it was the artillery, but it was too soon. Instead, the damned Smoke Jaguar *Fenris* had found her again. She'd tried to cut contact, but the OmniMech was too fast. It had come down barely a hundred meters in front of her, firing its extended-range particle projection cannon even as it discarded its single-use jump pack.

Clan OmniMechs had a more manufactured, modular look than the normal Inner Sphere BattleMech. Minka's *Exterminator*, from a far distance, could be mistaken for a man. The *Fenris*, just as tall as the *Exterminator* but twenty tons lighter, just looked like a machine.

As the static discharges of the ER PPC hit flickered out, Minka checked her damage indicators and frowned; machine-like or not, it was deadly. She raised both arms and triggered her four medium lasers, but the bolts flicked past the angling 'Mech harmlessly. She cursed and squeezed the trigger for her long-range missile launcher. Ten LRMs rippled out of the launcher in the *Exterminator*'s chest, angling up and then down. Minka prayed to Blake that her aim had been true, guiding her munitions against the Smoke Jaguar's armor.

Her prayers were rewarded; a clutch of missiles ate at the armor on the *Fenris*' chest. The 'Mech shook the damage off like a dog shakes off water, twisting around to come right at her.

Then the ground around it exploded in dirty black puffs of smoke and flame. Thunder shook the ground hard enough she felt the impact transmitted up to her cockpit through the *Exterminator*'s frame. The sound shook the 'Mech as well as the artillery fell.

When the smoke cleared, the *Fenris* was down with a mangled knee. Sparks shot from its hip actuator as well. The Smoke Jaguar MechWarrior, true to his reputation, was still trying to drag the 'Mech closer to her, determined to keep fighting.

"Blake protects the just," she whispered, and settled the targeting ring for her lasers over the *Fenris*' heart. The recharge indicator was nearly green.

"Reload, standard HE!"

It was an unnecessary shout; the guns' automatic reloaders would already be sucking the ready rounds into the firing magazine. Two of each gun's crew, wearing the heavy exoskeletons, would already be heaving the next set of stacked shells into the ready round hopper, per the firing orders already published. In a well-oiled machine, the humans would be just as smooth as the machines. In the Fiftieth...

Enrique stood to see over the lip of the pit. "Rashid," he said, keying a private channel on his helmet.

"Acolyte?" the young loader replied. He stopped and turned toward the pit, round held firmly in the exoskeleton's arms.

"What's the load queue say for the next rack?"

"Five rounds HE," ibn Ibrami said immediately.

"Right," Enrique said. "HE rounds are marked how, Acolyte?"

"Solid copper ring, Acolyte," ibn Ibrami said without hesitation.

"Good answer," Enrique said. "Now look down." He watched the boy look down to see the paired copper and yellow rings on the smoke round he was carrying.

"I'll get it right, Acolyte," ibn Ibrami said doggedly. He turned and trudged back the way he had come. Even with the exoskeleton's whining steps, his determination was clear. He was tired, they were all tired. But he refused to give up.

"I know you will," Enrique said, then keyed his helmet mike off. "I know you will," he whispered.

Turning the other way, he lifted the electronic binocs he wore around his neck and looked where the rounds had fallen. Smoke lifted from several damaged machines, but he couldn't tell if it was the fall of his rounds or fire from the nearby Com Guard 'Mechs and tanks. Regardless, the white-painted Com Guard machines were moving away from the impact zone.

And the Clan 'Mechs...

Enrique crouched down, took the fire direction noteputer in hand, and keyed the orders. Then he toggled his helmet radio. "Battery, battery fire. Repeat!" Then he opened his mouth wide, to equalize the pressure when the compression wave from the guns firing in tandem washed over him.

Blake forgive him, but he loved the sound of the guns. He ignored the sensation of his organs moving and concentrated on the shot timer on the noteputer screen, ready to call the splash warning.

Minka Woloczak looked at her tactical map screen and knew it was hopeless. Too many red icons for Smoke Jaguar 'Mechs stood between her *Exterminator* and the position her Two had been assigned to hold. And now the Smoke Jaguars were jamming long-range comms, so she couldn't even tell her second-in-command he had control of the Level II.

She told herself Paxton was a good MechWarrior. He'd lead the Two as well as she would have.

But that still left her on the wrong side of the battle.

"—splash, 30 rounds HE!" came the artillery's voice again. It was full of static and she missed most of it, but she got that much. Minka set her *Exterminator* walking backward, eyeing the sky in front of her. On her screen a small icon pulsed behind her, the small firebase the artillery was firing from. She touched the map near that post, setting a nav point.

Right now, that artillery post was the only Com Guard outpost she could reach.

Enrique was holding the noteputer out to Acolyte Flores when the precentor's Cobra VTOL exploded. The impact was of a class with the guns firing, but it smacked him against the side of the pit because he wasn't expecting it. The noteputer clattered to the floor. He stared at the pyre that had been an aircraft and then spun at the sound of thunder from the sky.

The largest aerospace fighter he had ever seen was bearing down on his battery. It was already too close, close enough he could see the gray paint and the snarling smoke jaguar painted on the underside of the wings. The gigantic, delta-winged beast overflew the battery, bomb-bay doors open.

"Blake's black balls," Enrique whispered.

Shapes fell out, tumbling in the wash of the fighter's powerful engines.

They weren't bombs.

It was much worse than that.

They were Elementals.

"Local defense!" Enrique screamed. "Toads!" He shouted the bearing, clawing his way to his feet, glancing from the guns to the falling shapes of the Clans' giant, genetically-bred armored infantry. It looked like the fighter pilot had miscalculated, and the Toads—the Inner Sphere's derogatory term for Elemental armor—were going to come down a couple hundred meters away.

Acolyte Flores shoved him aside, still on her knees, hands scrabbling for the noteputer controller he'd dropped. He ignored her, instead rolling himself over the berm of the pit and sprinting for Two Gun. The controller would be too slow for something like this; Enrique needed to get his hands on the gun controls if they were to have a chance.

A couple of hundred meters—be generous and call it four hundred—was a lot or a little time depending on circumstance. Two guys with sticks? Four hundred meters was a lifetime. A guy with a sniper rifle? A few seconds. Toad infantry would cross that distance in less than a minute, bounding with their integral jump jets. That minute was the whole time Enrique Miranda and his battery had to stop them before they were in among the guns and killing them all.

"Move!" he told Acolyte Reyes, Two Gun's normal gunner. The girl, to her credit, climbed quickly out of the saddle. Enrique slid into with the ease of long practice, ignoring where his knees and elbows rubbed because the seat was set for Celestine Reyes and he was twenty centimeters and thirty years larger than she was.

He grabbed the gunnery controls in both hands and put them both hard over. "Load HE!" he shouted. "Zero distance, contact fuse!"

The gun traversed as fast as its motors would drive it. Enrique thanked the Blessed Blake's foresight that the guns were mounted on 360-degree carriages. As soon as the barrel aligned with the azimuth Enrique wanted, the recoil compensators slammed down into the Tukayyid soil. The barrel was still coming down, toward elevation zero or damn close to it.

The Elementals landed in puffs of jet exhaust. It only took them a moment to orient on the artillery position and bounce toward it. It looked like one or two of their "Points," what ROM intelligence told them the Clans called a squad. Five or ten of the monsters.

Even one, inside the wire, would be enough to kill them all.

Enrique risked a quick glance around him, at the other guns. Three of the other five were almost pointed where he was; Three Gun was on the right azimuth, but the barrel was still coming down. And Six Gun was just spinning in place, the barrel still pointed up at the original firing elevation.

It would have to be enough.

The barrel *thunked* down against its elevation screw. Enrique ignored the other guns and concentrated on the gunnery screen. It displayed the local defense, direct-fire targeting grid, which was not one he had ever before seen outside of training sims, but he'd done the sims. Unlike the crosshairs of a gun, the screen showed a rough oval projected over the topography for the estimated area of effect for the round.

Enrique resisted the urge to giggle; this was not artillery doctrine. They were never supposed to see the enemy. A Long Tom fought at ranges of kilometers, not meters. On his screen the Toads were just moving blurs, but he could tell them apart from the ground. He waited, timing them at the apex of their jump, then led them a little and squeezed the trigger.

The concussion of the Long Tom firing was twice what it had been when he was sheltered inside the fire direction pit, but he didn't care. The punishing impact rocked him in the too-tight chair, but he held his gaze on the site.

Enrique was used to thinking in terms of time of flight; at this short range, the impact was almost instantaneous. A blossom of dirty black smoke and flame exploded beneath the descending Toads; they disappeared into the cloud, but Enrique swore. He'd led them too far.

"Reload!" he screamed. Leaning out of the gunner's seat, he grabbed his binocs and tried to watch the fall of the other guns' rounds. All three of the other guns close to being laid in fired within five seconds of each other.

One Gun's loader had made a mistake; instead of the dirty bloom of an HE round, One Gun's shot exploded short, then covered the ground for sixty meters with firecracker explosions from the cluster shell. It could have worked, except it was two degrees off to the right of where the Toads had come down.

Four Gun and Five Gun fired within two seconds, and their shots made Enrique snarl in satisfaction. One of the rounds fell right among the clustered Toads, exploding and tossing them aside like children's toys. The other fell short, but the blast wave sent three of the suits that had been knocked down scuttling across the ground like turtles overturned on their shells.

Any normal men would have been turned to jelly. BattleMechs taking those hits would have been on their back, not destroyed, but certainly knowing they'd been hurt. But from what ROM reports said...

Enrique swore.

Most of the suits picked themselves back up again. Two waved to the others with their thick, laser-armed gauntlets.

Then they leaped into the air on jump jets. Enrique's eyes flicked to the reload indicator. Still red and crosshatched. "Where's that round?" he growled.

"On the belt now, Acolyte!" shouted Rashid ibn Ibrami. Enrique twisted around to see the boy stepping back from the conveyor that took the rounds from the magazine to the breech; Enrique flashed him a grin and turned back to his controls.

The suits were already coming down from their leap. They only had to jump one, maybe two more times before they could bring the artillery crews under fire. Which meant he had one or two more shots. He worked the controls, leading the Toads, but not as much as last time—

—the Toads fell toward the ground—

—he fired—

And the target area disappeared into the blue-black smoke of an HE round.

Around him, the other guns boomed.

A new icon appeared on the Long Tom's limited tactical screen, behind them.

Minka Woloczak crested the small rise where the artillery had set up to find them all facing away from her. One of the guns fired as her sensors cleared the rim, and her *Exterminator*'s computer automatically painted the impact zone. A cluster of small red icons were in that zone.

Elementals.

Minka pushed her thumb against the throttle that was already to its gate, urging the *Exterminator* to go faster even as she knew it couldn't. She felt a desperate, unexpected need to protect this artillery battery. She knew she was projecting her own sense of loss, unprocessed loss, that she would feel for her Level II onto these unnamed Com Guards, but she didn't care.

Minka had become a MechWarrior to protect people.

This was her chance.

The artillery park was barely a hundred meters across; she took care where she placed her 'Mech's feet, but once she was past the burning wreckage of a VTOL, she centered her course. Her sensors told her there were still eight Elementals active; it warred against all of her training to be worried about eight infantry troopers, but the Clans had changed all the rules.

Slowing her throttle, she settled her crosshairs on the lead suit and squeezed off a barrage from her LRMs.

Enrique cheered as the white-painted *Exterminator* went past, but he didn't get up from the gunnery controls. Instead, he twisted until he could see ibn Ibrami directly. "I want the next three rounds to all be flechette," he told the loader.

"Yes, Acolyte." The boy took two steps, then stopped. "Aco—"

"Copper and red-black," Enrique said. He waited for ibn Ibrami's nod, then palmed the side of his helmet. "All guns; load flechette." He glanced back to where the Com Guard 'Mech was engaging the Toads. "If you need to shoot near that 'Mech, do it. The flechettes won't hurt it."

Flores staggered up out of the pit and half-ran, half-staggered toward him. For the first time he noticed the line of blood running down her left temple. "We've got fire mission requests," she gasped, waving the noteputer.

"Proper ones?"

"It's Ncuthu himself," Flores said. "I recognize his voice."

"Give me that." Enrique took the noteputer. He scanned the fire missions, scowled, and looked back past where the *Exterminator* had appeared. He could see half-a-dozen skirmishes where the Clans were pushing the Fiftieth back. Dirty black puffs of smoke over the field told him some of the other batteries were still firing, but it wasn't enough.

"Okay," he told Flores. "Put all the guns except this one back on director control. You queue the fire. I'll put Two Gun back on battery as soon as the Toads are dealt with."

Enrique didn't like any of his choices. It was his duty to serve the guns and support the rest of the division, but also his duty to protect his crews. He trusted Flores and the fire director to calculate the fire. He didn't trust any of the rest of them to use their gun like a giant shotgun if the Toads got past the *Exterminator*.

Speaking of which...he twisted back around to face the nearer threat. "Reyes!" he called.

"Acolyte?" the Two Gun commander replied. She stood at his elbow, clear of the traverse but close enough to take over if something happened to him.

"Go help Flores with fire direction," he told her. "I'll take good care of your gun."

"Yes, Acolyte."

The orders given, he looked downrange. The 'Mech and the toads were between 150 and 200 meters away. Enrique twitched the gun controls, bringing the barrel a few degrees of azimuth back around to point toward the 'Mech's back.

"Nothing personal," he whispered.

Minka swore and swung the *Exterminator*'s left arm out wide, holding down the trigger for the paired medium lasers there. One of the bursts of light went wide, ahead of the bouncing Elemental, but the other amputated both the trooper's legs just above the knee. She didn't have time to celebrate her victory, though, as a pair of SRMs hit the heavy armor protecting her 'Mech's chest.

It had been a mistake to charge in, she knew now. She was too close, and the Elementals too nimble. She'd managed to kill or cripple three of them, but the remaining five just kept coming. Worse, they kept trying to get around her, to get in among the artillery crews.

She couldn't let that happen.

One of the Toads' lasers washed across her cockpit armor. It didn't penetrate, but her flinch. One of the Elementals saw the opportunity and took it, rocketing up and over her 'Mech on its jump jets. Two of its fellows followed.

Minka twisted her controls, wishing her 65-ton 'Mech was faster.

She wasn't going to be fast enough.

"You just stay over there," Enrique muttered. He saw the Toad come down behind the *Exterminator* and gather itself for another leap. Enrique fired before the Clanner could get off the ground.

The flechette round was the modern descendant of the ancient canister round; packed with antipersonnel darts, it normally exploded over the ground and fired its flechettes down. Fuzed for direct-fire, it became the world's largest shotgun. A bursting charge fired almost as soon as the round left the barrel. A flock of deadly darts washed across the pair of Toads behind the *Exterminator*'s right calf.

The pair of suits came apart.

An Elemental suit was a marvel of engineering, but nothing is impregnable. The powered armor had already been battered by the previous rounds and by fighting the *Exterminator*. Thirty meters worth of darts packed into about four square meters was just too much.

What didn't stop with the Toads pinged and sparked off the *Exterminator*'s leg armor.

"Yeah," Enrique said. "That's what I said."

The MechWarrior took care of the rest of them.

An acolyte who looked like he'd been young and clean when Jerome Blake was alive waited for Minka when she climbed down from the *Exterminator*. He glanced around, shrugged, and saluted when she stepped clear of the ladder.

"Acolyte Enrique Miranda," he said. "Thanks for the help, ma'am."

"Adept Minka Woloczak," she said, then grinned. "You shot my 'Mech."

"Should buff right out," Miranda said, grinning back. "Ma'am, any word from higher? We had a fire mission from Precentor Ncuthu, but nothing since." He turned and pointed. "I don't mind telling you, it doesn't look good."

Minka looked where he pointed. Her eyes saw far less than her 'Mech's sensors would have told her, but she could see enough. 'Mechs were moving back toward the mountains, 'Mechs that had to be what was left of the Fiftieth Division. Behind the skirmish lines were pyres and broken machines. Aerospace fighters on ground attack missions stooped on both sides.

"Nothing since they dropped," she said, finally.

"Then I'd love some orders, Adept," Miranda said.

"Me too, Acolyte," she told him. She felt a wave of exhaustion threaten to rise up, but she pushed it down. "But in the absence of orders, we follow the last order given, right?"

"Ma'am?"

Minka gestured. "Let's find you some wheels, Acolyte," she said. "And then let's go put some fire up those bastards' backsides. Maybe we can still make a difference." She grinned warily. "We stay here, more of the bastards will just fall out of the sky on top of us."

Mirana grinned back at her. "Sounds good, ma'am." He held up one hand. "Flores!" he bellowed. "Inventory for movement!"

"Yes, Acolyte," came a woman's voice.

"We have vehicles, ma'am," Miranda said. "We have to crew them ourselves, so we drive or we shoot." He shrugged, big broad dirt-stained shoulders going up or down. "Blake knows where we'll find resupply."

Minka clapped him on the shoulder. "Blake does know, Acolyte Miranda," she told him. "And he protects us all." She looked past the artilleryman, toward the Clans who were killing her friends.

"He will know his own," she whispered.

TWO ROADS DIVERGED

MICHAEL J. CIARAVELLA

DINJU OVERLOOK
DINJU PASS
TUKAYYID
2 MAY 3052

"I thought I would find you out here, sir."

Star Colonel Brandon Howell did not react to the respectful voice behind him, keeping his gaze fixed on the broad expanse ahead. The Dinju Overlook, a beak-like crest that stood at the far end of the broad canyon that was the Dinju Pass, which led directly to the silvery outline of the mining city of Dinju Heights, only barely visible in the distance.

If nothing else, we must win this upcoming battle to punish whoever was in charge of naming things on this benighted planet.

"As ever, you are correct," Howell replied, finally glancing at the younger warrior. Star Captain Jared Canto was a newcomer to the Jaguar Grenadiers, and well thought of as one of the *ristars* of the Clan. Star Colonel Howell believed it was a coup to have earned the younger warrior for his staff, and quickly appreciated how Cantos' thought process occasionally mirrored his own. For a Clan with such fervent Crusader leanings, such a mindset was to be prized.

"I suppose you heard much of that," Howell stated, referring to his recent conversation with the Khan of Clan

Smoke Jaguar, Lincoln Osis. Their discussion had been like many that came before it: heated and passionate from Osis, calm and controlled from Howell. Fire and Ice, he had heard it said, and believed it.

"*Aff*, Star Colonel," Canto replied, managing to not look abashed. "The Khan had several of us wait outside his command tent for when we were to receive our orders."

Howell nodded, still not turning to the other man. *And to make sure everyone else heard my objections without being obvious about it.* With great difficulty, the Star Colonel kept a sneer off his face, having learned long ago that such outward displays of emotion made him far too much like his fellow Jaguar warriors. He prided himself on his uniqueness, a trait he thought was far too rare in his own Clan.

He knew what the Khan called him behind his back: Bloodless. Lacking the fiery spirit that defined the Smoke Jaguar, the famed stalking predator of Strana Mechty, a creature—like the warriors of the Clan themselves—genetically altered from original Terran stock to become one of the most feared predators in the galaxy.

Yet he also knew there was a flaw in even the most carefully designed evolutionary plan. The ambush predator had its place, but was at a severe disadvantage when its prey was aware it was being stalked.

Which was exactly the situation they had found themselves in—attacking the planet Tukayyid as a proxy for control of Terra, the birthworld of humanity and the goal of all the Clans. The forces of ComStar, the quasi-mystical order of former Star League technicians that had chosen to stay behind when the Great Father had pulled the majority of the Star League Defense Force from the Inner Sphere, had chosen to defend this strange planet instead of risking damage to their homeworld. It was an oddly intelligent request from a group that had already proven unworthy of the great honor they had once held, remaining behind and being complicit in the fall of the golden ideal that had been the Star League, the pinnacle of human achievement.

His fellow Smoke Jaguar warriors dismissed the mystic technicians, thinking them nothing more than the last gasp of a bygone age, but Howell was more cautious about dismissing their foe. Since receiving official word of the upcoming battles, the Star Colonel had devoted much of his time to researching their mysterious opponents while putting his subordinates through a grueling training schedule for the upcoming conflict.

Howell allowed himself a small, satisfied smile at the thought: He trusted his people implicitly, having trained most of them himself, and knew they would never let him down when it counted. The only way the Jaguar Grenadiers could have maintained such an impressive position in the *touman*, and Alpha Galaxy itself, had been by ensuring they were some of the best of the best, second only to the Khan's own Sixth Jaguar Dragoons. It was just one of the reasons why the Khan suffered to keep him so close: While the two men would never truly like each other, they had developed a grudging respect that had served them both well in the past. The Khan enjoyed using him as the tip of the spear, assault troops in his campaigns, (Howell would never go so far as to say his Khan thought of him as expendable...) but he also knew the Khan would never allow him to take sole victory in any conjoined conflict, so Howell was fairly convinced he would always have talented reinforcements at his back.

While his forces prepared for the upcoming conflict, his research had proven less than fruitful. There was surprisingly little to go on, especially in regard to these mysterious "Com Guards." None of the reports from the other invading clans had said anything about engaging ComStar BattleMech forces, and any of the Clan forces that had encountered ComStar at their various HPG centers on captured planets had found them lightly defended at best, quick to surrender to the Clan invaders.

Still, that lack of knowledge concerned him greatly, and brought him back to the same concern: For all of their differences, both the Inner Sphere and the Clans thought of Terra as the homeworld of humanity, the crown jewel of the human systems. It held immense political significance, and holding the planet would raise its owner to a level of prominence that neither the other Great Houses nor Clans could match.

Despite all of that, however, and how the various Great Houses had grown in the various "Succession Wars" that had pervaded the Inner Sphere in the wake of the departure of the SLDF, none of them had managed to take Terra away from ComStar, despite the fact that there surely must have been multiple attempts, clandestine or otherwise. That seemed to indicate a level of political acumen or military prowess beyond what the rest of the Inner Sphere had managed, which immediately should put the cautious warrior on their guard.

After all, the Jaguar could be patient when it wanted to be...that was one of their greatest strengths. *When they choose to be,* he thought.

"Star Colonel, are you all right?"

Howell composed his features as he turned to the other MechWarrior, although he was still amused that he had allowed his thoughts to get away from him for a moment. The painfully young warrior watched his commander carefully, but couldn't help darting a quick look over the vista below, clearly curious to know what his commander was thinking.

Which means I should indulge him, Howell thought. "What do you see, Star Captain?"

To his credit, the younger warrior took a moment to consider his answer, coming up to stand directly beside his commander. As Cantos began speaking, a stray thought flitted through Howell's mind, that if the Inner Sphere forces that had to be somewhere nearby had a sniper watching, they could decapitate the Jaguar Grenadiers in a matter of seconds. The fact that he was able to draw another breath was a small relief, and Howell once again focused on the vista before him.

The Dinju Pass was a wide gorge that separated Dinju Heights from the surrounding landscape, serving as a dry moat that would provide an interesting tactical challenge. The gorge would slow down attacking forces, allowing the city's defenders to attack them at will, but would also provide the Smoke Jaguar warriors, with their range advantage, the opportunity to control the timing of the battle as they approached, allowing them to maintain an indefinite siege upon the city while they sought out weak points. The gorge also provided an interesting method to advance on the city;

the Smoke Jaguar forces could close to point-blank range under the cover of their fellow warriors on the opposite bank, then use their jump jets to leap into the city, sowing chaos when and where they chose.

When Canto had finished his analysis, the other man merely nodded. "An excellent analysis, Star Captain. However, I believe you might be missing an important piece of information."

"What might that be?" Canto replied, seemingly unfazed by the thought that his answer might be incomplete.

"You must remember that the Inner Sphere warriors chose this battlefield, probably long before we had ever heard of the world."

Canto's chin rose slightly, and he instantly revised his assumptions. "You think this may be a trap."

"Oh, I am sure it is a trap," the Star Colonel replied lightly. "I merely wonder what sort."

The younger warrior nodded. "You believe they are waiting in ambush for us?"

"Nearly certainly." The Star Colonel gave the young officer an appraising glance. "The question is, do we avoid the trap, or trip it for our own purposes?"

For a long moment, the younger warrior seemed to grapple with the wealth of possibilities, but the Star Colonel saved him from embarrassment by laughing heartily. "Do not trouble yourself, Star Captain. I do not intend to lay my tactical concerns upon your doorstep. I merely wish to hear another's thoughts on the matter."

Anything else that the two warriors were going to say was cut off by a flurry of voices behind them, and the two men turned to see Khan Lincoln Osis stepping out of his command tent, striding purposefully toward the staging area where his battle armor waited—a clear sign that the battle was due to begin. Howell nodded respectfully to the larger man, but the Khan did not deign to respond to it.

Keeping his voice even, Star Colonel Howell turned back to Canto. "Well, it appears we are about to find out..."

DINJU PASS
TWENTY KILOMETERS OUTSIDE DINJU HEIGHTS
TUKAYYID
2 MAY, 3052

Star Colonel Brandon Howell tightened his hands on the joysticks of his immense *Timber Wolf* OmniMech, stalking toward the entrance to the Dinju Pass. While checking in with the various Stars of his Cluster, he watched two Stars of his fastest OmniMechs line up at the wide mouth, ready to take point for the upcoming battle.

As he finished his preparations, the Khan's gravelly voice came clearly across the radio. "You are cleared to proceed, Star Colonel."

Ignoring the other warrior's disdainful tone, Howell switched to his own command channel. "Recon Stars, proceed."

He watched with quiet pride as his forces brought up their own reactors and his Stars entered the pass at full speed. For long moments, the radio remained silent as the two Recon Stars moved swiftly through the canyons, each one taking a different path forward.

When the next report came, it was from a surprising source. "Contact!" said Canto from where his Star was watching from an overwatch position well back from the mouth of the pass. "We have BattleMechs exiting the city."

This was surprising, that the defenders would be moving out so late. Surely they had seen the approach of the Jaguar forces: *Why would they not try to stop us before getting so close?*

Howell allowed himself a moment to consider the thought, and then switched back to the cluster channel. "Warriors, if they descend into the pass, you may engage, but do not slow down. We are going to take them at a run. I want all of our forces to hug the walls as you pass through, do not stop until you have reached the outskirts of the city on the other side."

There was a quick series of double *clicks* on the comm channel to verify receipt of the order. It was the same plan he had announced while approaching the pass, but he couldn't help feeling an increased sense of urgency he could not explain.

The first of his main battle line forces began running through the pass, following in the footsteps of the Recon Stars, cutting close to the high walls. In the distance, ComStar units in the pristine white of their order moved up to the edge of the city, firing down at the oncoming forces and then retreating back to cover among the buildings on either side of the street. While most of the initial fire seemed random, it was clear the damage would increase as they approached.

To Howell's extreme pleasure, his forces seemed completely unfazed by the incoming fire, rushing into the cauldron at full speed. A few OmniMechs suffered light strikes on their armor, but most of the shots did not connect. Some of his more experienced warriors fired back with their energy weapons, one of which hit a ComStar *Lancelot* with an extended-range PPC that nearly ripped off its left arm, but the others simply concentrated on closing the range. While the Clan warriors had the range advantage, the tight confines of the pass would make them easy targets if they slowed down.

However, while the ComStar forces had the advantage of the interior defensive position, they appeared to have been caught unprepared for the sudden thrust through the pass, which was also surprising. From how fast they were sending out forces, they clearly had planned for the contingency, but it was clear that there was something wrong with their overall strategy.

"Diamond Star, hold your position and provide covering fire. I want to get a count on the various forces we are facing." It would not be an easy task, especially from such a distance, but the missile-armed OmniMechs of Diamond Star would do best at a range in which the ComStar forces could not reply, and he was very interested in knowing just how much of the ComStar force they currently had focused upon them. "Ax Star, pull south around the outskirts of the City when you reach it; I want to ensure we are not flanked by opposing forces. Bold Star, take north."

A chorus of replies confirmed that both Stars had received their orders, and the OmniMechs began executing their maneuvers, using the canyon walls to avoid the majority of fire from the city defenders. Howell observed on his secondary monitor as his forces moved through the pass toward the city, and then refocused on the entrance to the pass itself. Cycling his own OmniMech into a run, he moved to lead his own command star through the pass.

Which was when everything went straight to hell.

Ax Star was the first one to report trouble, suddenly surrounded by heavy BattleMechs as soon as they turned a sharp corner of the rocky canyon. Quickly identifying their opponents as members of the ComStar 299th Division, they had clearly been placed here for just this eventuality, hidden from magscan and heat by the metallic elements in the walls.

"Full speed through the pass! We stop for nothing!" The Star Colonel felt a wrenching feeling deep in his chest, and fought to keep himself focused as he forced his unit into a dead run through the winding canyon walls. His first instinct was to rush in to assist his forces, but something still felt wrong.

It all came sharply into focus as his secondary monitor blossomed with the signs of additional fusion engines coming online. More Inner Sphere forces boiled out of camouflaged entrenchments like an army of ivory ants intent upon their prey, descending upon the Jaguar OmniMechs in a voracious swarm. From the careful way the initial forces had struck at the approaching Clan units under the cover of fire from their heavier compatriots, it was clear the ComStar leader had gained a keen appreciation for the Clan ways of warfare.

Switching to a private channel, he reached out to directly to Osis. "My Khan, I am receiving reports of ambushers within the pass from my recon elements. I am having them press through while we ascertain their locations."

When he replied, the Khan sounded dismissive. "No need, Star Colonel. I have my forces moving through the pass now. Keep moving forward, as you wanted, and we will crush them for you."

Howell allowed his lips to thin carefully, refusing to respond to the other man's mocking tone. The Khan had not thought much of his plan to run through the pass—considered the ideal striking location against the city—and he remained concerned.

"Star Colonel!" Cantos' voice held an unexpected note of excitement. "We have breached the city!"

Turning his attention back to the battle before him, Howell fired a volley from his right arm PPC before looking at his second monitor, watching as it ripped an armor plate from the shoulder of a ComStar *Wyvern* that quickly ducked back behind the building it was using for cover. "Report, Star Captain."

"Epsilon Star has slipped into the city. They are using hit-and-run tactics to break up the enemy defensive lines."

"Have them advance farther into the city and see if they can get a better look at what we are looking at. Do not have them waste time trying to analyze the data, just have it transferred directly to Diamond Star."

"*Aff*, Star Colonel."

"Also, try to get support to them if they can...if I were the ComStar commander, I would have a hunter/killer squad prepared for just this sort of eventuality."

His warning proved prescient, as he got an urgent message from Epsilon Star only a few seconds later. "Epsilon Star reports engagement...*Black Knight, Wyvern, Crab*..."

"Epsilon Star, pull back to rendezvous with Foxtrot. Confirm."

There was no reply, but the carats denoting the various Epsilon warriors on his secondary screen began retreating, clearly under heavy fire. On the secondary channel he heard Cantos spurring on the Foxtrot warriors, who apparently were also taking fire from the ComStar defenders to keep them from linking up.

For the briefest of moments Howell considered moving his Command Star up to support them, but quickly dismissed the idea, continuing his run toward the city. They were too far behind enemy lines, and his own duties were clear. "Diamond Star, do we have analysis on that data?"

There was a brief pause, and then Star Captain Chilean responded, his careful speech patterns what he had come to expect from the stolid warrior. "Star Colonel, we are reading the equivalent of two Binaries within the city. Additional forces may be hiding deeper near the city center."

Howell's brows furrowed in concern. *That makes no sense—if there are only two Binaries in the city, where are the rest of the ComStar forces?* The last thing ComStar would want would be to fight within the city itself, where the higher damage potential from the Clan 'Mechs would lay waste to tightly-confined city blocks.

Suddenly, a flash priority message cut through the channel. It was from Bold Star, now approaching the far end of the Pass. "Contact! Additional contacts!"

"Bold Star, report!"

"MechWarrior Voss of Hotel Star, Colonel. Star Captain Jihan is down, we have multiple ComStar BattleMechs in the Pass. We are currently engaged."

"Gregor Star is moving to assist, Voss. Can you hold?"

"We have sightings of multiple BattleMechs... at least twenty...two zero—" A burst of static Howell recognized as a near miss by a particle projection cannon erupted over the radio. "We will require reinforcements—"

"Negative, MechWarrior. Continue moving through the pass at full speed. Do not wait for reinforcements...we will cover you on the other end. Star Captain Cantos..."

Cantos did not need to be told his duty. "Iota Star, move down the central pass, provide cover for Gregor and Hotel as they rejoin us."

Howell switched back to his command channel. "My Khan, we have multiple additional ComStar BattleMechs in the pass. I suspect an ambush. I recommend you swing around to meet us where we can provide support."

The response seemed almost perfunctory, as he could sense his Khan's complete focus on the battle ahead. "Fight your own battle, Star Colonel! We will teach these Inner Sphere *surats* what it means to battle the Jaguar!"

Howell swore under his breath, careful to do so in a way that would not trigger his radio, before switching back to Gregor Star. "Star Captain Chilean, can you see the Sixth Jaguar Dragoons?"

"*Aff*, Star Colonel. The Khan is leading them into battle with the ComStar forces."

Once again, Howell cursed the Elemental's lack of caution. The nature of the pass negated the Clan range advantage if the enemy met them here—and at least one portion of the enemy units had been optimized to close with the Jaguars, creating a far more even playing field. Not only that, but as he had feared, many of those units were using their point-blank advantage to fight with physical attacks.

The powerful hand of a ComStar *Hunchback* stabbed into the hip of an *Adder*, stripping the lower hip and upper portion of the thigh straight down to the myomer fibers, then launched a kick that snapped the limb at the titanium bone. The savaged leg crumpled in on itself, sending the *Adder* crashing to the ground, where it strugged to rise again. The *Hunchback* stomped on to its next opponent, a *Stromcrow*, while the pristine *Crockett* following in its wake had no compunction about using its small and large lasers to lacerate the downed 'Mech.

Howell swiveled his torso in a vain attempt to bring his own weapons to bear on his lancemate's killer, but was an instant too slow. The *Crockett* leaped to the air to escape the barrage, its goal already achieved. This time, Howell did allow a choice epithet to slip out: The *Stormcrow* was destroyed, its torso a smoking ruin; the maimed *Adder* had lost nearly half of its armament; and the rest of the Star was completely focused on a single fleeing BattleMech while the additional ComStar forces picked them apart.

He quickly tried to find where the *Crockett* was going to land, eager to claim the BattleMech as his own target, but found himself surrounded by enemies and burning hulks that had once been proud Smoke Jaguar war machines. There was simply more threats than the invading force could deal with, and Howell could see the Clan mindset was causing them to get overwhelmed. The Clan warriors were being assaulted on too many fronts—both literally and mentally—to succeed against the onslaught. They had to pull back, reevaluate their strategy, and preferably bring up reinforcements to crush the Inner Sphere forces against the wall of the pass.

Unfortunately, Howell also knew his Khan too well...Osis would not call for reinforcements until there was no chance of victory, especially against an enemy he thought of as inferior. Even more so, he knew the Khan was also besieged at the moment, and probably in a desperate fight for his life.

"Canto, do you have a visual on the Khan?"

"*Neg*, Star Colonel," the MechWarrior replied. "When last I saw him, his Star was engaged against an Inner Sphere *King Crab*."

"Can you get reinforcements to him? Harassers or snipers?"

"*Neg*," the other man replied, the frustration in his voice evident even over the radio. "I sent harassing forces to break the enemy cordon, but the *surats* are refusing to break! I would have to devote my entire Trinary to breach their defensive lines, probably more. All attempts to provide fire from the top of the pass have also been ineffective: They have heavy units dug into firing positions on either side of the walls of the pass which immediately target any single unit in a crossfire. Their tactics are dishonorable..."

Howell heard what the other man did not say. *But effective.*

The reality was a stark one: Half-measures would not be effective here. If he was to relieve the Khan, he would need to do so with all the forces at his disposal. Unfortunately, that would also mean giving up their best chance for a quick victory in Dinju Heights. He would have to abandon the city to secure the pass, which would force him to fight his way back over here after ensuring his fellow Jaguar warriors were safe.

Howell stifled an instinctive sigh. Normally, the decision would be obvious: Victory was key, and he was within striking range of his objective. Unfortunately, the clear preparations by ComStar rendered his concerns valid, and forced him to reconsider all of his tactical deployments. Not to mention, what other surprises would the ComStar forces have within the city himself? As the preeminent Clan amongst Clans, the wily Anastasius Focht must have devoted significant forces against the Smoke Jaguar threat, knowing it would be the only way he could claim victory.

"Give the Khan what support you can, and hold the door open for them. I want to give him the chance to punch through to us as quickly as possible." About to give further orders, a flash of movement out of the corner of his eye caught Howell's attention. Instinctively reacting from years of training, he hauled back on his controls as a glittering nickel-iron ball the size of his head passed less than a meter in front of his cockpit.

"Additional contacts!" Cantos called out as he fired a burst from his extended range large laser. "The defenders are coming out!"

It was true: the ComStar defenders were pulling out of the city to engage them directly. The *Atlas* that had fired the Gauss round at him was now wreathed in smoke as it fired its long-range missiles at Howell's *Timber Wolf.*

Getting the solid tone as his crosshairs split the assault 'Mech's chest, he pulled the double triggers, sending a third again as many missiles winging out toward the ComStar brawler. The missiles contrails seemed to pass in the air, and he braced himself as the enemy salvo struck his arm and chest, ringing his torso in explosions. Howell managed a feral grin as his own missiles wreathed the *Atlas* in fire, although it was clear that the initial volley had done little against the other 'Mech's thick armor.

He sensed more than saw the rest of his Star begin to choose their own targets, but his own focus stayed on the *Atlas,* clearly one of the command 'Mechs for the city defenders. The immense 100-ton BattleMech, originally designed at the order of the Great Father himself, seemed to taunt him by its very existence, a reminder of all that they had lost when the Star League had fallen.

Carefully watching his heat, Howell switched his PPCs over to chain fire, firing each in sequence, and shot a burst of charged particles into the center of the larger 'Mech's chest, following up with a linked blast from his medium pulse lasers on his secondary target interlock circuit.

The lasers carved armor from the right torso, while the PPC left a glowing wound over the BattleMech's fusion heart. Neither strike penetrated the massive machine's armor, but it was clear he was beginning to have an effect.

In response, the *Atlas* reached out with its quartet of medium lasers, slicing into the *Timber Wolf's* center torso with a pair of emerald lances, boiling away armor as he quickly tried to cut to one side.

Howell was preparing to fire again when Cantos' *Ebon Jaguar* ran past him, briefly cutting across his field of fire. He almost chided the other warrior, but quickly saw the necessity. Cantos' target, a ComStar *Wolverine*, had jumped away from their engagement to combine fire against MechWarrior Kissil's *Stormcrow*.

The *Stormcrow* could usually hold its own against any comers, but it was currently bracketed by the *Wolverine* and a ComStar *Crab*, and had taken a critical amount of damage already. The *Crab*'s claw-mounted large laser lashed out and speared the *Stormcrow* in the lower thigh, cutting deep into the control runs for the leg and causing it to lock up. The medium OmniMech took a final shuddering step, then crashed to the ground. The *Wolverine* was about to capitalize on the downed 'Mech's misfortune when Cantos' LB-X autocannon peppered him, causing the *Wolverine* to turn back to the more immediate threat.

The *Timber Wolf* shook as another shot from the *Atlas'* Gauss rifle struck him in the left torso, nearly stripping the area of its armor. Knowing he had no time to concentrate on his Starmates, Howell reached out with both PPCs, heedless of the heat, and grinned as the scalding wave of hell's own fury reached up into his cockpit. Both PPCs hit, stripping more armor from the center torso and right arm as the *Atlas* fired back with its own medium lasers.

Howell's concentration was on the *Atlas'* broad chest, however. Was it his imagination, or did that PPC blast seem to linger on the center torso? Knowing he had only one chance, he risked tying all his weapons into a single target interlock circuit and waited carefully until his crosshairs locked below the *Atlas'* rictus-headed chin before squeezing the trigger.

As he fired his alpha strike, the *Atlas'* laser suite replied in kind, and his wireframe flashed red as the lasers sliced his left LRM launcher off his 'Mech. To his immense relief, none of the remaining missiles cooked off in sympathetic explosions, and his own missiles were already on their way. Nearly thirty missiles struck the ComStar BattleMech over the head and shoulders, but it was the other weapons that did the most damage. One PPC struck the *Atlas* in its heavily armored center torso again, while the other went wide, slashing over the right leg. Both extended range medium lasers cut into the center torso as well. One of the beams must have lanced deep into it, as the entire mammoth BattleMech seemed to shudder.

Howell cut to the right, attempting to gain a better angle on the approaching 'Mech as it fired its weapons again. LRMs seemed to shoot randomly off into the distance as the *Atlas* moved inside their optimum range, but the Gauss round smashed into his *Timber Wolf*'s right arm, turning the entire wireframe of the shoulder a dangerous amber. A large laser scored his left leg, with the other narrowly missing his cockpit, triggering the auto-tint to keep him from being blinded by the glare.

Howell took a careful breath, savoring the scorching heat in his cockpit before lashing out again with his missiles and medium lasers, as the PPCs would send him into an uncontrolled shutdown if he used them again so soon. His ER medium lasers carved more armor from the torso of the approaching 'Mech, but it was the spread of missiles that clinched the battle, setting off a chain of explosions across the *Atlas*' centerline. Some of the damage must have capitalized on the earlier PPC blasts, for with a screech of tearing metal he could almost feel in his teeth, the *Atlas* collapsed on its left side, clearly suffering the complete destruction of the meticulously balanced gyro that allowed a Mechwarrior's sense of balance to assist the 'Mech in staying upright.

Howell immediately searched for other threats, but it seemed he was momentarily clear. The loss of one of their heaviest 'Mechs had pushed the remaining ComStar skirmishers into retreat, pulling back toward the city limits, while the now-freed Jaguar 'Mechs used their range advantage to force them into full flight.

Glancing around, he attempted to keep track of his fellow warriors, noticing with despair the burning husk of Kissil's *Stormcrow*, as well as the lack of response from either Ax or Bold Star. It took him a moment, but he realized what he did not see: The Jaguar Dragoons.

With his heart sinking deep into his chest, he reached back out to Star Captain Chilean, knowing the other officer would have a better vantage point of the battle. "Star Captain, report."

"We remain engaged with the ComStar forces. It appears the majority of the heavy ComStar 'Mechs were dug into the sides of the Dinju Pass. The Dragoons are being severely pressed."

"Can you support?" Howell immediately regretted even asking the question, knowing Chilean's Trinary was significantly lighter than the opposition.

"We are attempting to hold the path out of the pass open for them, but it is taking all of our efforts. If ordered, we can press forward, but we cannot guarantee our connection to you."

Howell was easily able to read between the lines of what the other warrior was telling him. *We will charge into the gates of hell for you, but we will not be coming back.* As a commander, he had to consider such an option, but dismissed the thought as quickly as it came. There would be no point in such a maneuver, and if the Khan should manage to disengage, he would need those forces to ensure his own safe withdrawal.

"Hold your current position, Star Captain. Maneuver as necessary, but hold the exit open for as long as you can. Has there been any communication from the Khan?"

"*Neg.* I do have a connection to Star Captain Kellas of the Dragoons, however."

Howell vaguely remembered the name as one of Osis' Elementals. "Can you patch us through?"

"*Aff,* Star Colonel." There was a momentary pause that told him the other MechWarrior was still engaged with ComStar forces, forcing him to split his attention.

In a squeal of static, a hearty voice came over the line, one that could only have been produced by the barrel chest of one of the battle-hardy infantrymen. "Star Captain Kellas."

Howell was not surprised to hear the staccato chatter of autocannon fire in the background. A high-pitched screech from what could only be a damaged small laser on the Elemental's battlesuit cut a harsh note against the background din of the battle.

"Star Captain, do you have a visual on the Khan?"

For the briefest of moments, there was silence on the line, and he raised an inquisitive eyebrow at the clear hesitation from the Elemental. Traditionally, the hulking Elementals would show great disdain for their MechWarrior brothers, but very rarely hesitation. For an Elemental, and especially one of Osis' chosen, it was...curious.

"Star Colonel, we have lost communication with the Khan and his Command Star. When last spotted, what was left of his Star was surrounded by the enemy, and he was battling a ComStar *Firestarter*."

Howell felt a flush of emotion, as if his BattleMech had overheated, immediately hearing what the other warrior could not bring himself to say. The *Firestarter* was famous for its ability to kill infantry, even armored infantry, and the Khan would have had little chance against even such a light BattleMech. If he had been forced to take on the enemy alone, so deep behind the ComStar lines...there would be nothing left to find.

Still, proprieties needed to be maintained. "Star Captain, link up with my forward scouts as we push the ComStar forces back to their fortifications. I do not believe we will be able to drive them from their prepared locations yet, but I want to make every effort to find the Khan before we plan our next offensive."

"*Aff,* Star Colonel!" The order clearly surprised the Elemental, who obviously knew of the enmity between his new and former commanders, but he seemed willing to ignore it with the opportunity to potentially find the Khan.

Without hesitation, Howell switched to the main radio channel for the Clan Smoke Jaguar forces. "All forces, this is Star Colonel Brandon Howell. I am taking command as we continue to seek out the Khan. Continue forward, providing cover for your fellow warriors as necessary. When the Inner Sphere forces act dishonorably, do not hesitate to reply in kind. I intend to flush these Inner Sphere *surats* from the pass. We have been tasked with taking this objective, and I intend to do so in the Khan's name!"

The resulting responses over the main channel seemed to crescendo into a very Jaguar-like growl, and he smiled widely as the two commands moved forward as one, any past enmity wiped away by his quick assumption of command in the wake of the Khan's disappearance.

Not to mention that the ComStar warriors had confirmed all of his worst fears about their skill levels. They had held against the might of the Jaguar, and any chance for a surprise attack had evaporated with the ambush in the pass. Not only had the element of surprise been stolen, but they had clearly taken their measure from this assault, and would know the incredible threat the Jaguar provided against their own goals.

As he watched, a pair of ComStar *Archers* began firing their missiles as quickly as their launchers could cycle, clearly unconcerned about the heat buildup. For a moment he was curious, but then he nodded as he saw that the two missile carriers were not aiming at any particular Clan forces.

FASCAM. LRM-deployable minefields. The ComStar 'Mechs were saturating the narrow paths above the pass with submunitions, probably vibramines, intended to detonate when BattleMechs of a certain tonnage traveled over them. Knowing they were there, the Smoke Jaguar forces could avoid them, but that was not their purpose: The Inner Sphere warriors were using them as an area-denial weapon, forcing his forces to expend energy trying to avoid the mines, preferably so they could provide easy targets for long-range weapons.

Although he could not see the top of the pass any longer, Howell didn't doubt that the ComStar warriors had learned their lesson, and were doing the same thing on the narrow corridors his forces had originally used to attack the city. Any attempt to pass through them now would be a slow, grueling slog into the heavy weaponry of entrenched ComStar defenders. They were trying to cut off the two forces.

If *only* the Khan had followed Howell's advice, and the two forces had attacked in tandem! They could have broken through into the city, moving too quickly for the Inner Sphere forces, and where ComStar would not have risked mining the streets. Unfortunately, now they were forced take a more cautious route, all while the ComStar forces had the opportunity to call in more reinforcements. While he considered a Jaguar warrior to be worth any three Inner Sphere warriors, he was not foolish enough to bet his already-damaged forces against fresh reinforcements.

Even more concerning, he was beginning to get reports that some of the weapons fire was coming from ranges that were nearly comparable with Clan weaponry. That seemed to confirm his own observations: Some of the ComStar Battlemechs, including a handful that had not been seen in the Inner Sphere since the fall of the Star League, might be using Star League-era technology. It only made sense: If the Inner Sphere had any remaining access to such equipment, they would surely throw it at the greatest threat they had ever faced. It also partially answered his question as to why the other "Great Houses" had not taken Terra away from ComStar long ago: With access to such BattleMechs and equipment, plus the powerful Star League-era fortifications that still dotted the birthworld of humanity, there was little chance that the obsolete, constantly-repaired hulks that made up the bulk of the House armies could have had an effect.

Suddenly, the newfound caution in the Elemental's voice made sense. With the Khan apparently out of commission, and no word from the Smoke Jaguar's Loremaster, Howell was the highest-ranking member of the surviving command structure.

For the briefest of moments, he allowed his gaze to return to Dinju Heights, haloed in gold by the setting sun, and felt a stab of instinctive regret. Despite his confident words, he was no longer sure he could take the city in the fashion he would have chosen, knowing that he had just lost the best opportunity for a swift conquest. From the quick rundown he could see on his secondary monitor, the Khan's Sixth Jaguar Dragoons—correction, *his* Sixth Jaguar Dragoons—had taken heavy casualties in the pass, and would need to repair and rearm before they could press forward against the city again. His own Grenadiers were doing significantly better, but their numbers would be affected with this thrust, and he would soon have to pull them back as well.

Still, while they might not find the victory they had expected, there might be a new opportunity looming. If he could pull his forces back from the edge of this defeat, he might be able to turn the current stalemate into a victory for himself. After all, the Khan was the one who had brought them to this point, not Howell, and if he could convince the Khan's own forces of that, there was little chance he could not convince the rest of the Clan.

Perhaps it was time for new leadership to take over, to prepare for their impending victory over the Inner Sphere and their inevitable thrust toward Terra.

"Star Captain Kellas, I am ordering the Sixth Jaguar Dragoons to pull back out of the Dinju Pass any way they are able. My forces are holding the far side of the pass. Can you reach them?"

Once again, there was a hesitation, but this time it was born out of an intense sound of frustration. "*Neg*, Star Colonel. Opposition is too heavy in that direction. If we are to regroup, we will need to link back up with our BattleMech forces."

Which, of course, were behind them. Howell shook his head in what under any other circumstances would be amusement. "Understood. Proceed to disengage. We will rendezvous with your forces at Rally Point Charlie."

The Elemental confirmed that he had passed along the order, and Howell quickly switched over to his own direct channel to Star Captain Chilean. "I have ordered the Dragoons to pull back to Rally Point Charlie. Hold the pass for another ten minutes if you are able, then rendezvous with the rest of our unit."

"*Aff*, Star Colonel. And the Khan?"

Howell smiled tightly before ratcheting his OmniMech up to speed and heading for the thickest of the fighting, his own Starmates instinctively turning to support him in his charge. "We will give the Khan every chance to join us, but if he is no longer able, I intend to take this victory in his name."

Once again, the Star Captain confirmed the order. If he had any concerns about it, he wisely chose to keep them to himself.

Which is only right, Howell thought. *Today will be a new beginning for the Smoke Jaguars, and all of the Clans.* The Battle for Dinju Pass might not be a victory for the Clan, but it would still go down in history as a historic turning point for the Smoke Jaguars.

Howell silently vowed that no matter what happened, the name Tukayyid would go down in The Remembrance as one of the first steps towards the true destiny of Clan Smoke Jaguar.

After all, he thought, *the Jaguar can be patient...when it has to be...*

SHADOW OF DEATH

RANDALL N. BILLS

LOSIIJE VALLEY
BOREAL CONTINENT
TUKAYYID
FREE RASALHAGUE REPUBLIC
1 MAY 3052

The DropShip exploded.

Torian Nostra watched in shocked disbelief as eleven thousand, six hundred tons of war-forged machine, fifty meters above the ground, tore itself apart in an orgy of fiery destruction that briefly eclipsed the bright sun over the Losiije Valley.

Only recently grounded on the world of Tukayyid—three hours after the start of the contest between the Com Guards and the Clans to decide the fate of hallowed Terra—Torian's fingers remained clenched on the controls of his 'Mech. The scene burned into his retinas, as though he was a young child staring too long at the sun, despite a *sibko*-trainer's harsh fists to the contrary.

Eighty-eight Clusters from seven Clans were facing off against seventy-two Com Guard Divisions in the largest single conflict ever fought by the Clans, and the Nova Cats had just lost three entire Galaxies before the fight had even begun! Long seconds stretched to eternity as a pit opened wide within him.

Was that part of it?! The horror of it stretched his skin until it beat like a drum in rhythm with his heart, and his jaw ached as a snarl twisted his face. The abrupt metal rain across his position—the remains of several dozen of Alpha Galaxy's finest warriors—broke the tension, and he slumped momentarily at the release. Despite the half-kilometer distance, his 'Mech swayed as the destructive energy of the *Overlord-C*'s wreckage hammered into the prairie, setting flashfires as it carved out a blast crater, and undulated out across the battlefield.

Outside his viewport, a mere forty meters away, a *Stormcrow* raised its arm, vomiting metal flechettes from its LB-X autocannon at the swarming gnats of Com Guard aerospace fighters returning fire: the sheer chaos of battle engulfing the entire valley. The striking black camo scheme, with a swath of blue nebula and stars along the chest of the OmniMech, told him at least some of Alpha Galaxy had performed a hover-drop maneuver before the destruction of their DropShip. The pilot's smart and efficient movements spoke louder than a voice in his ear. Star Captain Mia Attwater. Her confident actions immediately brought him back to himself. *It was a Com Guard aerospace fighter pilot that destroyed the* Cat's Maw. *Nothing more.*

Torian manipulated his right-hand joystick and the right arm-mounted Gauss rifle of his fearsome *Shadow Cat* moved skyward. The golden targeting reticule on the forward viewscreen matched up with the bright, white spec of a Com Guard aerospace fighter arrowing across the field; his computer tagged it as a 30-ton *Spad*. Computer-aided math, along with his genetic predisposition and a lifetime of harsh training across worlds a thousand light years from this one, lined up a shot well ahead of the aircraft. The nickel-ferrous slug discharged in front of a wave of electromagnetic energy and flew true, smashing into the craft, tearing away slabs of armor that flashed as they gyrated toward the ground.

The first smile of the Trueborn Nova Cat warrior blossomed since he'd touched down. His left hand moved the throttle forward and he sped across the field, gaining better positions to eliminate the fighters harassing their position.

The burden would come to claim him soon enough. For now...the hunt.

CONGRESS-CLASS FRIGATE *TRUE VISION*
UNINHABITED STAR SYSTEM
PERIPHERY
2 JANUARY 3050

Light from the nearest star, ten AU below their feet, washed the stark docking collar chamber in harsh shadows as their eyes fought its orange wavelength. *Or perhaps my eight decades are finally catching up to me.*

Though it was difficult to stand among the best and brightest of their leadership and not feel the Clan's ageism press against him, Severen Leroux kept an impassive face, but chided his self-deprecation. As the DropShip with its unusual passenger bled off the last of its velocity before docking, his eyes roved over those gathered for the reception.

Leo Showers. The Smoke Jaguar Khan stood easily among the others, his well-muscled body seemingly relaxed, his mane of black hair swept back off the tattoo on his forehead as it cascaded into small plaits that fell around his shoulders.

His piercing light-green eyes momentarily caught Severen's, and a flash of something sparked before Leo fixed his gaze on the docking collar. *I am not at all surprised, Leo, by your audacity in meeting this enemy in secret.* He begrudgingly conceded the boldness and intelligence required to seize on the offered transmission. *But we all underestimated you, didn't we?* Leo's resplendent uniform of the ilKhanship spoke of that underappreciated political acumen. *The eyes. It's always in the eyes, and even I forgot it.*

After nearly a quarter of a millennium, the Smoke Jaguar Khan had been the one to lead the Clans back to conquer the thousands of Inner Sphere worlds. The arrow forged by the Founder was drawn and ready to be loosed at the heart of the corruption that had destroyed the original Star League.

And if the Periphery worlds they'd just finished conquering in preparation for the start of Wave One Operations into the so-called Great Houses were any indication... *I've always trusted your visions, Biccon. How could you let us down in our time of greatest glory?!* Severen's chest constricted with the disappointment of being a reserve Clan; he refused to look at his Oathmaster standing at his side.

To keep his thoughts at bay, he contemplated the rest of the company. One of the oldest men of the group (*still young by my standards!*), the Khan of Clan Jade Falcon filled his Clan's black, green, and yellow uniform admirably. Elias Crichell adjusted his jacket three times in the few moments Severen watched, then ran his hand back through his luxurious white hair.

He preens almost as much as their namesake. Severen worked to keep a sneer from his face for such ostentatiousness before a new thought intruded. *Unlike Leo Showers, all know of Elias' political savvy.* If there was one more individual most responsible for leveraging the accidental discovering of the Clan Homeworlds by ComStar's *Outbound Light* JumpShip into the Grand Council voting for war, it was Elias. He stood alone. *He has no need of support. And could convince a Blood Spirit to accept a Dark Caste in their midst. I must remember that.*

Almost directly across from Elias stood Khan Karl Bourjon and his saKhan Theresa Delvillar; her long, dark dreadlocks almost seemed a flourish next to Karl's tight cap of light brown hair. Theresa kept her eyes down as she spoke quietly, but the Ghost Bear Khan stood impassively listening—hardly speaking a word versus her steady stream—arms crossed as though an immovable object for today's unusual proceedings. *He is one filled with the spirit of his totem.*

The final occupant of the room—beyond a Point of requisite Elemental guards—stood with a smirk on his face. Instead of a full, resplendent Clan Wolf uniform, Garth Radick wore a field uniform of green shirt and mottled gray and green cargo pants tucked tightly into brown boots, with the magnetic slips clamped on the bottom that kept them all firmly in place as the WarShip parked at the nadir jump point of the system.

Clan Wolf did not even send their Khan. You play a dangerous game, Ulric. You failed in the Grand Council and in the Trial of Refusal to stop this invasion. And you use every moment to slight the ilKhan and his supporters. Yet you have chosen to fight in our return, and you even beat the Smoke Jaguars in their Periphery timetable. What are you up to? You can only play the lone wolf for so long.

Then again, the ilKhan had thrown around his own slights, as he'd not invited either the Steel Viper or Diamond Shark Khans—the other two reserve Clans—to this strange meeting. *And we are only here after much adroit wrangling of egos.* Anger roiled Severen's stomach at his companion once more, and he momentarily closed his eyes. Breathed out deeply. *Including my own.*

A *clang* rang through the chamber as the DropShip met the docking collar. This close to the pressure equalization, Severen's ears popped, and the sound of exchanging air hissed while the entire assembly seemed to stand taller. *As though we are fearful? Of one man? From an organization that only controls a world?* But even his own words echoed falsely. *But the world they control is the most important jewel in the universe.*

The docking hatch slowly cycled open, and Severen's saKhan, Lucian Carns, carefully walked into the meeting. Glancing around at the assembled leadership of the Clans, he marginally nodded his head to acknowledge the presence of the ilKhan, and then stepped aside to allow his passenger entry.

An old man with a heavily lined face, a black eyepatch, and white, shoulder-length hair stepped onto the *True Vision*, his white uniform shocking against the vibrant colors of his awaiting audience.

The surprised looks that flashed across the assembled Khans' faces spoke volumes. In a culture where growing old meant failing as a warrior, this man was ancient. *Perhaps older than I am.* Then again, his Nova Cats had always been considered odd amongst the Clans. That their Khan outpaced everyone else by two decades only cemented such eccentricities in their minds.

As some of the Khans' faces settled into sneers of contempt, Severen studied the strength in the man's bearing, despite his age and the obvious weight of leadership. More importantly, the eyes...or eye, in this case. Always pay attention to the eyes. *This Precentor Martial Anastasius Focht is far more than he seems. He is...a dangerous man—*

"AAAHHHHH!" The animalistic howl that erupted at his side caused Severn to jerk to the right, and actually lose his left foot's magnet strip. Horror at the breach of protocol crawled up his neck and onto his bald pate as his Oathmaster's small, wiry frame launched off the deck and shot forward in the micro gravity. Even the two Elemental guards behind Focht froze, along with everyone else, at the shocking maneuver.

Before anyone could react further, she had twisted in midair—his mind cataloged the oddity of her clutching magnetic slips in her hands—tucking herself into a ball as she slammed into Focht's chest. The speed and ferocity of the maneuver toppled the man backward, momentum levering him off his own mag slips and tilting him downward, before they tore free.

Bunched up, as though a feline straddling her kill, they neared the deck, and she maneuvered her left foot onto Focht's neck, right leg tamping tight to the right-side of his chest, while she reached forward past his head to slam her magslips onto the deck, securing them in place.

"This is the black cloud!" she howled, looking over her shoulder at Severen and then onto the rest of the Clans. "He will destroy us, as I have foreseen and as I have foretold!" The feverish light in her eyes seemed to glow as the Precentor's face began moving from red into purple under the constriction of oxygen.

Shame burning his skin—even as foreboding prickled along his arms—Severen moved forward, having finally reattached his left foot to the deck. "Oathmaster—what have you done?!" He tried grabbing her, and she hunkered down, as a feral beast did to protect its kill. Fire seared his arms, her fingernails clawing him as she batted away his attempts to seize her.

"Remove her!" the deep voice of ilKhan Leo Showers bellowed. The two Elementals moved forward, and for a moment, despite their towering size and strength over Biccon, she managed to retain her position choking the life out of the ComStar ambassador.

"We will be destroyed!" she screamed through foam-flecked lips. "The black cloud will destroy us all! You must listen!"

Finally, one of the Elementals chopped down across the back of her neck, instantly sending her into oblivion. They pulled her off the ambassador, letting her momentarily float as they helped the Precentor Martial to his feet.

Severen was torn between watching two events. The Precentor Martial for a frown or creased brow to indicate this explosive situation had soured a potential powerful relationship between the Clans and the controller of all Inner Sphere faster-than-light communications before it had even begun. And at the unconscious form of his Oathmaster, dragged through the air by her hair toward who knew what.

He shivered as those feelings of forebodings and shame continued warring within him. *What have you done, Biccon? What have you done?*

NORTH LOSIIJE, LOSIIJE VALLEY
BOREAL
TUKAYYID
FREE RASALHAGUE REPUBLIC
2 MAY 3052

The magnetized sandstorm occluded sensors and cut vision to less than a hundred meters. Torian saw a shadow flit toward him and let fly with a Gauss slug, which tore a furrow in the ferrocrete of the long, lonely highway before skipping off into the sandy curtains and beyond his sight.

"Star Commander?!" his immediate superior's voice was filled with urgency.

"*Neg*, Star Captain," he said sheepishly. "I thought..." he couldn't bring himself to say it.

After less than forty-eight hours on planet, already the Clans knew this fight would be far different than anything they'd expected. The uncertainty of the terrain, combined with the strange storm, strung out the moving Nova Cat column, allowing the Com Guards to strike when least expected. Much less the horror of losing so much of Alpha Galaxy on day one. The secret he carried burned as a fire brand on his skin. If he had ever doubted in the last few weeks, the truth of the Oathmaster's vision towered ominously over the sky.

"Understood," came the soft response. Torian breathed a sigh of relief, fingers clenching over and over against the hard plastic of the right-hand joystick and left-handle throttle, feet nervously tapping pedals that caused his *Shadow Cat* to move slightly to the left and right as it loped through the landscape, waiting for the next attack.

The hours of the day dragged on as they moved forward, ever closer to the cities of Joje and Trost. The targets they must capture to win their portion of this fight.

When will I see my sign? When will my time come? The hours frayed the nerves as the weight settled more firmly across his shoulders.

MERCHANT-CLASS JUMPSHIP *VISION'S PRICE*
NADIR JUMP POINT
ALTENMARKT
(CLAN WOLF CONTROLLED)
10 FEBRUARY 3052

Torian Nostra sat cross-legged on the deck of his Khan's quarters, microhooks along the back of his pant legs adhering to the patch of floor prepared for this moment.

They were mere weeks away from the Trial of Possession to be fought against the Com Guards, with ancient Terra as its prize. The thrill of it boiled in his veins. Combined with the awe of sitting in a circle of a vision quest with the other three warriors and his Khan: heady emotions undulated until he felt he floated in a warm ocean, the sun kissing his skin, a salty breeze a caress of contentment and pure joy.

In the center of the gathered five, a small flame flickered in a crucible. *Not the roaring fire of a traditional ceremony. But we Nova Cats always adapt.*

Severen's visage swept over them, his mien capturing their attention with its power. "I have watched you for years, my warriors," he began, voice barely a whisper.

Torian leaned forward. He dared not miss a word. The visions and portents of the last few days had been paramount no matter where he looked. Or what work he did biding their time as their JumpShip traversed the stars toward waiting Tukayyid and the planet of their coming victory.

"Your hearts are pure. Your skills renowned. Your visions long ago calling you to the attention of myself and the Oathmaster."

Torian struggled to keep a smile from his face—noted others losing that battle—as the compliments landed one after another. *The Oathmaster watches me?!* He nearly crooned with the joy of it all.

"I come now to you to share a burden that only the Oathmaster and I have shared. An axial moment is before us, upon which our entire existence revolves. You will be required to do a hard thing. To bear a secret and accomplish a task that would shatter lesser warriors."

His Khan paused, the room utterly silent but for the ebb of commotion outside of the berth vibrating through the plating of the deck. They seemed set apart from their fellow warriors in this moment. Initiated into something greater only they could see and understand. But Torian's elation eased toward concern as that silence stretched and the pain in their Khan's eyes reached out to draw them in.

Severen opened his mouth and as the words passed the terrible burden to these gathered few, the weight and the horror bore them down until only the whites of their eyes shown and their teeth bared in snarls as the darkness and terror threatened, and only the small, flickering flame on the deck—mirroring the light of Torian's own visions within— kept him from running into the bulkhead until it burst his head in relief.

LOSIIJE LAKE, LOSIIJE VALLEY
BOREAL CONTINENT
TUKAYYID
FREE RASALHAGUE REPUBLIC
4 MAY 3052

Torian watched the strange fish swim beyond the ferroglass. Its primary-colored yellow and green markings stood out powerfully against the pure blue of the lake, especially as early morning sunlight slanted down through the top of the calm waters.

"Go!" The command roared through the comm. The entire Trinary, hidden in the depths of Lake Losiije, surged forward— the fish swimming amongst the OmniMechs after the long hours of waiting in the water's depths, scattered away— clawing up out of the lake.

Water cascaded down his viewport as the bright sunlight burst across the view of the shoreline now in full sight. Torian brought his Gauss rifle onto target and pulled into the trigger, firing a nickel-ferrous slug at a Com Guard *Thug* standing perfectly still. The round shattered armor, making the 80-ton 'Mech shiver. Of the dozen BattleMechs in immediate view, only two others moved in response to the ambush.

Despite the secret he bore and the moment he knew would soon arrive, he relished lashing out at the hated enemy that had ravaged so much of his Clan already. He sent another Gauss rifle round toward the powered down *Thug*, while a brace of incoherent beams from his medium lasers stabbed at the armored vehicles at the machine's feet. One beam slashed a furrow through the ground before connecting with a J-27 ammo resupply truck. A massive explosive swept Com Guard personnel unto death in its embrace, tossing the *Thug* to the ground in a smoldering heap, the powerful shock wave even causing Torian to struggle in the shallow waters at the edge of the lake for a moment.

He immediately lined up for another shot against a *King Crab* whose own Gauss rifles were dealing damage with vicious precision. But the tables had already been turned, and this battle, at least, would be a quick and decisive massacre in favor of the Nova Cats.

CONGRESS-CLASS FRIGATE *TRUE VISION*
STAR'S END
15 JANUARY 3050

Severen stood in the hatchway of the small berth. Hesitant. Fingered the shallow scratches on his arm. He took a deep breath of the redolent stink of warriors too long on a WarShip that had spent the better part of a year crossing a thousand light-years, and then waited through the initial months of battles his Clan was denied. He shuffled his feet, fidgeting for a moment more before slapping a hand on his thigh at his timidity.

He decisively stepped inside Oathmaster Biccon Winters' assigned quarters, turned and dogged the hatch closed before facing her again.

The diminutive woman sat facing him, as though expecting the visit. She bore the ugly bruises on her face and bare arms as a badge—as would any Clanner—and her eyes still carried the depth of...*knowing*. Of *understanding* that only an Oathmaster of Clan Nova Cat, with her powerful visions, could acquire.

Eyes matched force for force before Severen conceded the moment; after all, he was the one who had come calling. The foreboding of that moment of her assault on the Precentor Martial had only grown, despite attempts to vanquish it, impelling him here.

"I see your bruises are healing from your failed Trial of Refusal."

She raised her chin, as though to show them off further. "SaKhan Carns felt a need to be...extra strident in his victory over my attempts to stop the invasion."

Severen cocked his head, as though unsure how to proceed. After all, he believed as his saKhan did. *Then why am I here?*

"For generations," he began, voice loud to his ears, "we have bred and trained ourselves for this moment. The Founder crafted us, and drew us, and aimed us at this crux in time. We are here to punish the *stravag* House Lords and their evil that destroyed the Star League."

Silence met his words.

"We are a sword forged in the fire of our righteous cause, quenched in the blood of thousands of warriors."

Silence, as her eyes seemed to grow bright as stars, burrowing into his skin.

"We are here to conquer and to raise the flag of the hallowed Star League once again—"

"Why are you here?" Biccon spoke.

Expecting an assault against his words, he felt caught off guard at her flanking maneuver. Exposed. Naked before the eyes of the finest Oathmaster the Nova Cats ever decanted.

He opened his mouth again, and to his chagrin, nothing came out.

She slowly stood and moved toward him, her sinuous grace evoking the nova cat, her eyes as large and unblinking and knowing as any feline. He towered over the bruised, small woman, and yet he flinched as she reached her hand out to place it on his chest. An electric spark bound them as one, goosebumps dimpling his flesh and standing his hair on end.

"You have come because you see," she practically whispered, and yet the words echoed like a shout in his ears.

He shook his head, opening his mouth and once more, could find no words, as a tingling ran along his scalp and swept down his spine, a storm of energy that almost made her touch painful on his chest.

"You do not want to see. You want to rush off to the glory that beckons you along the path the other Clans run down with abandon. But you *do* see, my Khan."

She closed her eyes, and Severen nearly trembled in relief, feeling as though 'Mech-scale searchlights had turned away from him. But her face transformed into the statuesque woman of prophecy that stood at the end of the Nova Cat's Chronicle of Battles only a few months before, and her voice pitched as though to carry across the frenzied dancing field and she recited, word for word—intonation for intonation—the vision that he'd ignored, as they all had:

"I saw the cat attacking by the hundreds, flanked only by the bear, the wolf, the jaguar, the falcon, and the shark. Our enemy still stood divided, and had not yet fallen—I knew that we would earn glory early in the war. I saw a burning rain of

fire that struck from the sky in wanton destruction of people and resources—I knew our enemy would stand fast against the Clans. I saw a black cloud threatening the cat—I knew an older enemy than the Inner Sphere sought to overwhelm us."

Her words evoked a call from deep within. Severen had doubted. For the first time in his life, he had doubted his Oathmaster. Despite decades of unerring service and visions that had ultimately led the Nova Cats through the Revival Trials and into the Inner Sphere...still, he had doubted.

She opened her eyes and once more, their searchlight intensity speared straight into his soul; he rattled within the husk of his body, trying to escape, but knowing the jail was ironclad. "The shadow of death hangs over all of the Clans. It hangs over the Nova Cats. And...you...know it."

Despite the years of command and his towering presence, Severen's legs buckled and he slid to his knees. His stiff-necked warrior pride fought a moment longer in the hardest decision of his life. But he slowly bent his neck, and felt the cooling balm of her hand rest upon his brow.

"I believe..." he whispered. "I finally believe. But no one else will. The Founder's call to glory is etched into every blood cell. Into our very souls. You carry that conviction imprinted on your body from my own saKhan. Even now, its siren song pulls at me."

He couldn't bring himself to look at her, ashamed of his previous actions that had so fully ostracized her; ashamed of his own weakness, even now.

"There is yet a path out of this valley of death," she continued. "I see something, yet still darkly. There are decades ahead for the Clans as we enmesh ourselves in the fight for the soul of mankind. Decades that will see the broken corpses of most Clans discarded along the way, forgotten to history. If we are to survive, I believe we will need to morph into something...different. Something new."

He swallowed past the dry mouth and the unease of pinpricks running along his skin. Looked up as Biccon pulled away her hand. "How can *they* believe that?"

"Why did our ancestors follow the Founder?" The hurt in her eyes contained an ocean of sympathy. As though she'd seen something not yet in his focus. And was there to share the burden when it arrived.

"Because it was right."

"No."

"Because he was a leader that would make things right."

"No."

"Because..."

"No," she interrupted kindly, eyes once more burrowing into his, forcing him to search deep inside himself. Decades of teaching and history rolled through his memories, and nausea slowly climbed until he panted with the pain of it. It felt blasphemous to even speak such things, but she drew them out as though a surgeon drawing poison from a wound.

"Because the Star League soldiers had almost been destroyed. The Pentagon Worlds were in flames as the Civil War destroyed the Great Father and turned his dream to ashes. And there was no alternative. They followed the Founder because...there was no other option but death."

"Such is the path of most enlightenment," she responded gently, sharing the pain of *knowing* in this moment.

At any other time, Severen would balk at such tenderness. It was un-Clan like. And yet, in this private moment, as he shared just a brief glimpse of the vision she'd borne as a mocked pariah...his awe of her expanded to new depths.

"There will come a time," she said, nodding as his understanding finally synched with hers, "during Operation Revival, in months or in years, I do not yet see, when the Nova Cats—when all of the Clans—will face this ComStar. And in that moment, we must be blooded as we have never been in our history. And when our glory and our *touman* have been crushed in the blood of our broken warriors, and our dreams are as cold and dead as the Great Father—then maybe, just *maybe*, as our hollowed Bloodname forebearers before us, we can find the path to transformation. And survive."

For the first time in seventy-two years, tears welled and fell as Severen bowed his head, wracked with grief at the unholy burden placed upon his shoulders.

JOJE, LOSIIJE VALLEY
BOREAL CONTINENT
TUKAYYID
FREE RASALHAGUE REPUBLIC
6 MAY 3052

Sweat slicked Torian Nostra's face as he breathed in his own stench. With only a few hours of sleep captured in snatches over the last several days he ached with weariness. And yet, the moment he'd been waiting for had arrived. A sign he'd seen in his vision. Another might have missed it in the chaos of battle and sleep deprivation. Yet to his eyes it stood out as though a beacon.

"Star Commander," a voice spoke across the comm. "We have found a way in!"

Torian tore his eyes away from the feline graffiti splashed across the side of the decrepit building and toward his Starmate, Jix, and her *Huntsman* OmniMech that had just kicked in the wall. The partial collapse showed a 'Mech-sized tunnel running off toward the distant city of Joje and the impenetrable walls that had thwarted the onslaught of the Nova Cats for long hours.

"Our Star can come up behind the walls and wreak havoc. We can yet carry the day, Commander."

"*Aff*," Nostra responded absent-mindedly as his hand reached forward and toggled on the communications scrambler he'd secretly installed on his 'Mech during the in-system burn over a week ago.

Jix died in the flash of a Gauss round fired point blank into her cockpit, and a second warrior was assassinated just as quickly as his Star stood momentarily frozen. His final two subordinates overcame their shock and began returning fire as he danced death among his remaining Starmates. *My friends.*

He kept the horror of his actions at a distance, enraptured with the shared burden placed upon his shoulders by his Khan and Oathmaster, as he sprinted in a tight circle, throttle nearly full, weapons blazing as he wove between the two. Armor exploded and burned away in rivulets as the knife-fight of such a short-range combat exploded in abject brutality.

He knew he would die in this moment, as the portents had foretold. But he would carry these final two warriors to death as well. And in doing so, would ensure the Nova Cats would crush themselves against the walls of Joje. And in the death of all he had known, yet still would the Nova Cats survive.

Somehow, somewhere, somewhen, long from this day.

A thunderous explosion blew through his cockpit and he had only a flash of agony, buoyed by the death of his final Starmate and the completion of his task, before blackness swept it all away.

LOSIIJE VALLEY
BOREAL CONTINENT
TUKAYYID
FREE RASALHAGUE REPUBLIC
8 MAY 3052

Hannibal. Khan. Charlemagne. Patton. McKenna. Kerensky.

The litany ran through Severen Leroux's mind. An anchor keeping his body erect on the DropShip ramp as the last of his bedraggled survivors clawed their way off the blood-drenched soil of Tukayyid in preparation for liftoff. His right leg trembled from the bruising during a PPC strike that had almost ended his life, and his left arm was in a flash-cast for the shrapnel that had torn off most of the flesh; he'd refused the medical drip to dull the pain, as it was his to bear for what he'd done.

Never had the seven decades of his life weighed more heavily or caused more doubt than in this moment. He stilled the trembling through sheer force of will and stood ramrod straight, raising right fist to his chest as the last horribly battle-scarred BattleMechs trudged up the ramp.

Each metal avatar raised a limb in salute.

It was almost more than he could bear.

Tukayyid would ring down through history. Just as those mighty generals were remembered through all time for their supernal acumen, so too would the campaign for Tukayyid.

But there was another list. Just as heralded, if for opposite reasons. *Crassus. Zhao. Burnside. Luchesi.* Generals whose incompetence and blundering had earned them a mocking place in history.

An *Arctic Cheetah* limped onto the ramp as the last survivor. It was hardly recognizable underneath the damage; its entire left torso and left arm were gone, while the right arm dangled in a web of burst myomer muscles and shattered internal structure. Yet somehow the warrior made the 'Mech stand taller as it passed his Khan.

The ache of two years, and its furious capstone of the last eight days, burst in a torrent that swept through him, and for a moment tears threatened and his leg tremor returned. *My name will be added to that list. I will be derided till the end of time as the worst Clan commander in history.* The pride of seventy years of Clan upbringing surged and fought to tear free from the chains he'd placed on them two years ago.

He struggled for breath as he closed his eyes, on the verge of shaming himself further by collapsing in front of his warriors. *Fifteen 'Mechs. Of three Galaxies, of the finest Nova Cat troops, my warriors...fifteen survived.* The death of the four he'd initiated into his cabal to aid in these events carried extra pain, despite the paramount need for their demise, as even a whiff of this truth would turn the other Clans on them in a frenzied Trial of Annihilation. *All by my hand.*

And yet...

He breathed in the sweat and blood and burned metal and alien fauna of this cursed planet. The confidence of a shared vision with his Oathmaster calming the raging beast within. Despite doubts. Despite the horror he'd orchestrated upon his own Clan—and in a way, upon all of the Clans—calm eased a balm across a shattered ego and wrenched soul and bruised body. The assurance that he *had* shared that vision. That it would come to pass. That without this terrifying humbling of his Clan, they would pass away as dust into the forgotten pages of history.

He also believed the Oathmaster's declarations that at another pivotal moment in time—perhaps years and years from now—the Nova Cats would be called to choose a completely new path. A path that would lead to their salvation. And they would only be ready for it by this catastrophic loss of bodies piled up as high as DropShips and left to rot under an alien sun.

And if my name must be derided for all time among unbelievers...

Severen opened his eyes, the tears unshed, and turned away from the universe to *his* warriors and *his* Clan and to *his* friends, his gait strong under the crushing mantle of the weight he would bear into the grave and history and beyond— all so that his people would survive.

THE BURDENS OF HONOR

BLAINE LEE PARDOE

**GHOST BEAR FORWARD POST
WEST OF LUK
TUKAYYID
FREE RASALHAGUE REPUBLIC
1 MAY 3052**

Adam sat before his large, leatherbound book and carefully painted letters on the page with slow, meticulous strokes. The lantern hanging from the single hook inside his portable dome danced off the green walls as he worked. He had spent much of his life in the field, or so it felt. This was different. Now he was with the Ghost Bears, a bondsman, captured and made prisoner years earlier. This was a test of his mettle, his patience, and his cunning.

He heard his bondholder, Star Commander Cymril Tseng, enter the dome behind him and felt his looming presence as he finished a stroke, pleased that his hand did not pause or tremble. He had become so familiar with Cymril he could even smell his sweat.

"Your contribution to the Great Work is quite full," the Star Commander said. "Have you finished this part of the story yet, *quineg?*"

"*Neg,*" Adam replied, putting the quill down to allow the page to dry. The book had nearly a thousand pages, each one intricately filled right to the borders with ornate formal lettering of *kanji* and *kana*. "Such tales have are complicated, and the hero I write about has much to learn. I have not found the right ending for it yet."

Clan Ghost Bear placed emphasis on the arts; warriors were encouraged to pursue the creation of great works to honor their clan. They referred to such art as the Great Work. It was one of the things he respected about the Ghost Bears. They were more than genetically constructed and finely-honed warriors. The Great Work gave them a hint of humanity. The book Adam wrote was his...but it was also much more. *It is my grip on the calm of a* samurai; *my last vestige of sanity over what I have endured.*

Adam had been *Tai-i* Adam Kaningamu two years earlier, a loyal servant of the Dragon and hero of the Draconis Combine. Then the Ghost Bears had come from beyond the Periphery, and he and his fellow MechWarriors had gone out to face them. On Constance, he had fought with distinction and honor, and had been made a bondsman to Cymril Tseng, who had bested him in battle.

Since then I have walked a different path, a unique journey. Adam had considered *seppuku*, taking his honor with him into the afterlife. The clan called it *bondsref*, but it was the same thing, a ritual suicide. It would have ended his shame at having been made a prisoner of the Ghost Bears.

A nagging voice in the back of his mind told him that this was the best way to serve the Dragon...that his path was different than most men. He could have been left to die or worse, Dispossessed, but instead, he was still alive.

So Adam did the unthinkable—he'd adapted. He forcibly became part of the Ghost Bears, but the spirit of the Dragon still burned in his soul.

He had come to respect the Bears. They were not so different from the MechWarriors of the Combine. Honor reigned in the Ghost Bears, more than the other Clans, or so he was led to believe. Ritual defined life in the Clans, and he struggled for a time to master them. Even how they spoke required rethinking everything he knew. He worked hard to rewire his thinking to a Clan mentality, without losing who he really was inside. *The Dragon is still with me, but it is covered in the pelt of the Ghost Bears.*

"It is a shame none of my people can read Japanese," Tseng said. "I should like to read the story you are writing someday."

"Perhaps when this invasion is over, Star Commander," Adam said, marking the page with a swath of red fabric he had taken from *Sho-sho* Riku Kondo's fallen *nobori* and slowly closing the book.

"Then it may be soon," Cymril said with a wide grin. "This fight will seal our victory over the Inner Sphere."

Adam nodded obediently. "I am bound to you and your fate, Star Commander," he said glancing at his bondcord. "As you have said many times, I serve the Ghost Bears. My free will is not mine, but that of the Clan."

His was the life of indentured servitude. Everything from his former life had been lost. Even his beloved *wakizashi*, presented by the Coordinator himself, was now worn by his bondkeeper. His rank, his family, his past—everything had been taken from him in his new life of servitude. All that was left was his secret devotion to the Combine. *The Dragon always prevails, regardless of the tests life puts on its servants.*

Cymril put a beefy hand on Adam's shoulder. "You have deemed yourself honorable in the eyes of the Ghost Bears. The time may yet come when I sever that bondcord. These Com Guards are an unknown quantity. All able warriors may be needed in this battle."

Com Guards. Hai! *My grandfather was never fooled by all of their mysticism and techno-chanting—he always said they were a danger. Now we see the full extent of what they were hiding. Their forces were much larger and well-equipped than anyone realized.* "Indeed. The extent of their army is a surprise to me as well."

"No matter, we shall defeat them here. We have no choice at this stage. And when that happens, Terra will be open to our people. The Ghost Bears will be the ilClan...mark my words."

"*Aff,*" Adam said slowly. "It is as you say, Star Commander." He held his emotions in check. While a part of him admired the Ghost Bears as warriors, the thought of the Clans taking Terra, the cradle of mankind, was unnerving. *It is the moral center of humanity, a powerful symbol. These may be the descendants of the Star League, but they are not what General Kerensky took with him into the Periphery.*

He had trained, as if he were a raw recruit, learning to fight all over again. Adam had shed his Combine upbringing and suppressed his years of experience to learn to fight as a Ghost Bear warrior. *I fought a little in the Fourth Succession War and earned great honor in the War of 3039. None of that matters to the Ghost Bears. Those wars are not part of their culture. Here, I am only as good as my last victory. Here, my past is but dust in the wind. Here, I am but a novice.* His retraining on the trail of the Ghost Bears had done something he had not anticipated...it had humbled him.

Adam had lost his last name and all that was tied to it when he had become Cymril's bondsman and a Ghost Bear. Last names, Bloodnames, were revered, drawn from a list of long-honored dead affiliated with his clan. Trueborns, those birthed in iron wombs, genetically engineered from the most successful warriors, were the most honored in the clan. Adam quickly came to learn he was lower on that pecking order. *Never did I realize that being born naturally to a mother and father was a curse.* The Ghost Bears used the word Trueborn as a noun and an adjective, sometimes uttered "*freebirth*!" as a curse. It was a constant reminder of where he fit in within the Bears. *How can natural birth be seen as a burden?*

Yet he did fit in. He had made friends. Charlotte Hall, the green-eyed warrior of Fury Star, had spent long, sweat-drenched days training him. She had recently won her Bloodname trial, and it had ratcheted up her arrogance. She looked down on Adam without even knowing she did it, but was still friendly to him, teaching him the ways of the Ghost Bears. Even Cymril took extra measures to make sure he felt as if he belonged.

"These Com Guards," Adam asked slowly, "What do you know of them?"

"Little to nothing," Cymril replied, "which is cause for concern, at least with me. Our leaders are confident that an untried army in antique BattleMechs is no match for us. I feel a sense of foreboding, though. We have learned a great deal fighting the Free Rasalhague Republic and the Draconis Combine. Spheroids can be ruthless, cunning, and lack honor when it suits them. This army we face, we know nothing about. Our Khans are confident, but I have learned much in the last two years. Overconfidence can kill."

There was a hint of hesitation in his voice, something Adam had not heard often from the Star Commander. *He suspects deceit from ComStar, which is more than prudent.* Cyrmil had the haughty superciliousness of a Ghost Bear, but kept it in check.

"Star Colonel Vong seems, dare I say, 'hesitant' about the enemy we face," Adam replied.

"Perhaps," Cymril replied. "If he is too much so, there will be challenges to his position and he will be replaced. It is the way of our people."

Adam nodded. *There is always someone vying for your position, and will take it by force if they can.*

"Tseng replied. "We are a proud people, but generations of selective breeding can only take us so far. In fairness, some of the Inner Sphere units we have faced have proven themselves almost our equals." It was a stark admission from Tseng, and one Adam appreciated. *He is not like most Ghost Bear commanders; he understands both the strengths and weaknesses of his own people.*

"Tukayyid is a test for the Ghost Bears, if not for the Clans as a whole," he mused.

Tseng nodded. "Our test begins soon. Our Delta Galaxy, along with Beta, will make a drive on our primary objective, the city of Luk. If these Com Guards are hiding any surprises, we will uncover them quickly, given the speed with which we are being sent in."

"There is an old saying...no plan survives first contact with the enemy," Adam said.

Tseng chuckled. "I am aware of it. But our people have a saying of our own, 'Even a poor plan, executed with brute force and speed, can be made into a victory.'"

Adam allowed a thin smile, but only for the Star Commander. *It is the way of the clans, speed and overwhelming firepower. ComStar may not play that game. We shall see how our clan fares...*

OUTSKIRTS OF LUK
3 MAY 3052

Star Commander Tseng's Fury Star advanced quickly through the outlying neighborhood. The first three days had seen the Delta Galaxy forces persistently annoyed by a series of well-coordinated hit and run attacks. One had been by more than a dozen fast-moving Beagle hovercrafts, which did little but melt away at armor and slow the advance. At first, the Com Guards seemed to refuse a stand-up fight. That changed when they hit the outer neighborhoods of Luk, at the edge of the Holth Forest.

ComStar's 91st and 12th Divisions had made the city a seemingly never-ending series of ambush locations, minefields, and pre-ranged artillery targets. Beta Galaxy was struggling to hold the 12th Division at bay, presuming Delta Galaxy would have better luck in the city. Luck proved not to be in the mix in the battle for Luk. The 88th Striker Trinary had nearly been wiped out just trying to enter the city, and the Elementals of the 78th Elemental Support Binary had become bogged down by formations of ComStar tanks and infantry, all firing from well-prepared positions.

The tall buildings in the sector assigned to the 413th Striker Trinary, who Tseng reported to, were larger than their 'Mechs, casting long dark shadows in the streets. He was forced to exercise caution, knowing the enemy could strike from anywhere. The civilian population had been evacuated by ComStar to minimize casualties. *In this we are aligned with these Com Guards. We are Ghost Bears, we do not kill innocents—we are their shield.* At the same time, this was not the kind of fighting he favored. Speed was armor to the Ghost Bears, and the city of Luk was a slow and deadly grind.

He had already downed a *Wyvern* and had left a Demon assault vehicle a smoldering hulk, though his right leg now carried a crater where a Gauss round had found its mark.

Urban battles were brutal, but this one seemed more so. The Com Guards seemed to be everywhere and nowhere. *We should be wrapping up this assault, instead we struggle block-by-block.*

His sky-blue-and-white-streaked *Summoner* suddenly quaked as a blast of autocannon rounds tore into his right side. He twisted to face the foe, but his attacker had faded behind a block of office buildings. "Fury Star, contact, right flank. Composition unknown. Diamond formation, point on me."

Warrior Charlotte Hall moved her OmniMech beside his. "I took a nasty laser barrage a few minutes ago," she said. "These cowards shoot and run." As if to emphasize her point, a squad of ComStar infantry bathed her in manpack particle projection cannon fire. Charlotte blasted at the building they had fired from, her lasers flashing in the distance.

Before he could concur, an artillery barrage landed on his Fury Star's point. The concussions of the explosions made his chest vibrate under his coolant vest. Shrapnel rattled against his 'Mech, punching through his left leg near the knee—yellow damage indicators demanded his attention. Juking hard to the right, he tried to move behind an office building, only to have it explode next to him, spraying his cockpit canopy with bits of ferroconcrete and steel.

"*Stravag!*" he spat. *We cannot stay here to die a little bit with each barrage.* "Fury Star, we are advancing to the east. Follow me."

Racing up a wide boulevard, a white *Thug* appeared from around a corner. Its pair of particle projection cannons flashed white-blue, both hitting his left side and arm. His *Summoner* twisted to the left under the impact and he felt the armor slough off onto the street.

Cymril returned the favor with his extended range PPC and LB 10-X autocannon. Both hit, with his autocannon also riddling a building behind the *Thug* with two or three wild rounds. The hulking white ComStar BattleMech fell back, out of line of sight. "That *Thug* belongs to me," he said through gritted teeth.

An explosion next to him showed Charlotte Hall's *Stormcrow* in a series of explosions from missiles, bits of her armor peppering his own OmniMech. "That *Longbow* is mine!" she snapped. Cymril saw it on his sensors for a moment, but like his own target, it had drifted behind cover.

They are baiting us...and it is a mistake. "Do not advance too far, Fury Star. Keep close enough to support each other."

"Bah!" Lawrence, another Fury Star warrior, replied. "They shoot and hide like rabid *surats*. These are no match for us. They pilot relics—some are even considered museum pieces."

"Heed my orders, Lawrence," Cymril said as he swung to the right of his position in an attempt to flank his opponent. "Keep within 150 meters proximity." He trotted his *Summoner* two blocks down and came up on the larger *Thug*'s left side, then unleashed everything he had. His long-range missiles went hot instantly and spiraled in on the stark white 'Mech's arm and legs, a dozen yellow-orange explosions blooming all over it. His ER PPC also tore into the arm of the hulking BattleMech. The burn-hole glowed crimson for a moment as his autocannon cratered the armor on its upper body.

The temperature in his own cockpit went from warm to balmy in a millisecond, but he ignored it, crossing the open street as the *Thug* returned a pair of PPC blasts at him. One missed, the energy discharge racing past his missile rack by less than a meter. The other savaged his left arm near the shoulder, rocking him hard in his command seat as he adjusted his stance to compensate.

He saw the other BattleMech on his sensors a moment before its large caliber autocannon blasted a ragged string of holes across his *Summoner*'s upper body. A *Hussar*, painted white with light gray streaks, had fired and was already running away at nearly 90 kph. It was not the standard SLDF *Hussar*, this one packed a deadly punch.

They lack honor, two against one. So be it.

Tseng's tactical display showed Lawrence's *Mad Dog* was still unleashing hell at the far flank. Charlotte had closed to deadly range with the ComStar *Longbow*, but was paying for her aggression. Cabral's *Ice Ferret* was down, his ejection seat transponder pinging—so he could still be alive—though punching out in a city was a dangerous proposition. Roman

Tseng's *Hellbringer* was badly damaged and fading back toward the center of their formation.

Cymril's mind picked up the details in a second as he swung his *Summoner* around the corner for another attack. He caught a glimpse of a ComStar Zephyr hovertank, a blur of white and gray, diving for cover the moment he saw it. *They are everywhere, like rats, nipping at us. This is not an honorable battle worthy of the Ghost Bears.*

The moment he rounded the building, a wave of missiles and a brilliant PPC blast from the *Thug* consumed his OmniMech. He struck back with a growl, his own PCC blasting the *Thug's* damaged arm, taking it off at the elbow joint. The BattleMech lurched at the loss of weight, sparks flew from the elbow as myomer sizzled on the hot metal.

Another autocannon blast hit his rear...the *Hussar*! His weaker rear armor was not enough to resist the damage. His LRM ammo cooked off under the stabbing energy beam, shaking the *Summoner* hard. The *Thug* fired as well, its remaining PPC missing by a half-dozen meters.

Cymril drifted his targeting reticle onto the cockpit and unleashed his autocannon. The LB X-10 found its mark, blasting the ferroglass with a stream of shells. The *Thug* lurched hard, then fell, crunching into the side of a building on the way down with the sickening sound of grinding armor and snapping myomer.

Tseng grinned, but only for a moment. Another blast hit his rear torso from the speedy *Husssar*. This shot melted the remaining armor, punching into the heart of his *Summoner* and its fusion reactor. The housing was compromised, his damage display blared the story. The temperature spiked in his cockpit and seemed to hang there...a hint that his reactor insulation was also damaged. He pivoted in place to target the *Hussar*, but it was already gone again. Then came a blast from his flank—the wounded *Thug* had risen and hit him in his damaged right side.

He tasted the salt of sweat on his upper lip. Roman Tseng's transponder wasn't signaling anymore—not a good sign, especially in an urban combat environment, where damage and death were often at close range. Charlotte Hall was fading back toward his position—her *Stormcrow* crumpled like a crushed can of energy drink. Another rumble of artillery shook the ground and filled the air with a fine powdery mist. A near miss, but still too close for comfort.

"Star Commander..." Hall managed, struggling to find the right words. Defeat did not have a strong vocabulary in the Clans.

He understood her feelings even if she could not form the word. *We are Ghost Bears. Retreat is not in our nature, not unless it is for our advantage to do so.* In all his battles in the Inner Sphere, he had *never* given up ground. A spray of missiles caught him before he could move into cover, rending his chest armor into mangled chunks of charred, smoking metal.

"Fury Star, fall back," he said grimly.

Lawrence came on the tactical channel. "Fall back, *quineg*?" Disbelief hung with each word.

"*Aff*, you heard me correctly, Lawrence," he said firmly. "Combat drift back to Waypoint Bravo."

GHOST BEAR REAR AREA
THREE HOURS LATER

Adam saw the return of his bondholder's Star and was awestruck by the damage they had taken. Charlotte's *Stormcrow* was blackened from head to foot, her torso armor peeled open, twisted and gnarled. Lawrence lost his grip climbing down, collapsing in a limp heap at the feet of his mauled *Mad Dog*. His 'Mech's cockpit was caved inward, the ferroglass breached in several places. His skin was pale, and there was blood splattered on his neurohelmet's faceplate. Medics moved in and carried him off. Adam knew he wouldn't be piloting a 'Mech anytime soon. *To have piloted his OmniMech back in such a condition is a testimony to his breeding, but more to his character.*

Cymril Tseng's *Summoner* had a green, oozing wound; coolant, the blood of a BattleMech, leaking out onto the hot, charred armor that remained. His missile rack was a twisted stump on the shoulder of the once proud 'Mech. As Tseng climbed down from the cockpit, Adam could see the shimmer of his sweat. He knew the smells of battle, the aroma that only damaged BattleMechs could emit, and it stung his nostrils. They mingled with the smells of urban combat in the distance, a hint of burning garbage and charred wood and plastics.

He had seen the Ghost Bears fight before; the first time had cost him his freedom, the others had been as a spectator to the carnage. Damage was not uncommon, they were ferocious warriors. This was different. *I have never seen them so badly mauled.* It was a hint of how savage the fighting in the city was.

The Com Guards are not the cakewalk we were led to believe. The Bears were a proud people that flirted with arrogance from time to time. His parent unit, the Walking Panzers of the 68th Striker Cluster, had only known victories since he had been made a bondsman. Yes, warriors suffered individual defeats, but never the unit. Adam would normally have cradled an inner rejoicing that they had been handed in Luk. Instead he kept silent, running his hand across his head and through his cropped black mohawk to the tight chonmage near the back and stared at the damage with wonder. *How do these people handle defeat on the field of battle?*

"Star Commander," Adam said as his bondholder approached. "What happened?"

"They did not fight with honor," Cymril snapped. "Minefields, sniping attacks...these are unworthy of Trueborn warriors." He turned to the lead Technician for his Star, who was surveying what was left of the OmniMechs. "Torq, we need to get refit. How long to repair them?"

"Too long," Torq replied.

Cymril's nostrils flared and for a moment, Adam thought he might strike the Technician. "Choose your words carefully. We need to return to Luk and retake it."

Torq shook his head to hide the fear in his eyes. "We can repair the cockpit on Lawrence's *Mad Dog*, it looks like mostly armor replacement. Your *Summoner* will take days from the looks of it, and I'm out of LRM pods on top of that. We were able to cobble together an operational *Timber Wolf* for Cabral, who made it to our lines a few hours ago, but it is only marginally battle-ready. I have a new *Stormcrow* and a repaired *Kit Fox* that you can take out. That is it for replacement 'Mechs, sir."

Charlotte Hall moved into the conversation, her body glistening with sweat and red hot with anger. "I have had time in a *Kit Fox,* Star Commander, if you wish to take the *Stormcrow.* That leaves us short a warrior to pilot Lawrence's *Mad Dog* though, assuming they can repair it." She shot Torq a fiery glare and the Technician left the tight circle, barking commands to his techs. No one wished to be on the receiving end of one of Charlotte's furious stares.

For a long moment, Cymril Tseng said nothing, looked at no one. It was as if he stared out past Adam and Charlotte at his once proud OmniMech, now a battered shadow of its former self. Then his gaze fell on Adam again.

"Your wrist," he said calmly, now in control of his anger.

Adam lifted his wrist. Cymril took out his survival knife and cut the bondcord, letting it fall to the ground at their feet. "Normally, I would assemble the warriors and walk you through the ritual...but these are pressing times," he said in the closest thing Adam had heard to an apology. "Adam of the Ghost Bears, the time has come for you to be a warrior for your people. By cutting this bondcord, I restore your free will and elevate you to warrior. We will ride into battle together. Today you are a Ghost Bear warrior, an *abtakha* of our Clan—a rare and frightening thing to behold."

Charlotte's harsh voice spiked through Adam's rush of emotions. "*Neg,* Star Commander—he is old, far too old. He should be sent to the ranks of the *solahma* to fight. There is no precedence for such a relic to fight as equals." There was no hint in her voice that she cared that she had insulted him.

Adam understood, he knew Charlotte well. The taunts of "*solahma*" had followed him from the moment he had been made the Star Commander's bondsman. *Age is not a weakness, but a strength.* His memories returned to his former commander, *Sho-sho* Riku Kondo, and his former life in the Home Guard. They were memories he still clung onto, refusing to let them fade. *These Ghost Bears do not appreciate that age and experience trumps youth and impatience. They relegate their older warriors to lesser duties, yet these are warriors that have lasted long in a martial society.*

Adam said nothing, but looked where the bondcord had been on his wrist. *I am old only by Clan standards.* He was 51, and more than able to fight at least one more battle. *The Coordinator would not set me aside, not as long as I could pilot a BattleMech and serve the Dragon.*

Before he could speak, Cymril did. "This is the proxy battle for Terra, Charlotte! If we lose here, the Smoke Jaguars or some other Clan may take the title of ilClan. Would you prefer the Jade Falcons become the ilClan, *quineg*? Rather than face that, I will bend our rede and break our rules if I must. Adam *will* fight. He will prove himself a true Ghost Bear."

Charlotte recoiled, both physically and in tone. "Very well, Star Commander. You are right, victory is all that matters."

"We will rest, and give the technicians some time to do their jobs," Cymril said as he removed his coolant vest. "I will put us on the roster for deployment in the morning. Luk will be ours, and Adam will prove himself worthy of our Clan."

Adam drank in his words but said nothing, only nodded. He bent over and picked up his severed bondcord, twisting it in his fingers. A memory came to him, almost as if he were suddenly aware of a dream he once had. *"The Dragon cannot be taken from you..."* For all of this time, his bondcord had been a symbol of his honor. His ability to choose his own path had been taken from him, as had his last name and his past. Now he was being made whole again.

My path is now my own again...

GHOST BEAR FORWARD POST
WEST OF LUK
TUKAYYID
FREE RASALHAGUE REPUBLIC
4 MAY 3052

Adam waved at Cymril to enter his domed quarters. "Throughout history, samurai have shared tea before a great challenge—the *chanoyu* ritual. In the field, it was hard to find any of the components, and my formal utensils were lost when I was made a bondsman. I apologize for this not being equal to the full ceremony. I hope you will join me."

He took the heated kettle, recovered from someone's blasted kitchen, and poured hot water into a bowl, crushing the green tea leaves into it. His moves were slow, deliberate, and meticulous. Once the tea had been prepared, he poured it into two cups...handing one to his former bondholder.

Adam lifted his tea to his face, breathing in the aroma and closing his eyes. For a moment he was not on Tukayyid—he was with the Home Guard, in a time when he did not even know of the Ghost Bears. He felt a wave of relaxation wash over him. As he cracked open his eyes, he sipped his tea and savored it.

Cymril was more deliberate, taking a full swallow. "I am unfamiliar with this ritual. Am I to do or say something?"

Adam cracked a thin smile. "No words are necessary. We share this drink, as honorable warriors. It is designed to relax us, provide focus." He did just that, letting himself bask in his memories of his life as a MechWarrior in the DCMS.

The hulking Ghost Bear warrior took another sip, remaining silent for a full minute. He set the cup down on a field desk. "I appreciate you sharing this with me, Adam. This battle we face today is important."

"As is this ritual," he replied, slowly drinking the rest of his tea. Drawing a long, calming breath, he turned his full attention to the Star Commander. "I thank you for cutting my bondcord."

"Adam, you have served well as a bondsman. No task I gave you was beneath your pride. You accepted your role with great dignity...never once complaining or objecting. In doing so, you honored me. You are one with the Ghost Bears now. I am counting on you in the coming fight. I need you to fight with the full fury of all you have experienced as one of our people."

"I will be true to my nature," he said slowly. Turning, Adam picked up the book he had been writing in, his own Great Work, and wrapped it in a thin sheet of ballistic cloth. Carefully, he secured it inside his survival kit.

"Why would you take it with you?" Cymril asked. "It is a piece of art."

Adam did not meet his gaze, but made sure the straps were secure on the kit. "It is a story, and one never knows when a story is about to come to an end."

Turning, he faced Cymril Tseng, locking his dark eyes with him. "Let us go and face battle together."

ONE HOUR LATER

Adam could see the *Mad Dog* had been hastily repaired. The dull flat gray armor replacement plates stood out against the light blue and gray of the original paint job. Black burns on the paint still showed. The replacement cockpit panel still had a protective plastic sheet on it. As he stared up at it, he could not help wondering if he might meet the same fate as Lawrence, its previous pilot.

Cymril came up alongside him, holding his neurohelmet and looking up. "Today, you fight as a Ghost Bear, Adam," he said proudly. He held out his hand, and in it was a metallic wristband, with a chip mounted on it. "Your *codex*...it is clean, but today you will start to fill it as a Ghost Bear warrior."

Adam felt a swell of pride rise in him, but didn't let it show. *I have endured a great deal to see this day come...but it still feels wrong.* ComStar, for all of its quirkiness, had never done anything to provoke him to want to kill them. As a bondsman, he had been a third-class citizen with the warrior caste. Now that had been erased, forgotten.

Adam had not forgotten, though.

"I will not fail in my duty," he finally said, starting the long climb up the leg of the *Mad Dog*. As he entered the cockpit, he noticed it was not pristine; the air smelled of sweat and old, spilled coolant. He noticed that some of the internal cockpit plates had been cut and made to fit, clearly taken from other 'Mechs. Adam had always known the Ghost Bears were rich in terms of equipment. Now they were salvaging other damaged 'Mechs. The realization quickly came to him...*they had not planned on the battle lasting this long.* He suppressed the urge to grin.

Settling into the cockpit, he initiated the startup sequence and connected his coolant vest. The fusion reactor throbbed under him as the controls came to life in a myriad of colors. He had piloted the Combine's best BattleMechs in his career, but none compared to the raw firepower and precision engineering of this Clan 'Mech.

Adam fell in line behind Cymril's new *Stormcrow* as they set out for Luk. While he could not see the city itself, there was a thick black cloud of smoke hovering in the distance, marking their destiny.

TWO HOURS LATER

Adam settled his targeting reticle on the distant white/gray *Exterminator* that had blasted him a few seconds ago. The moment he got a target lock, he unleashed forty long-range missiles. They arced high, up over the rooftops of several buildings, then plunged downward, raining carnage on the ComStar BattleMech. He lost his target lock and was unable to determine how many warheads had hit. *These Com Guards are smart...they stay on the move and use the city to their full advantage.*

He was responding to attacks rather than leading them... firing only at those Com Guards that targeted him. The rest of Fury Star was far more aggressive—and paying a price for it, one charred armor plate at a time.

"We held this neighborhood yesterday, now they are crawling all over it," Cymril spat on the tactical channel.

"Star Commander, that *Lancelot* is mine!" snapped Cabral.

"Then take him, Cabral," replied Cymril. "Charlotte—sitrep."

"My right leg is still attached, but barely," she said in an exhausted tone. "I may need to redeploy at the edge of the city." Redeploy was her way of saying "retreat," and Adam knew her plight was indeed dire for her to even hint at it.

"Do it," Cymril said. "You are of no use to the Bear if you are downed."

Adam's *Mad Dog* registered a laser blast hit; he felt armor shift and melt on the 60-ton OmniMech. A Magi tank had poked out enough to fire, then pull back behind the rubble of a parking structure. He blasted back with his large pulse lasers, sending crimson bursts at the tank. One weapon found its mark, catching the flank of the vehicle before it was out of line of sight.

The tactical channel crackled for a moment as another voice, that of Star Captain Stunner Tseng, came on the comm. "Attention, 413th Striker—we are falling back to sector G as in Gamma. All forces, rendezvous at sector G."

"Sir," Cymril responded. "We have fought to take this part of Luk. We would be turning it over to the enemy."

"Look to the east, sector three, Cyrmil," the Star Captain replied.

Adam pivoted as well and saw a massive cloud of smoke rising in the distance...thick, black, menacing. "Our reinforcements, the Seventh Bear Guards, are in the Holth Forest, and ComStar set it on fire."

Adam stared at the massive pillars of twisted smoke as they rose higher into the sky. It was an inferno, and if they didn't move, it would cut off the 413th Striker Trinary.

"*Stravag*..." Cymril cursed. "Fury Star, we are going to fall back. I will cover your redeployment."

Adam remembered when he had done that same thing, two years earlier, with Whirlwind Company. It had cost him everything but his honor. "I will remain with you, Star Commander."

Cymril didn't reply, but was immediately bathed in three coalescing PPC bursts from a white-gray Burke tank that emerged from the rubble of a building. The excess energy arced over, searing paint on his OmniMech. His *Stormcrow* reeled, falling into a building on the left, grinding armor as it crashed down into a smoke-and-dust-filled hole.

Adam moved between the tank and the fallen *Stormcrow*, only to have a Com Guard *Crab* poke out and fire its large lasers into his already damaged center torso. Flashing crimson warning lights bloomed as a ripple of heat rose in his cockpit. His gyro had been badly seared, as had his fusion reactor. Adam returned fire with his pulse lasers, stitching burn marks along the oblong body of his foe.

His *Mad Dog* fought him, reeling from the damage it had taken. He took a wobbly side-step, then collapsed hard onto the street, churning up ferrocrete as it hit. More warning lights flared as he was thrown around on the command couch. Sweat stung his eyes, and he saw his gyro was all but destroyed. Jamming the foot pedals and joystick, the OmniMech groaned but did not move, and he saw his gyro had taken more damage in the fall. The *Mad Dog* was dead.

Through the dust and haze, he saw Cymril right his *Stormcrow*. Then a salvo of laser beams from several blocks away lit the Ghost Bear OmniMech in neon fire. Globs of molten metal splattered Adam's downed 'Mech as the *Stormcrow* started to topple again. The canopy blew, and Cymril's ejection seat rose high in the air.

Adam popped his canopy and tossed his coolant vest, then grabbed his survival kit and slung it over his shoulder. The cool air felt good on his hot skin. Staggering over the debris in the street, he headed toward where Cymril had landed, up against the side of a building. When he got there, he saw the Star Commander's left ankle was broken, the white bone poking through a hole at the side of his foot. Cymril was in agony, and Adam worked to get the restraining straps off.

"Leave me," Cymril said through gritted teeth.

"*Neg*," Adam replied. "You are my responsibility now." Casually, he reached down to the Star Commander and pulled the *wakizashi* Tseng wore at his hip, sliding the blade and sheath under his own belt. *Where it belongs...*

There was a grinding sound behind him, and Adam turned around. Looming over them was a stout white egg-shaped 'Mech with brilliant blue horizontal stripes—an *UrbanMech*. Stenciled high up near the cockpit door was the Epsilon symbol and the warrior's name: *Adept Allen Steiner*. The sight of the name made him do something he had not done in a long time—chuckle.

I was in the DCMS, and made a Ghost Bear bondsman. I have fought and lost and now face surrender to someone named Steiner, fighting for the Com Guards... The irony was not lost on him.

Adam helped Cymril up onto his one good leg to stand and waved as the *UrbanMech* lowered its autocannon to train on them. "We surrender."

"*Stravag!*" Cymril cried out. "I do not!"

Adam grinned slightly his former bondholder's frustration. "You do," he said firmly, then turned back to the *UrbanMech*. I am *Tai-i* Adam Kaningamu of the DCMS! This man is my prisoner!" he yelled at the top of his voice.

Cymril's body tensed, and his eyes widened as he realized what Adam had said. "This cannot be," he growled.

Adam lowered him to the ground and looked down at him. "I assure you, I am quite serious."

COMSTAR FIELD HEADQUARTERS
TUKAYYID
7 MAY 3052

The ComStar ROM agent Christine Rosenfeld stood with crossed arms, glaring down at Adam, who was sitting in the sterile isolation room. Her black hair was devoid of any sort of style, worn short. Her white uniform was the only thing that gave her face any color, and even then, it was pale.

"So, you claim you are *Tai-i* Adam Kaningamu of the Draconis Combine, and that you've been living as a bondsman for the last two years to the warrior you brought in with you?" Her voice was calm, level, but oddly threatening.

He almost answered, "*Aff*," but caught himself. "Yes."

"This...creates a problem for ComStar," the agent replied. "We have an arrangement to repatriate any prisoners taken during this battle to their respective Clans."

"He is not *your* prisoner," Adam corrected. "He is mine."

She nodded curtly once. "So you say. The problem is, we do not know for sure that you are really you. Adam Kaningamu is listed as missing in action, presumed dead."

That thought disturbed him only for the impact it must have had on his family. *All this time they thought me gone... dead...having joined my ancestors.* He had not thought much of the grief and now relief they would feel with his return to the ranks of the living.

He eyed the ComStar ROM agent with a sneer creeping onto his face. "Who would claim to be a Ghost Bear bondsman who was not?"

The question gave Agent Rosenfeld a rare moment of pause. "An intriguing question. To be blunt, someone from another intelligence agency attempting to perform some sort of deep-cover infiltration. It is not my job to discern a motive—only to find the truth."

Truth is always a matter of perspective. "You may take my blood if you desire it."

"Not necessary. We have already made arrangements to validate your identity." There was a slight, ominous tone in her voice that Adam presumed was designed to intimidate him. It failed.

I have been through more than you can comprehend. It has not broken me—it has only made me stronger...

**COMSTAR FIELD HEADQUARTERS
TUKAYYID
8 JULY 3052**

Sho-sho David Vivas entered his cramped quarters along with another man, whom he could tell was from the Combine, and no doubt an ISF operative. *They all have that look, brooding, intense, emotionless.* His black uniform was devoid of any hint of who he was, save his name badge—*Malik Feff*, no doubt a false name.

Vivas had been on Shirotori, training new recruits, when ComStar had requested his presence for a security matter. It was urgent enough that the DCMS had arranged for his trip—and his escort.

Adam rose to his feet. Their eyes met, then his gaze drifted to David's right hand, which was clearly a bionic replacement, then up to his collar, which showed his rank. "I see you have been promoted, old friend." He did not betray his happiness to see the other man; it would be inappropriate with strangers present.

Vivas studied his face carefully. "We believed you dead...if you are who you claim."

"What do your own eyes tell you?"

"My eyes can be misled." He glanced at Malik Feff, who nodded grimly, then continued. "I had feared you had died on Constance. The Ghost Bears wiped out the Home Guard. If you are who you claim; your actions allowed me to fight on for five days. I lost this—" Vivas held up his hand. "—fighting the Smoke Jaguars on Luthien. My actions earned me a promotion. My daughter, Ichika, fought with me in the battle as a MechWarrior."

Adam cocked his head. "The David Vivas I knew did not have any children. He *did* have a mother, Ichika, who is a fabled MechWarrior, his inspiration for joining the service."

A smile rose on Vivas' face. "Only my friend would know that. My mother, Ichika, served in Takashi Kurita's Dragon's Claws, and I fought beside her on Luthien. She died there, defending the Coordinator."

ISF agent Feff still betrayed no emotion. Adam returned the grin. "I grieve for your loss David...we have much to discuss."

The ComStar ROM agent Rosenfeld entered the room. "My apologies, *Tai-i* Adam Kaningamu, but we had to be sure."

"Of course, we will still need to...*debrief* you, at some length," Malik Feff said.

Debrief—neg. *Interrogate is more like it. Worse, he looks as if he might enjoy it.* "Where is Cymril Tseng?" Adam asked.

"We have him in a secure cell," Feff replied.

"Good," Adam said, putting his hand on Vivas' shoulder. "I need to speak with him." He paused. "And I want my *wakizashi* and my survival kit."

Cymril Tseng rose to his feet and glared at Adam as he entered the stark room, flanked by ROM agent Rosenfeld and Malik Feff.

"Thanks to the likes of you, we were only able to fight to a draw on Tukayyid," he said with venom in his voice. "Thanks to the likes of you, we lost Terra."

"There is no shame in losing a fight that was unwinnable," Adam replied. His next words came to him as if from a long fading dream. "For a warrior people, you failed to perceive that the Com Guards outmatched you in strategy."

Cymril ignored his response. "You have betrayed our people," he finally said, sitting back down, his shoulders slumping.

"They were never *my* people," Adam replied flatly.

"You fought as a Ghost Bear, then turned on our clan. My clan."

Adam took a confident step forward. "Your honor compelled you to make me your bondsman. I accepted that because there was no alternative. I did everything you asked. When you cut my bondcord, you gave me back my free will. This is how I chose to exercise it."

Adam reached into his survival kit, pulling out the book he had worked on for so long. He carefully handed it to Malik Feff.

"What is this?" the ISF agent asked. Cymril also looked at the book with a puzzled expression on his face.

"The Ghost Bears are a highly artistic people, but they do not study languages," Adam replied. "I worked on this for two years. In it you will find profiles of all of their warriors, details of their logistics network, computer systems, et cetera." *He never knew I had been preparing for this moment from the start.*

A look of surprised awe on his face, Feff held the invaluable book with delicate reverence.

Cymril turned his head and lowered his gaze to the floor. "You lack any semblance of honor."

"No. I am nothing but honorable," Adam said, turning to the ROM operative. "I release him to your custody."

"When the fighting is over, he will be returned to the Ghost Bears—" Rosenfeld began.

"*NEG!*" Cymril roared. "You would have me carry this disgrace back to the clan I failed! I brought a traitor into our midst. I am no longer worthy of the Ghost Bears! I am *dezgra*—I have no home now."

Feff leaned forward. "The Draconis Combine will gladly take him as our...guest." There was something in his tone that made Adam shiver...but then he realized any ISF operative would have had the same effect.

Adam looked at the Star Commander seated on the edge of his bed, beaten, dejected, his face red with fury and rage. There was no joy over the outcome of their relationship, nothing to rejoice over other than returning home to fight again for the DCMS. A feeling of pity came over him. Cymril Tseng was not a bad person; he simply lacked understanding of his enemies...he lacked *perspective*.

"Cymril..." Adam started, his mind still formulating his thoughts. "We tried this your way. Now we will try it my way."

Turning to Feff, he rose to his full stature. "He is *my* responsibility now. I make him my bondsman. I will make him a son of the Dragon. He will walk a new path—one I will lay before him."

Glancing down at the bed and the hulking former Ghost Bear on it, he thought he saw a flicker of acknowledgement in response...and perhaps, a bit of hope.

ALWAYS MOVING

STEVEN MOHAN, JR.

KOZICE VALLEY, NORTH OF DIAMOND SHARK ASSAULT OBJECTIVE
TUKAYYID
FREE RASALHAGUE REPUBLIC
3 MAY 3052

Old-growth lodgepole pines and Douglas firs crowded the Kozice Valley, giving way to cottonwoods at the river. The evergreens' dark needles choked out most of the day's sunlight. Gloom filled the woodland.

Along with several hundred BattleMechs.

When ComStar had attacked, three enemy divisions had punched into the Diamond Shark rear. Star Colonel Seth Davis had broken his bid to rush Gamma Galaxy to the new front, but was too late. Khan Ian Hawker's supply lines were severed, and he was cut off from his LZ.

Now the battle was a desperate free-for-all. Ian had no choice but to fight his way through the mess.

He glanced down at his map display and saw a jumble of icons spread across the screen in knots of six or three or *two*.

Ian had lost all operational control.

He was just one more warrior fighting for his Clan.

A savage smile curled across his sharp, vulpine face.

Fine.

He saw a flash of pale white through the trees.

He would fight the *stravag* Spheroids any way he could. All by himself if he had to.

As if some dark god were watching Ian for His own ironic amusement, a trio of bone-white machines chose *that* moment to shoulder their way through the trees.

Ian split his fire right and left, painting the wide, milk-white carapace of a *King Crab* with emerald light from his right-arm large lasers and adding a long rattling gout of fire from his Ultra AC/5.

He simultaneously directed autocannon fire paired with his *left*-arm lasers and a volley of long-range missiles at the *Black Knight* emerging from the trees on his left.

In an effort to hold his heat load in check, he held off on his quartet of pulse lasers.

Which left him nothing to engage the *Wyvern* arcing around to flank him on the left.

He backstepped his *Dire Wolf* through the forest, trying to keep the two big machines in front of him—and delaying the moment when the faster *Wyvern* could come at him from his unprotected left.

The shark is the ultimate pelagic predator, he thought.

Passage 152 of the Diamond Shark Remembrance always came to Ian during times of stress.

This was definitely one of those times.

Ruby laser fire strobed, cutting through the darkness like the flicker of summer lightning.

He angled away from the *King Crab*, presenting fresh left armor to the enemy pilot. The Diamond Shark Khan gritted his teeth as the Spheroid 'Mech sliced into his left leg with its large pulse laser, stitching ruby darts of light into the *Dire Wolf*'s armor until it melted and ran like water. Dollops of molten composite ignited the scraggly grass at his machine's feet.

Ian ran through fire.

The shark ceaselessly patrols the blue depths.

He kept moving right, shrugging off the Spheroid's attacks, trying to string out the 'Mechs on his left.

Twin Gauss slugs missed left—one wide.

One *close*.

Its black eyes gather the ocean's meager light as it endlessly searches for the scent of blood.

His right oblique had boxed out the *Wyvern*. The medium could not engage until the *Black Knight* cleared its solution.

Ian kept moving.

Until he pushed through a copse of cottonwood trees and found himself pinned against the sheer rock face of the valley's eastern wall.

Or the tremors of a thrashing fish.

The passage's words were powerful. *Reassuring.*

But right now *Ian* felt like the thrashing fish.

Far from the blooms of plankton that anchor the web of life near reefs and shallows, the ocean deeps are vast blue deserts.

He was *trapped.*

The predators that survive in these barren waters must forever be on the lookout for prey.

The *Crab*'s large pulse laser exploded a cottonwood tree immediately to Ian's right and burning splinters of wood rained down. The enemy pilot punched a pair of Hovertec Streaks into his *Dire Wolf*'s torso, shattering armor.

But its other pair of SRMs missed left.

The two missiles slammed into the valley wall, shattering gray slate and filling the air with a cloud of rock dust.

For a heartbeat, Ian Hawker's BattleMech was invisible.

Fragments of rock peppered his *Wolf* like a hard rain.

He ignored it.

And surged forward.

To survive, the shark must be always moving.

He closed with the *King Crab*, moving inside its LRM's minimum range and making it hard for the *Knight* or the *Wyvern* to engage without risking a blue-on-blue. Ian pulled into his triggers, pouring laser fire into the 'Mech's left arm, slicing into the elbow.

Armor bubbled and melted.

The shrill cry of Ian's heat alarm blared. He slapped the override and held his shot.

The *King Crab*'s left arm fell free, and the ComStar machine staggered right, overbalanced by the loss of seventeen tons on its left side. Ian let his lasers cut out, and jinked right, hitting the *Black Knight* with a flight of LRMs before passing behind the shelter of the *Crab.*

Then he tore into the off-balance machine with his autocannons, cutting deeply into the *King Crab*'s left leg, flensing armor until the 'Mech's gleaming titanium femur was revealed.

The *King Crab* tried to turn, to bring its torso-mounted SRMs to bear, but Ian moved right too, adding his lasers back into the mix.

The limb finally gave way, and the assault machine's wide, ungainly head smashed into the earth.

Ian was still overmatched by the surviving ComStar BattleMechs. He could have crouched down behind the fallen *King Crab* and taken pot shots at the *Black Knight* and the *Wyvern*. Or he could have used the downed assault machine as cover to withdraw.

Instead, he stepped out from behind the *King Crab*.

He did not fear Spheroid warriors. They were dilettantes *playing* at war.

Ian's genetic heritage had come from the best warriors, carefully distilled by Clan scientists. As a child he had been subjected to hard—even brutal—training. His whole life had been devoted to the ways of combat. He was a Clan warrior, untainted by love or family or freedom.

All of which were just different words for *weakness.*

It did not matter if these Spheroids had some small numerical or weight advantage.

These freebirth filth would never defeat a Trueborn warrior in a stand-up fight.

So Ian Hawker stepped out from behind the fallen *King Crab*, pounding the *Black Knight* with lasers and autocannons and corkscrewing missiles.

He saw a sun-bright flare out of his peripheral vision and glanced left. SaKhan Barbara Sennet's *Summoner*—painted matte green with blue and silver checkerboard trim—descended on a pillar of fire. She was taking the *Wyvern* under fire with her extended-range PPC as she came down.

Ian did not like his saKhan. She was a Warden who believed the Clans' duty was to protect the Inner Sphere, rather than conquer it. How any Clan warrior could believe such a fallacy was impossible for Ian to understand. Trueborns were superior to freebirths.

Still, Barbara herself was a Trueborn warrior, decanted from an iron womb. She might be misguided, but she was still a daughter of the Clan eugenics program.

This battle was no longer governed by the rules of *zellbrigen*. It had become a melee the moment Seth Davis had broken his bid.

So he let Barbara Sennet take on the *Wyvern*.

And he turned to pummel the *Black Knight*.

With the *Summoner*'s appearance, the ComStar pilots realized they were outmatched, and began backstepping away, firing as they retreated.

Always moving, Ian thought, recalling the line from the Remembrance. He suited his action to those words, stalking his *Dire Wolf* forward, employing his two AC/5s on the *Knight*'s chest, abrading armor. He held off on his lasers, allowing his heat levels to fall.

For a moment, he thought he had the *Black Knight* beaten.

Then his right-arm autocannon guttered out. He had drawn down to the bottom of his ammunition bin. Cursing savagely, he watched the heavy disappear into the forest, wounded—but still alive.

This was the consequence of their broken supply line. Ian's troops would be running low on munitions.

Still, it had been the right choice to engage the three ComStar divisions. A glance at his mapscreen showed Gamma was beating back the Spheroid assault. The Diamond Sharks had won this battle, and once they reestablished their supply lines, they would be able to rearm and press their assault on Kozice Prime and Urcunat.

Ian turned to look at Barbara Sennet's *Summoner*. The *Wyvern* had used its speed to escape. Ian expected his saKhan to charge into the forest after the ComStar medium. Instead, the 'Mech's torso was tilted back, as if it were gazing up at the sky.

Ian turned to follow Barbara Sennet's gaze.

DropShips streaked across Tukayyid's pale blue sky. The vessels were as white as moonlight, each one painted with a BattleMech climbing a mountain. It was the emblem of the Mountaineers—ComStar's Fifth Army.

The Mountaineers had originally fought the Smoke Jaguars, but they must have beaten the cats if ComStar was deploying them here.

As Ian watched, he saw a BattleMech crouching in the open bay door of a hovering *Overlord*, its knees bent, as if it was a paratrooper awaiting the signal to jump.

The sky was suddenly filled with a handful of machines the color of bone.

Then dozens.

Then *hundreds.*

Ian realized he needed to pull his forces back before Fifth Army cut them off and his surviving forces were encircled.

And *destroyed.*

Always moving, he thought. *Always moving.*

A cold chill wriggled down Barbara Sennet's spine as soon as she looked up and saw ComStar dropping behind the Diamond Shark lines.

They were beaten. It was as simple as that. ComStar's Precentor Martial had beaten them. The Mountaineers had both numbers and position on the Clan force.

There was only one chance.

And *that* was a desperate chance.

She just hoped her Khan would listen.

She shifted her transceiver to Ian Hawker's private UHF channel. She was glad the frequency was line-of-sight. She thought her chances of convincing him would be better if no one overheard.

"My Khan, order Omega Galaxy to relieve us. Quickly, before Fifth Army can consolidate their position."

"*Neg,*" he snarled.

"We have a small window of time. Some enemy 'Mechs can be hit as they fall. And it will take time for ComStar to organize. If we hit them hard *now*, we can save the balance of our forces."

"Omega Galaxy is filled with filthy freebirths." Ian's voice was heavy with derision. "They are little better than the dirty Spheroids we fight. *Neg*, saKhan Barbara Sennet. Alpha and Gamma will have to save themselves."

"My Khan—"

"That is my final word on the subject."

Barbara said nothing further. Ian Hawker was a brilliant tactician and a fearless MechWarrior.

But his bigotry would kill them all.

She glanced down at her transceiver for a moment.

Then she reached forward and adjusted her selector switch, shifting frequencies.

Star Colonel Adrine, CO of the 3rd Shark Regulars, pushed her *Vulture* down the Kozice River, her heavy 'Mech submerged in the rushing, thrashing water up to its hips. The rapids buffeted her low-slung cockpit. It was dangerous to use the river to transit the forest, but it was the fastest way through the trees.

And right now, her cluster needed to get to the battered remnants of Alpha and Gamma Galaxies *fast*.

The Star Colonel came to a sharp right bend in the river and hit her radio squelch button twice. Her cluster immediately stopped at the sound of the double click.

Mostly the river moved down the valley's center, but this sharp turn carried it toward the eastern wall and out of sight. Adrine glanced down at her mapscreen. It showed the river hugging the valley wall for a good six, seven klicks.

And *deepening*.

The darker blue on this part of the map promised a depth of ten meters.

Just about deep enough.

The map showed the river opening into Lake Kozice— was *everything* named Kozice here?—that was a natural chokepoint along the valley's north-south axis. A crescent of forest curled around the lake, but Adrine was willing to bet her *Vulture*'s left arm the woodland was crawling with a ComStar division just *waiting* to ambush the battered Clanner force rushing south to link up with their DropShips.

All of this made her feel dirty. She might be a freeborn warrior.

But that did not mean she preferred the dirty tactics of a melee.

She aspired to something better than a Spheroid's careless existence.

Adrine studied that enormous bowl of water to the north.

But to achieve victory, she would use whatever tools fate had seen fit to give her.

Precentor Mari Rennery, CO of Fifth Army's 323rd Division, waited quietly in her *Highlander*, her fusion engine banked to minimize her heat signature, her force positioned well south of the tree line, so the Diamond Sharks would be caught in the forest long before they detected the 323rd and the 299th on magres.

She did not want the fish to wriggle off the hook.

Rennery had helped smash the Sixth Jaguar Dragoons a few days before.

And she'd gotten a taste for crushing Clan units.

The Precentor had deployed her division—Negative Communications—in a staggered line abreast running east-west, using trees as concealment. Behind her, the 299th Division—Courtesy Through Words—was held in reserve. Both divisions faced north.

Waiting for the fleeing Clanners to race into the teeth of her trap.

And be destroyed.

So when she heard the whipcrack of lasers, the rippling explosions of missiles, and the rattling roar of autocannon fire, she was bemused. She had expected to see movement as the Sharks approached. Rennery expected to see flashes of blue amongst the red-brown trunks of lodgepole pines. And she had *not* expected to hear the sound of missiles and autocannons.

We cut off their supplies.

The Clanners were supposed to be nearly out of projectile rounds and missiles.

That was when she heard the panicked cries coming from the Level III guarding her right flank.

They weren't engaging the retreating remnants of Alpha and Gamma to the north.

They were engaging someone else to the *east.*

Demi-Precentor Sandra Turley waited for a glimpse of Deathstrike blue, or a flicker of motion. Then she glanced right and saw BattleMechs rising from the lake like some horrific zombie army.

"*Blake's Blood,*" she swore under her breath.

This wasn't the blue of Alpha Galaxy and it wasn't the green with blue and silver accents of Gamma. *These* machines were a dark metallic green with blood-red trim. A strange red and green pattern climbed up their right legs.

But they were sure as *shit* Diamond Sharks.

She could tell by the grinning shark teeth painted on their cockpits.

A *Mad Dog*—called a *Vulture* by the Clans—turned toward her, stitching ruby fire into her *Flashman*'s chest armor. The machine's right-arm pulse lasers missed.

But its left-arm weapons were right on target.

The *Mad Dog* followed up the laser attack with a one-two punch from its torso-mounted LRMs. Missiles shattered armor all across Sandra's front.

She answered with her trio of Selitex Radonic large lasers, scoring two hits on the Clan machine.

All of which was great.

Except her heat levels *spiked.*

Bastard must have gotten one of her heat sinks along with the armor.

The *Mad Dog* came right back with another alpha strike.

How are they doing this? she thought frantically.

And then, *Of course.*

The Clanners were coming out of the lake.

The superior heat transfer of half-immersed 'Mechs allowed them to cycle their weapons faster.

Panicked calls from Sandra's people crowded her comms channel. "*This is Turley!*" she roared. "All units, execute a fighting withdrawal to the hundred-meter line, then reset and reengage. Turley, out."

A little distance would give her Level III a chance to adjust to the Clan attack and it would pull the Diamond Sharks out of the lake, so they'd be on a more even footing as far as heat went.

Next, she called her CO. "Three-Twenty-Third Actual, this is Second Battalion. The Sharks are attacking my position in regimental strength. Over."

Mari Rennery's disbelieving voice emerged from Sandra's speakers. "Say again your last, Second Battalion. Over."

"I say again, the Clanners are hitting our right flank with an understrength regiment. I have ordered a fighting withdrawal. I will reform our line 100 meters from the shoreline. Request immediate reinforcement. Over."

Sandra was outnumbered two to one, and those were *Clan* warriors she was facing.

She needed *help.*

And she needed it *now.*

So Mari Rennerly's next words were unwelcome. "Standby, Second Battalion."

Sandra clenched her jaw, swallowing back a string of profanity. "Wilco, Precentor. But be advised, we cannot *standby* for long—not without reinforcement."

Rennery came back at once, her voice icy. "Copy that, Second Battalion. Three-Twenty-Third Actual, out."

Sandra reached the hundred-meter line and positioned herself behind the dark skirt of a spruce, for all the good it would do it would do her, and waited for the Clan force to come.

The 323rd was nicknamed Negative Communications.

Got that *right*, she thought bitterly.

The freebirth Spheroids were falling *back*. Adrine had turned the ComStar flank.

But they were *not* panicking. The enemy was backstepping, not turning and fleeing. And they were returning fire. This was a fighting withdrawal.

Not a rout.

Which was bad. The Third Shark Regulars had numbers on the battalion holding the ComStar right. But if the Precentor in command reinforced the Level III, then Adrine's cluster would be quickly outnumbered.

She could not give the Spheroids time to regroup.

Adrine had to press *now*.

And press *hard*.

"Regulars, this is Third Shark Actual. Feeding Frenzy. Out."

She was ordering a savage, no-holds-barred assault. She was ordering headshots aimed at cockpits. She was ordering coordinated attacks. She was even ordering *physical* attacks. If *zellbrigen* had not been dead before, it *was* now.

This was not warfare.

It was murder.

This is what ComStar wanted, she thought grimly.

Well, they were about to.

She charged the *Flashman*. The ComStar heavy had fifteen tons on her *Vulture*, but Adrine had got the first shot in, and she had launched alpha strike after alpha strike, allowing the lake water to carry away her excess heat.

By Adrine's count, the fleeing *Flashman* had lost at least two double heat sinks. It had to be struggling with heat load right now, especially since all its major weapons were lasers.

She cleared the tree line, shouldering aside the tall lodgepoles and the gnarled cottonwoods. She sighted in on the walking, ovoid-shaped 'Mech and engaged with her large pulse lasers, stitching fire into the forest. She held off on her mediums to keep her heat load from spiking. Adrine was not really trying to take out the *Flashman* anyway.

She was going for the trees.

The retreating ComStar machine hit back with its large lasers, again forgoing its mediums.

The two volleys had nearly cleared the trees between the two 'Mechs. Now with an open field of fire, Adrine pulled into her primary triggers, hitting the *Flashman* with a one-two punch of LRM-20s. The missiles ran straight and true, racing toward the ComStar machine. The *Flashman*'s Buzzsaw AMS took some of them.

But not all.

The surviving missiles punched into its right leg, smashing armor all up and down the sturdy limb.

Then Adrine launched an alpha strike with her lasers.

Like a shark tearing flesh from its victim, she severed the *Flashman*'s leg entirely.

The heavy toppled backward, punched right out of the fight.

Adrine stalked toward her fallen foe.

She was not done yet.

Sandra Turley fought her way back to consciousness. Her five-point safety restraint bit cruelly into her shoulders and breasts. A stiletto-sharp pain on her left side told her something was broken—probably a rib. And her skull pulsed with agony.

She struggled to get the *Flashman* up.

Sandra couldn't stand, but if she could kneel on the left leg and prop herself up on her right arm, she could bring her left arm and her torso-mounted weapons to bear.

The crippled *Flashman* fell back, and pain stole her breath away. For a moment she lay there, sweating and gasping for air.

All of Sandra's actions had been textbook. When your flank is turned, execute a fighting withdrawal to a defensible position and then reform and call for reinforcements. That was doctrine. Every ComStar field officer knew that.

But the Clanners had come on too fast.

They had cut into her battalion before she could reset her line.

"Three-Twenty-Third Actual, Second Battalion. The Diamond Sharks have broken my line. I say again, my line is—"

She didn't get the rest of her report out.

The *Mad Dog* stalked up to her and brought one splayed food down on the prone *Flashman*'s cockpit, crushing the ComStar pilot beneath sixty tons of fury.

That descending foot was the last thing Sandra Turley ever saw.

And after she was dead, the Clanner machine went off to search for new prey.

"The Diamond Sharks have broken my line." The report chilled Mari Rennery's blood. But what came next told her just how dire the situation was. "I say again, my line is—"

The words just cut *off*.

Rennery knew Turley had just been killed, and Second Battalion was likely in headlong retreat.

She had been flanked. Her force was about to be split in the middle, her two divisions cut off from each other. Worse, if Alpha and Gamma pushed forward, she would be encircled.

She could execute a facing movement, pivoting right to face the new threat. But if she did, she'd be opening her left flank to Alpha and Gamma. No, there was really only one choice here.

"Three-Twenty-Third, this is Three-Twenty-Third Actual. Fall back by battalions. Two-Ninety-Ninth First Battalion, move up on the right to cover our withdrawal. Out."

She didn't like retreating.

But she had to preserve her force.

Adrine saw it at once. The *surats* were falling back. She had just opened the door for Alpha and Gamma.

Now if they could only get through.

Ian Hawker saw a ghostly *Cyclops* push its way out of the trees. It was angled left, so the Clanner could see the "*31*" painted on the SRM box on its torso. This was one of the Static Hurlers of ComStar's Eighth Army. The Sharks had managed to crush the 85th Division.

But not the 31st and 56th.

The *Cyclops* was often used as a command 'Mech. This might be the division commander himself.

Good.

A battle was like an ocean current rolling through the depths, and he was like a great, pelagic shark riding those dark torrents. His force would hack their way through the ComStar defenders. There was a lake to the south. If he could reach it, he could withdraw in good order. He would not be forced to rise from the water until he was under his DropShips' guns.

Always moving.

The Khan stepped forward and laid into the *Cyclops* with his pulse lasers. He *would* have followed up with a salvo of LRMs and a punishing gout of autocannon fire while his heat load dissipated.

But he had no more ordinance. All he had were lasers.

This was the price of allowing your supply lines to be cut.

Ruby fire splashed across the ComStar machine's torso, blackening the ghostly paint job and melting the Starshield Special underneath.

The *Cyclops* hit back, cutting into Ian's *Dire Wolf* with its Twin DO Type 20 lasers and following up with a Gauss slug that missed close to his right. The assault machine held off on its missiles—probably because it could not get a shot through the trees.

Ian Hawker decided to use his weapons while he still had them.

He stepped forward and fired all his lasers, sending a storm of ruby darts and emerald beams cutting into the *Cyclops*'s torso.

This time he got lucky.

His lasers cut right through the already-damaged armor and into the missile stores beneath. No one had cut the *ComStar* supply lines. The enemy machine had *plenty* of missiles.

And they all went up at once.

There was a moment of rippling explosions, and then a massive fireball engulfed the *Cyclops*.

Ian did not see the pilot eject.

He also did not see an alert on his IR sensors. The flare of heat from the dying *Cyclops* blinded his thermal sensors.

The first indication that he had a pair *Lancelot*s on his right were when they cut into his left arm. Multiple beams of emerald fire sliced into the limb.

Then the ComStar machines' PPCs sliced away his arm at the elbow.

It fell with a massive *crash*.

Half his remaining firepower had been cut away.

Ian staggered sideways, fighting to regain his balance. A storm of lasers sliced past him, just to the left—the *Lancelot*s must have been holding off on their PPCs to manage their heat.

Ian backstepped, firing his lasers again and again and again—no sense worrying about heat *now*. He hit the closer *Lancelot*, but it was just a holding action, and all three pilots knew it.

The Diamond Shark Khan was running.

Always moving, he thought desperately.

He had to regain control. As he backstepped away from the ComStar machines he was joined in retreat by an Alpha Galaxy *Kit Fox*, its blue paint burned away—along with most of its armor. He came across a fallen *Vapor Eagle*, the humanoid 'Mech lying face down in a stream like a drowned man.

It was not until a retreating *Kingfisher* engaged one of the *Lancelot*s that Ian realized he *had* no line. *All* his people were retreating.

There was no safe place to fall back to, no line to reform.

Safety lay only six hundred meters away.

But they were never going to reach it.

Adrine watched icons with Diamond Shark tags falling back. The Spheroids had already won this battle. Now the Clanners were on the verge of being *crushed*. Both Alpha and Gamma Galaxies could be destroyed to a man.

And if her Clan were humiliated, with two front-line Galaxies utterly savaged, it was conceivable that there would *be* no more Clan Diamond Shark.

Adrine was a freeborn warrior destined never to win a Bloodname nor rise to command anything beyond her freeborn Galaxy.

But she *was* a Diamond Shark. This she knew in her heart. Adrine did not care what *surat* Trueborns like Ian Hawker said. She *was* a Diamond Shark.

So she surged forward, charging alone into the 56th's rearguard.

She gave no orders, issued no stirring speeches.

But her people followed. First, they came in ones and twos. Then they came in Stars and Binaries. Soon all of them were charging after her, all that remained of the 3rd Shark Regulars, following her to their doom.

OVERLORD-CLASS DROPSHIP *REQUIEM*
KOZICE VALLEY
TUKAYYID
FREE RASALHAGUE REPUBLIC
3 MAY 3052

Dripping with sweat, his muscles burning with fatigue, Ian Hawker guided his wounded *Dire Wolf* up *Requiem*'s ramp.

The 'Mech felt strange. The severed left arm had unbalanced the machine, and there was something wrong inside the right-leg assembly. A tremor ran through the limb every time he took a step. He felt these wounds in the control sticks beneath his hands, felt them in the way the assault 'Mech shuddered as he worked it up the steel ramp.

But as bad as this was, none of it was as bad as the bitter, metallic taste of defeat.

Once he had managed to clear the ComStar line, he had drained half his canteen. But no matter how much water he drank, he could not wash away that harsh taste.

He had led his Clan to a humiliating rout. And the *only* thing that had kept his Diamond Sharks from being obliterated was the Third Shark Regulars.

Freebirths.

He had been saved by *freebirths*.

How could the universe be so *unjust*?

Ian stepped his machine onto the steel deck of *Requiem*'s cavernous cargo bay. He marched the *Wolf* up to its alcove, backstepping the machine into its berth and holding it motionless until the clamps closed around its legs and arms.

Well, around its *arm*. The left arm could not be secured.

It was gone.

He looked out at the vessel's deck. *Overlord*s could carry a battalion of BattleMechs. This enormous ship should have been filled with clanking, striding machines, moving to their berths as they waited extraction from this benighted world.

Instead, *Requiem* was not even a third full—a testament to the devastating losses ComStar had inflicted on his Sharks.

Ian popped his hatch, hearing the faint *hiss* of equalizing pressure. He stepped onto the bright orange gantry elevator, hands curled around the steel railing.

The elevator began its smooth descent.

Ian looked out over the DropShip.

Requiem was named for a kind of shark, a family that included the fearsome tiger shark. But as the elevator sank toward the deck, he remembered that the word had another meeting. Before requiem had been a family of sharks, it had been some kind of Spheroid religious ceremony meant to placate the souls of the dead.

As Ian looked out over the vast emptiness, he wondered which was the more appropriate meaning.

By the time he reached *Requiem*'s wardroom, Ian had convinced himself that none of this was his fault. The blame lay with Barbara Sennet.

And the Smoke Jaguars.

Ian had led the counterattack in the Diamond Shark rear against three ComStar divisions. He had rescued his force. If the Jaguars had managed to take their objective—or even had inflicted a reasonable amount of damage before being defeated—there would have been no ComStar Fifth Army to drop behind Ian's lines and turn the tide of battle.

And even after that happened, the remnants of Alpha and Gamma Galaxies had fought with the courage of Trueborn Crusaders. They would have found a way to win, if they had not been distracted by the freeborn filth from Omega Galaxy.

If Barbara Sennet had not ordered the Third Shark Regulars into the battle.

The Jaguars were beyond Ian's ability to punish.

But Barbara Sennet was *not*.

He pushed into the room where shipboard officers took their meals. It was abandoned. *Requiem's* officers and crew were at launch stations, preparing for takeoff. The room's lights had been secured, the only illumination coming from a holographic map of the Ghost Bear invasion corridor. Amidst a sea of stars labeled with the Bear logo, was a single star labeled with a gray diamond shark swimming before a bright blue gemstone and a trio of crimson arrows.

This faintly blue A-class star was labeled Nyserta.

It was the Diamond Sharks' lone holding in the Inner Sphere.

Barbara Sennet stood alone in the dark space, peering at the map.

She was a dark-skinned woman, the lines of her face severe. Her afro was crushed down, pushed out of shape by long hours beneath a neurohelmet. A crust of salt from dried sweat lined the pits and neckline of her pale blue t-shirt.

She looked as tired as Ian felt.

For a moment, he felt a tiny bit of empathy for her.

Then he savagely suppressed it.

This woman had betrayed him.

This woman had betrayed her *Clan*.

"You disobeyed my direct order." His voice was hard.

She did not look up at him. Or respond to his fury.

"We will have to withdraw our forces from Nyserta," she said, studying the Diamond Shark star system and its Ghost Bear neighbors.

"Did you hear me, *saKhan* Barbara Sennet? Do you think I will tolerate your disobedience? If you do, you are badly mistaken."

She reached into the holographic display and flicked her fingers, expanding the diagram. *Now* the stars showed emblems of the military units posted there.

"After our losses on Tukayyid, the Ghost Bears badly outnumber us in this region of space. We cannot hope to defeat them. We must save what we can."

"*We did not need the Third Shark Regulars*!" shouted Ian Hawker, infuriated that she would not listen.

Finally, she looked up at him. "It is not only the imbalance of military strength that forces our hand. It is also our humiliating defeat on Tukayyid that makes us a target. It is *your* failure that has brought us to this place."

Ian Hawker sputtered, so angry he could not form words.

"We are now a Home Clan." She gently shook her head. "There is nothing we can do about it."

"I will *destroy* you," he snarled. "You *and* the Third Shark Regulars."

"The Third Shark Regulars are *already* destroyed." Her voice was freighted with grief. "I promised them a place in the Remembrance. It is far less than they deserve. Nevertheless, I will see it done."

"*Neg*," he said.

Barbara leaned forward and tapped her noteputer. The lights snapped on and the star map snapped off.

She stood straight, pulling her shoulders back. "As for me, you may try to destroy me if you wish. But many of your Crusader allies lie dead in the Kozice Valley. Destroying me might not be as easy as you think."

"I still have supporters," he growled. "You do not have the backing to bring me down."

She tilted her head, as if considering this assertion. Finally, she shrugged. "Perhaps. What *is* certain is that our Clan is on the verge of extinction. As weak as you have made us, a Trial of Absorption is likely. If you and I struggle for power, we will only end up destroying our own people."

"I will never—" snapped Ian.

She cut him off. "Would you like to find yourself a Ghost Bear? A Snow Raven? How would you like to be adopted into a *Warden* Clan?"

Each question was like a blow landing. Ian opened his mouth, but could think of nothing to say and promptly shut it again.

She looked steadily at him. For a moment, there was no sound in the wardroom but Ian Hawker's ragged breathing.

"You will remain as Khan, and I will remain as saKhan."

"I will not surrender my Crusader beliefs." His tone was emphatic.

She raised her eyebrows in a kind of shrug. "Very well. The Clans are bound by the Truce of Tukayyid. And *we* are bound to lose our only Inner Sphere holding. So it does not matter what you call yourself, Ian Hawker. Your own failures of leadership have made us Wardens."

Range boiled in Ian's belly. He wanted to wrap his hands around her neck and strangle the life out of her. But he said nothing.

What could he say?

"I will continue my work with Merchant Factor Angus Labov," she said. "Trade will make us stronger. It will give us the opportunity to rebuild. If we are fortunate, and some other issue distracts our fellow Clans, we Diamond Sharks might evade a Trial of Absorption."

Ian Hawker thought carefully about her proposal. Her *deal*. The word tasted filthy in his mouth. If he accepted this arrangement, there would be a thousand other deals. This would become the Diamond Shark way of life. Markets and lines of credit and amortization and all the other filthy terms that went along with Spheroid business dealings.

He hated it.

He hated the very *thought* of it.

Aff, he would maintain his title. And she was right, a battle between the Sharks' Crusaders and Wardens would only pave the way to their absorption.

But he was a warrior. How could he live as the de facto head of a mercantile enterprise?

As if reading his mind, she said, "Logistics is the soul of warfare, Ian Hawker."

"*Warfare* is the soul of warfare."

She nodded slightly, as if acknowledging his difficulty with the deal. "It is at times like these that I turn to the Remembrance for guidance. Are you familiar with Passage 152, Verse 6, my Khan?"

Ian Hawker's head jerked up at that question. He stared at her. That was the passage *he* always turned to. How could she be quoting it back to him?

"Passage 152 tells us that we must accept change," she said.

"*It says no such thing*," he snarled.

"'*To survive, the shark must be always moving*,'" she replied.

Ian Hawker heard that passage with new ears. *Always moving.*

Always *changing.*

Despair swept over Ian like a crashing wave.

This warrior with the heart of a money counter had just delivered him a defeat worse even than the one he had suffered on the world below.

THE LIONS OF PREZNO

BRYAN YOUNG

More than a thousand years ago, in the days when humans only had Terra to call home, they struggled to connect. Communication that can now take place between planets thousands of light-years away could barely happen between continents. Parts of the world were still unknown to humanity, and traveling across it was a struggle at best, an impossibility at worst.

In 1898, a railroad was conceived by the colonial invaders of Africa to connect the ports of the Indian Ocean to the interior of the continent. As the construction crossed the plains of Tsavo, two maneless lions attacked in the night, eating workers alive. For months, the progress of the railroad slowed, and the legend of the lions grew.

The workers named these lions the Ghost and the Darkness and it was everything they could do to survive their brutal attacks. The lions would strike in the night, tearing men from their tents as they screamed. By the time the other workers and the guards heard the cries, the lions had faded back into the darkness, ready to kill again.

They would appear randomly, covering more ground than anyone thought possible. Some said it had to be an entire pride of lions, rather than just two.

But that's all it was.

It was said that before the British lieutenant-colonel overseeing the operation finally killed the fabled predators, the Ghost and the Darkness had claimed as many as 135 victims.

This story is about lions and invaders of a different sort, and tells the tale of the White Lions of ComStar's 394th Division and the 5th Battle Cluster of the Jade Falcon invaders looking to cross the Prezno Plain to victory during the Battle of Tukayyid...

PREZNO PLAIN
TUKAYYID
1 MAY 3052

"What is it?" Star Colonel Diane Anu, a thin woman with raven black hair, said into her comm.

"They came from nowhere, Star Colonel, sir," the Mechwarrior, Marja, reported.

"Who came from nowhere?"

"ComStar forces, but we cannot be sure which outfit. By the time we knew the attack had occurred and the smoke settled, they were gone."

"Where did they go? Even with stealth technology, 'Mechs do not just disappear entirely, MechWarrior."

"Unknown."

The Star Colonel growled as she thought. "It would be fitting for these *dezgra* Spheroids to be using the ancient tools of assassins rather than fight us honorably."

"Yes, sir."

"Where is the Star Captain?" Diane asked. Star Captain Nedra was a fine warrior and the leader of Trinary Alpha. She should have been the one giving the report.

"She took the lead, and her *Summoner* was hit first. We are working on extracting her from her 'Mech."

"Any other losses?"

"MechWarriors Tyne and Pithra were both killed."

Diane Anu took in a deep breath and held it, trying to calculate all the possibilities. She had just lost three 'Mechs to an enemy they could not even see. She needed more information. "Find these ComStar *surats*. Report back as soon as you have word. And when you find them, destroy them."

"*Aff,* Star Colonel."

The static on the line vanished as Marja clicked off and Diane boiled with frustration.

Of course it was a trap. Why else would ComStar let the Jade Falcons land on the Prezno Plain relatively unmolested if they did not have something bigger planned for them?

The Prezno Plain was a massive patchwork of tall grasses, fields of grain, and clumps of trees, most established as orchards. The patches of arbored areas that dotted the landscape were perfect for ambushes. Aside from the trees, there was nowhere to hide. Just wide-open spaces. ComStar was just as vulnerable on the open plain, so Diane could not blame the fools for their line of attack. If they were going to win, it would be by resorting to *dezgra* tactics. But they would not win. The Jade Falcons—*neg*, all the Clans—would never let that happen.

She only wished it had never come to this. If the Clans were somehow brought low by these battles, the influence of the Inner Sphere would not serve them well. Diane knew her position was a minority among the Jade Falcons, though, and would still fight with every measure of her ability to see her Clan succeed. If this was their wish, she would grant it by being the sharpest blade she could be.

She took another deep breath and paused for a moment, trying to conjure ideas about what ComStar was really planning. That deep level of thought, research, and introspection had been the only way she had been able to get through everything from her *sibko* all the way to her Bloodnaming. She could see the battle strategies laid plainly like the inner workings of machines, and she could see the machines themselves for what they were, able to push them to their maximum and overcome when others could not.

Glancing down at the various readouts on the console of her *Summoner,* Diane took in as much information as she could. The layout did not offer much. She could see the horizon in every direction, and the only 'Mechs she saw up close were the units of her Command Star. Now she noticed something unusual; off in the distance was a puff of smoke. That must have been where Alpha Beak One had been ambushed. On the other side of the horizon were the specks that consisted of Alpha Beak Two. The Star of 'Mechs that composed Alpha Eye had faded into the distance behind her for the march to the bridges of Robyn's Crossing and Plough Bridge. But the bridges were still dozens of kilometers away, and ComStar would make covering that distance a very long, hard march.

If she were planning the defense against the Jade Falcons, Diane might have put the entirety of the 'Mechs at her disposal in fortified positions on both sides of the bridges that led over the Prezno River, one aimed at Olalla and the other Humptulips. That was the most honorable and sensible way to do things. But she also understood that, from their perspective, ComStar was fighting for their very way of life. They would resort to anything to keep it.

She supposed there was a sort of honor to be found in that.

Diane ran through a number of other scenarios in her mind and wondered if it was all a feint. If they could slow the Falcon advance even slightly, they would be able to secure their fortifications even more. The only option would be to ignore the hit-and-run attacks and push through.

"Golden Talons," Diane said into her comm, addressing all of the warriors beneath her, "tighten formation. Alpha Beaks One and Two, fall back toward command position. Alpha Eye, close ranks behind us. If ComStar is out there in small units, I want us to hit back overwhelmingly."

"*Aff!*" came a chorus of shouts through the comm.

But in their affirmative cries, Diane read concern as well. They were walking into something unknown. And the sneak attack had put them on edge. No matter how trained a Clan warrior was, there was always some concern over the direction of the next attack.

The command line chimed over Diane's comm. "Star Colonel Diane Anu here."

"This is Star Colonel Kael Pershaw."

"What can I do for the representative of our Khan?" Diane had wondered why saKhan Vandervahn Chistu had selected Kael Pershaw to act as his representative and help command the battle, but she did not question the decision. If he was the mind that was trusted to see them through this conflict, so too would Diane trust him.

"Stop your Cluster. We are going to hold fast here for the night. ComStar is too well dug in, and we still do not know exactly what we are up against."

"I believe that we are being harassed by small hit and run groups, striking and then pulling away," Diane said. All of the available data added up to that conclusion, and she had no reason to believe otherwise, though she did yearn for more data.

"It looks to me like we are facing the entire ComStar 11th Army out there," Pershaw replied. "And until we know more, that is how we are going to proceed. We do not want to engage the enemy on their terms, and walking into their trap is exactly what that would do."

"*Aff,* Star Colonel."

Diane harrumphed after the Star Colonel—a twisted man, more machine than warrior—clicked off the line. She did not like the assessment, but she would abide by it. Diane knew Kael Pershaw had a difficult a time being taken seriously by the rest of the Clan. Like she had to rely on her superior knowledge of BattleMechs, Pershaw had to survive by his wits. And if Kael Pershaw, who was overseeing the whole battle, saw something Diane did not, then maybe it was worth listening to him.

"Golden Talons," Diane barked to the 5th Battle Cluster, "there has been a change in orders. We camp here tonight while the Khan decides on a new plan of attack."

"*Aff!*"

Night on the Prezno Plain fell hard and fast. It was daylight, and then the colors of the sky shifted from orange to blood red to blue. And suddenly, darkness came upon them.

MechWarriors Kory and Daswin of Star Colonel Diane Anu's Alpha Eye Star One had drawn the first watch.

Kory pushed her *Kit Fox* around the next leg of their sentry circle, but she did not see anything out there. With magres,

IR, or anything else. There was simply nothing out there at the moment.

But she knew that was not true.

"I tell you, there is nothing out there," Daswin said from his own *Kit Fox*. Most members of their Star piloted a *Kit Fox*; though their loadouts were different, they all shared the same basic OmniMech.

"You heard what happened earlier. They attacked and vanished. They are out there," Kory told him.

"'Mechs do not just vanish."

"Surely ComStar wouldn't abandon stealth technology if they had it. And if there are no 'Mechs out there, what got MechWarriors Tyne and Pithra killed?"

"Tyne and Pithra were weak, then."

"They were not weak; the Inner Sphere forces are dishonorable."

"That much is true," Daswin admitted.

Kory pressed her 'Mech further forward, alert for any blip on the scopes, any irregularity on her HUD, anything at all.

But the black night on the Prezno Plain was quiet.

The only activity came from the staging ground for the rest of the Cluster, some distance away. The other MechWarriors in their Star slept in their 'Mechs, all aimed in an outward circle, ready and waiting to launch a counter-attack if an initial attack materialized.

Kory would sound the alarm and the Jade Falcons of the 5th Battle Cluster would all roar to life and put the ComStar 'Mechs down with prejudice. Then, they would be able to move on to their objective with no further delays.

That it had already taken a day to crawl forward from the dropsite confused Kory. They were Jade Falcon. Why take things slowly? Even if ComStar had overwhelming forces, an OmniMech was worth five Inner Sphere 'Mechs, and a Jade Falcon was worth any ten ComStar MechWarriors.

It was not even a contest.

Kory covered the next leg of the circle around the encampment and could not understand why the thermal image of her HUD flashed from dark blues and purples to white hot in an instant.

A malfunction?

That idea held until her *Kit Fox* rocked with the impact of a missile salvo.

"*Stravag!*" she said, firing into the white heat of battle with her large laser, hoping she could hit anything.

"Ambush!" Daswin cried out.

She glanced down to her scopes and saw Daswin as a bright spot on her radar, but his dot quickly flashed from green to yellow to red.

Daswin screamed through the comm and, when the line went dead, Kory knew she would have to face off against the ComStar threat alone until the rest of the cluster could be rallied. She shouted her location to the rest of the Cluster and transmitted the pertinent data.

Upon checking the damage readouts—her center of mass flashed yellow—she cycled through her viewscreen options, hoping to find one that would give her an edge and really show her what she was up against. They must have been jamming her; every single one showed a muddled mess.

Kory gritted her teeth as she pushed her 'Mech forward toward the origin point of the attack and lashed out with her large laser and LB-X autocannon. They were her longest-ranged weapons, and she knew the attacking ComStar forces were not close. If they *had* been close, they would have been spotted by the initial scout sweeps when they had pinpointed this area for the pause of their march.

Bringing her *Kit Fox* up to top speed, she closed the distance, but the wall of white heat began to fade.

She fired again into the night.

Her *Kit Fox* buckled with another impact, and Kory found herself in sudden pain. The cockpit had taken another hit—or series of hits. Missiles and lasers focused in on her, enough firepower to estimate there were five ComStar 'Mechs out there. Minimum.

Blinding pain radiated up from her left leg. She could not move it, and when she reached down, all she felt was wetness. She couldn't feel by touch whether the dampness was sweat or blood, but it did not have any bearing on her mission whether or not she had lost her leg. She still had enough life left in her to continue returning fire, and that was what she would do.

Firing her large laser again, she hoped to take at least one enemy down. If she could disable a ComStar 'Mech, those above her might be able to question the MechWarrior and find out what sort of force the Jade Falcons were actually facing on the Prezno Plain.

But the bright beam flew wide into the night.

As it faded, the white heat of the 'Mechs vanished from her scopes. They had disappeared again.

At the edges of her field of vision, she saw new marks coming from her six. The rest of the Golden Talons responding to her call.

But there was nothing left to respond to.

ComStar was gone.

Vanished.

Dawn arrived much slower than night had come, taking its time to brighten Prezno Plain. Soft dew covered the grasslands and meadows, and the trees around them cast long shadows from the morning sun.

Star Colonel Diane Anu stood in the center of the circle of Golden Talon 'Mechs, all still facing outward. With her were the Star Captains and Commanders in charge of the various Stars in her Cluster. "What is the report on the two MechWarriors on watch last night?"

Star Commander Joyce, a sturdy woman with deep mahogany skin and green tattoos in geometric patterns on her face, stepped forward. Kory and Daswin were in her Star. "MechWarrior Daswin almost perished in the attack and is recovering. MechWarrior Kory is also with the scientist caste. They are doing everything they can to replace her leg. But she will see no further fighting on Tukayyid."

"Regrettable," Diane said with a sigh. "They were excellent MechWarriors. Elite among the very best. We have lost a Star's worth of 'Mechs so far, yet we have not truly engaged with a single ComStar warrior. In both cases, they have retreated before we could catch them."

"It is cowardly," Joyce said.

"But what do we do?" Star Commander Jo Thastus of Bravo Nova Two asked. She had her frizz of black hair pulled into a tight bun, and her well-muscled arms were crossed over her chest. "Our MechWarriors will jump at shadows around every tree if these attacks continue."

"I do not disagree," Diane Anu said. "However, our orders from Kael Pershaw insist that we slow our advance and check those very trees. They have more information than we do, and say that the ComStar 11th Army is out in these plains in force. Tell me, Jade Falcons, is it ever wise to allow the enemy to choose the field of battle?"

"*Neg!*" they all responded.

"What happens when they take us out slowly, one by one?" Star Commander Helga, of Charlie Nova Two, asked. Her head was shaved on one side and her blond hair had been dyed Jade Falcon green on the other.

"We will not let that happen. But we will use what we have learned so far. Star Commander Res, report on the findings of your Elementals of Delta Strider."

Res, easily the largest man there, stepped forward. His dark skin offered a sharp contrast to his penetrating ice-blue eyes. Being an Elemental, he had muscles the size of most MechWarrior's heads.

He nodded at Diane. "Star Colonel, we investigated the area, and found they had crafted a subterranean cavern where they could fit between six and eight 'Mechs. The debris tells a story of how they covered it over with dirt and trees, and struck when the time was right."

"That would explain Kory reporting they had come from nowhere," Joyce said.

Jo Thastus waved a hand. "But where did they *go*?"

"According to the report my MechWarrior gave before the medics took her," Joyce brought a hand to her chin, deep in thought, "they were heading toward our target, further consolidating the forces arrayed against us, trying to keep us from crossing the Prezno River and taking Olalla and Humptuilps."

"Sound thinking," Diane Anu said. Looking around, she realized she was the smallest of all those in her command. She had earned their respect. She did not command the 5th Battle Cluster for nothing.

"But what if these are merely harassing attacks to slow us down and cover further preparations they make at our target destinations?" She was not really interested in a response to that question. It was rhetorical, and her Star Captains and Commanders all knew it. She had a habit of thinking out loud in front of them, and that was part of what had earned their respect. They knew her mind was keen and sharp when it came to strategy, and she never used more force than necessary, which made her a very effective bidder.

In this battle, though, she was a pawn that had been bid on behalf of their Clan, and had no ability to bid for herself or those under her.

That worried her as much as anything.

"This is what we know," she told the crowd around her, "the ComStar forces are *dezgra*. But they are cunning and fierce. The dishonor of our foe is no excuse for losing. If we must rise above it, we will. We are Jade Falcon!"

"*We are Jade Falcon*!" they repeated.

Diane raised a fist in the air. "The march continues. Though we go slow, we also go mightily. Back to our 'Mechs. Those bridges will be ours."

"*Aff*!"

The ground rumbled with the force of each Star of 'Mechs in the Trinary moving out. Diane could not feel it inside *her* 'Mech. Her *Summoner* stabilized those tremors from ever reaching her, but she knew what it would have felt like to be on the ground when an entire Cluster pushed forward.

She smiled.

The formation she had chosen to employ was tight-knit and would travel close together.

She had heard reports from Kael Pershaw that the unit harassing them was ComStar's 394th division. "The White Lions" they called themselves. And Diane Anu, obsessed with research, history, and the natural world, knew enough about lions to know they picked off sick and weak prey first. If her Trinary stuck together, there would be no easy targets for them to ambush. If these lions really were trying to pick off the weakest and most isolated, they would probably focus on the edges of the advance, meaning Diane's forces might meet less resistance than the Jaegers or the Falcon Guards. If the Lions *were* trying to pick off easy targets, the edges would definitely be easier than the main column.

Diane had tried to convince Kael Pershaw to increase their march speed, but he failed to see the wisdom in that. For Pershaw, the idea was simple. Slow and steady wins the race, and the faster the Jade Falcons advanced, the more likely they would run into a wall of ComStar 'Mechs. An enemy force on one side or another would stagger their units anyway, but according to Pershaw, going slow would give the Falcons an edge when it came to redeploying to deal with the ComStar threat.

The Star Colonel sighed. She tried to set aside the madness that had brought them to Tukayyid for this proxy battle in the first place. The Inner Sphere had no standing to negotiate with the Clans for a battle like this, but neither should the Clans have been waging the battle in the first place. But, if they were going to be conquering Terra anyway, perhaps there was some wisdom in not battling for it outright. *What good is control of a planet you are duty bound to protect if there is no longer anyone living there because the fighting was too intense?*

In the end, Diane hated to admit that the proxy war was sensible, as she wished they didn't have to fight it in the first place. It was likely that all of the Warden-leaning Star Colonels across all the Clans felt the same way.

But here they were on Tukayyid and no force in the galaxy, from the Inner Sphere to the Periphery, would change that.

All they could do was press on.

And that is what Diane Anu did.

She moved her *Summoner* forward, leading her Command Star at the head of the Golden Talons.

If the ComStar forces wanted to pretend to be a pack of lions, they would learn that the Jade Falcons were hunters with claws of their own.

"I want every copse of trees checked out as we move," Diane told those in her command. "If we are going to move slowly, we will be thorough, and rob ComStar of the ability to get the drop on us."

"*Aff*," her MechWarriors replied.

The Talons were a well-oiled machine. The best the Jade Falcons had to offer.

Every time they came to a new grove, a different Star took a turn, acting like a sort of bomb squad. They probed the orchards, checking for traps and hidden 'Mechs. It baffled the entire Cluster as to how ComStar had done it. They had not had *that* much time to build their traps before the Clans had agreed to descend on Tukayyid.

After the first potential hideout they came to, the one Alpha Eye had razed, they got word that the Falcon Jaegers, under Marthe Pryde's command, had been hit. They had lost three 'Mechs, which set the Golden Talons on their guard.

Diane could not explain the difference, but there was an electrical current she felt between the MechWarriors in her command. They were on edge. The slow movement of the convoy, the crawl of their advance toward their targets, it all added up to an apprehension that permeated everyone.

The second potential trap came, and Alpha Beak Two, led by Star Commander Hoyt, went out, taking their turn in the proverbial minefield.

As they finished up, finding nothing, another message came through the radio. It was Kael Pershaw to report more lost Jade Falcons to the ComStar hit-and-runs.

"Did they return fire?"

"Some. The ComStar forces faded before the Guards could launch a sufficient counter-attack."

Diane sighed as she relayed the news to her Cluster, telling them there was definitely a problem. The Lions were picking off Falcons one or two at a time and suffering no losses. According to Kael Pershaw, not a single ComStar 'Mech on their flank had been taken down by a Jade Falcon.

With the low losses of ComStar so far, even Diane Anu began to worry about the Lions in the shadows.

Another outcropping appeared on the horizon. Diane raised an eyebrow. "Bravo Nova Two. MechWarrior Calston, your Star is up. Investigate and clear so we can move on."

"*Aff,*" he replied.

In his 30-ton *Kit Fox,* MechWarrior Calston took the lead toward the trees. With the other *Kit Fox,* two 80-ton *Gargoyle*s and a 65-ton *Loki* trailing behind him, Bravo Nova Two fanned out as they approached the grove. All the while, they were under Diane's anxious, watchful eyes.

Every spot on their march today had come up empty, but the caution had been required, thanks to the reports from the other Clusters. But how would Bravo Nova Two approach the task? Would they attack with aplomb and sweep the trees easily? Or would they approach with trepidation and fear?

Diane knew the answer as soon as they arrived.

Aplomb.

MechWarrior Calston moved right into the trees and the rest of the Star followed, hoping to flush any ComGuards out like a dog rousting birds from a bush. Any lions that took flight would find themselves under fire from the waiting hunters.

Smoke and dirt billowed into the sky, and it took a moment to notice where the missiles were coming from.

A pair of ComStar 'Mechs erupted from the grassy area *beside* the trees, unleashing a barrage of missiles and lasers, all of it aimed directly at the *Kit Fox* furthest from the group. Diane's computer tagged the Falcon 'Mech as belonging to MechWarrior Hevlin. Between the surprise attack and their ambush away from the Cluster, they got a second volley off.

The rest of Bravo Nova Two took a moment to realize what was happening and turned toward the attack. But by that time, MechWarrior Hevlin's lacerated *Kit Fox* fell backward, taken out of the fight.

"Open fire!" Diane commanded, and the Cluster obeyed.

More fire came from the Lions—more than Diane would have guessed possible from two 'Mechs. The cluster of red dots on her radar display informed her there *were* more there, she just could not see them.

The dots began to pull back, running in the other direction. Looking up to her view screen, Diane saw them fleeing through the smoke.

"Bravo Trinary, pursue," she told her warriors. "Find out where they are going."

"*Aff!*" MechWarrior Calston said, immediately switching directions in his *Kit Fox.*

Diane shifted her attention to the 'Mechs further away from the conflagration. "Golden Talons, push forward. We are going to take those bridges."

"*Aff!*" they called and the cluster, still behind Diane, pushed forward.

"MechWarrior Hevlin," she called to the battered and smoking *Kit Fox* at the edge of the copse as they moved past the orchard. "Status report. Still alive?"

"*Aff,*" he said, his voice strained. "They cracked my cockpit, but I live. They will pay for this."

"Make them pay, MechWarrior. That is an order."

"*Aff,* Star Colonel."

Forward the Golden Talons marched while Bravo Nova Two pursued their attackers.

MechWarrior Hevlin would do his best to extricate himself from his 'Mech. If the support convoys could patch it up, they would. But there was no time for Diane Anu to worry about it.

"MechWarrior Calston, report. Are they dead yet?" But looking at her scopes, she knew what to expect.

"They are gone, Star Colonel. They had a head start and faster 'Mechs."

"No excuses. Next time we catch them."

"*Aff.*"

But Diane knew there was nothing to be done about it. There was still something going on she and the rest of the Jade Falcon command had not been able to figure out.

They still did not have all the information.

So, onward—slowly—they marched.

The slow advance continued.

The Jade Falcons stopped and started at the command of Kael Pershaw. Meetings were held and decisions made. More information was learned as they found it.

And then, they marched again, and more ComStar Lions would roar as they struck from ambush, and more Jade Falcons would fall.

They would debate again.

And then march forward.

And finally, on the third day, things changed with a call on the comm.

"Congratulations," Kael Pershaw's voice said. "You have made it to within a dozen kilometers of the bridges. But you have a problem. One only you can solve, Star Colonel."

"And what problem is that?"

"There is an emplacement of ComStar forces ahead of you. They are directly in your path, and they are dug in."

"This is not a problem. The Golden Talons will handle it," Diane replied, already formulating a plan. She would send the faster 'Mechs ahead to engage and bombard the emplacements, giving the heavies time to launch a direct attack. After that, the Elementals would go in and sabotage everything they could.

It made sense, given the distance they still had to cover. And the last thing she needed was to waste any more time after their crawling toward the objective.

"I know you will. I also have more intel about the forces that slowed our advance."

"*Aff?*"

"There was no movement in force. Our air reconnaissance confirms that our advance was slowed by no more than a few dozen ComStar BattleMechs, employing *dezgra* tactics. I wish we had pushed forward faster."

Diane held her tongue for a moment. Then cocked an eyebrow. "We can only move forward from our current position. No sense in wondering how to strike from a position previously held."

"Well said, Star Colonel, well said. Now let us strike these Lions hard and fast, and show them how Jade Falcons truly fight."

"*Aff,* Star Colonel." Hunting big ComStar game was exactly what Diane Anu had in mind.

She took to her comm and barked orders. "All right, Talons. The bridges are in our sights. We are going to take them both, but standing in our way is an emplacement of ComStar forces. They are dug in, but they do not stand a chance against us. The worst is behind us. They have nowhere else to hide or flee, and we know who wins this in an honorable, stand up fight, *Aff*?"

"*Aff,*" her MechWarriors replied, "*Jade Falcons!*"

Diane smiled when she heard their resolve.

The cities of Olalla and Humptulips would soon be theirs.

They would be the victors on Tukayyid.

And then, soon enough, on Terra.

THE ICARUS LAMENT

CHRIS HUSSEY

EASTERN TALLPINES
WALDORFF V
STEEL VIPER OCCUPATION ZONE
8 NOVEMBER 3051

Star Commander Avedis grinned in satisfaction. It was the only time during the entire Trial he let himself smile, despite having numerous reasons to do so. The Trial of Position to be a Star Captain in Gamma Galaxy came down to him and Point Commander Rudella.

From the beginning, Avedis had held the upper hand. Rudella's *Shadow Cat* outweighed his *Battle Cobra* by five tons, but possessed the same speed profile. If she desired it, her 'Mech could sprint past Avedis', thanks to its integrated MASC system. Those advantages meant nothing if not used—or, in Rudella's case, abused.

The Trial was nearly over. Avedis had already skillfully amputated the *Cat's* right arm, removing the extended range medium laser and one of its long-range missile 15-packs. After that brutality, the two began a chase through the Eastern Tallpines, where Rudella's speed advantage was blunted. When she did engage her MASC, the speed became a detriment. Desperate to flank Avedis, Rudella smashed through the trees with little care. By the time the dueling duo emerged from the woods, the *Shadow Cat* was crisscrossed in numerous scars and carved canyons from his ER large and ER medium lasers, while his *Battle Cobra* was little worse for wear.

The future Star Captain Avedis gave his lone smile, watching in amusement as the *Cat* charged forward, once again using its MASC, with a burst of speed that belied its 45 tons—only to stumble to an ungraceful stop as the MASC circuitry in the OmniMech's myomers, pushed beyond its limits, locked up. Avedis knew Rudella's speed advantage was now gone, soon to be followed by her challenge for this position.

His targeting reticule pulsed green as all four weapons beeped a lock on the immobile 'Mech. Avedis pressed the firing stud, assuring his victory. The wave of heat assaulting him was just a minor inconvenience as three of his four laser beams struck the *Shadow Cat's* left leg. The rays of focused light carved a line from knee to hip, boiling off the remaining armor, then severing the already damaged myomers and finally the structural underpinnings, sending the leg tumbling to the ground. The final beam, one of the medium lasers added the final insult, cutting a gash across the *Cat's* cockpit as Point Commander Rudella and her 'Mech fell—literally and figuratively—into defeat.

Avedis stared at the fallen 'Mech, memories dancing in his mind, each popping to the forefront, then twirling back while another took its place, only to wait its turn to come back around in the waltz again.

The fallen *Shadow Cat* triggered them all. The 'Mech was known for its speed, something his former Clan, the Ice Hellions, revered, and well known for. But Avedis was no longer a Hellion. Taken as a bondsman three years prior by a Steel Viper MechWarrior who taught him striking fast and hard wasn't the only way to win. Thinking, planning, and knowing not only when to strike, but *how* to strike could overcome any gross advantage an enemy might have, such as speed.

It was a painful lesson. His fierce pride in the Hellions made Avedis a difficult bondsman and a constant pain for his bondholder, Star Captain Roxanne Running-Elk. It wasn't until she was severely injured while defending against a bandit caste raid that Avedis learned the true steel lying within the Vipers. It was then he dedicated himself to prove that he, not born of Viper *sibkos*, could be a true Steel Viper.

Avedis still felt the pangs of separation from his home Clan from time to time. But returning to the Hellions meant defeat of a different kind. Not only for himself, but for his Clan. What better way to prove to the Steel Vipers the superiority of the Ice Hellions than to have one of their own rise in the ranks?

No, I must not think in such circles, Avedis chided himself. *I was born Hellion, but I am a Viper now. I am a Star Captain in Gamma Galaxy, and I will serve my Clan proudly.*

As Avedis left his cockpit to check on the welfare of his defeated opponent, he looked toward the sky. Smoke from Rudella's *Shadow Cat* rose in front of Waldorff V's distant sun, allowing him to view the perfect circle. His thoughts traveled beyond the star, into the deeper space beyond. His mind imagined all the worlds of the Inner Sphere; those already conquered by his fellow Clansmen and those that lay waiting to be liberated from their archaic bondage to these House Lords.

Soon, he would be part of this glory. The ilKhan had recently released the reserve Clans to aid in the invasion in the fifth wave. For the Steel Vipers, it began with the Jade Falcons ceding Waldorff V.

Avedis turned his gaze back to the fallen *Shadow Cat* and the slowly emerging form of Rudella. *And for me, it begins with my new rank and title.*

ALAENI FALLS
JABUKA
FREE RASALHAGUE REPUBLIC
7 DECEMBER 3051

Steam flashed, mixing with the cascading waters of the massive Alaeni Falls. The cloud burst red for an instant as the ER large laser from Star Captain Avedis' *Battle Cobra* pierced the wet, blue veil, striking the *Wolverine* fleeing into the caves behind it.

Though the frigid waters helped mask the heat signature of the FedCom 'Mech, Avedis knew that even if it did escape into the rocky passages beyond, it and the other fleeing Commonwealth 'Mechs had nowhere to run. Khan Natalie Breen's Command Star awaited them in the tunnels to deliver the killing blow. The last bits of resistance on this world were less than an hour from falling.

Avedis keyed his comm channel to the rest of his Trinary. "We halt here. They have fled into the falls. They seek refuge, but will find only defeat and humiliation. Our work here is done. The Khan's Trinary shall enjoy the rest of this meal."

"But Star Captain, should we not pursue? Are these not our rightful *isorla*?"

Avedis knew that voice; it was Star Commander Rudella. After his victory over the former Point Commander, he was impressed enough in her abilities that he had petitioned Gamma Galaxy's commander to allow her to test for his previous position and should she prove victorious, place her within his Trinary. Impressed by his boldness, Galaxy Commander and saKhan Zalman agreed. It was one of many rapid moves Avedis made to show the worthiness of his new position. Whether training sim drills or battle planning meetings, the newly minted Star Captain spoke his mind and shared his opinion fearlessly.

The shining moment for Avedis and his Trinary were their actions on Twycross. Retaking the world the Jade Falcons lost to the Federated Commonwealth forces was critical to show the seriousness of the Vipers, eager to make amends for being relegated to a reserve Clan. On the windswept world, his Trinary struck the crippling blow to drive the FedCom away.

Everything culminated in the battle plan for Jabuka. Avedis' Twycross actions had caught the attention of Khan Breen, but when it came to the bidding and planning of what would drive out the FedCom forces, his counsel convinced the Khan of what was needed to be victorious. As his reward, Avedis' Trinary was placed under Alpha Galaxy for the invasion of the planet.

It had proved to be a shrewd move, as Avedis and his warriors racked up kill after kill, culminating now with the shepherding of the last bits of the pathetic 19th Lyran Guards straight into the waiting arms of his Khan.

"*Neg,* Rudella. These kills are for the Khan. Our *isorla* is being allowed to partake in this attack. Only Alpha Galaxy was involved in this assault. For our Trinary to be here is a great honor. To herd these *surats* into the trap, an even greater honor. The road to Terra is long, and now that the Vipers are nearing the tip of the spear, there will be more than enough rewards for us."

"Well done, my Khan." Star Captain Avedis strode with purpose to the blond-haired woman standing among a quartet of other warriors, conversing. She turned at the loudly spoken words. Still dressed in her MechWarrior's garb; tight, emerald green shorts and matching battle vest. Her hair shaved short on the sides, but curved high and back in a messy mat thanks to her neurohelmet. The uniform matched all those around her, only the emblems on the vest giving any clue of difference from the rest.

Avedis wore the same. Thin and muscular, his brown hair rested as a disheveled flattop. The hint of a tattoo peeked out along his shoulders from underneath his vest.

Khan Breen's eyes narrowed as she smiled. "And to you and your Trinary, Star Captain." The other warriors in the circle ceased talking and turned to Avedis. He felt the resentment in their stares.

Alpha Galaxy warriors upset over a Gamma joining their party. And made worse by not being born of a Viper sibko. "Thank you." Avedis gave a curt bow. "You honored me and my warriors by allowing us to be part of the attack."

Breen gave only a slight nod back to him. "Your counsel and planning helped seal our victory." The Khan turned back slightly toward the other warriors. "Besides, had it been disastrous, it would be fitting that you and yours suffer the humiliation."

The warrior quartet chuckled. Avedis knew they must belong to her Command Star, or at the very least, her Trinary.

He smiled with them. "Agreed. Then it is good that did not happen. Did you enjoy the treats we sent your way in the falls?"

Breen nodded. "We did indeed. They fought so poorly; it is a wonder they were able to climb into their cockpits." Breen gestured toward one of the warriors. An olive-skinned man with angled muscles, accentuated by the tight fit of his vest. "Gamal here cornered and felled one of their assault 'Mechs in less than a minute as it struggled through a narrow passage."

Avedis met the man's eyes. "How...honorable—" he let the word hang to imply just the right amount of sarcasm and disdain, "—to take it down so quickly, sparing them the embarrassment of their very existence."

It worked. Avedis saw the anger burn in Gamal's eyes at the dig. Avedis let a smile flash for just an instant.

Khan Breen chuckled, knowing what he had done. "We all played our part and did what was ordered."

Stepping back, Avedis gave another bow. "I serve my Clan and my Khan."

"And you serve it well." She looked toward Gamal and the other warriors. "Every battle may be important, but not every battle must be some great testament to our honor. If it brings us closer to the realization of Kerensky's vision and our rightful place on Terra, then we have indeed acted with honor."

The Steel Viper Khan strode to a table in the hall and vaulted herself up on top. Raising her arms and shouting to the rest of the assembled warriors. "You have all acted with honor this day! No matter what role you served, what part you played. Your victory here, and every victory since our ilKhan chose to call us forward, shows that this is where we should have been all along!"

The crowd erupted in cheers as Breen jumped down, striding back to Avedis and the others. The Star Captain saw the wry smile and sly wink Khan Breen gave him as she walked past to the hall's exit. Like they had agreed prior, Avedis dismissed himself from Gamal and the rest, heading through the crowd, taking his time—the allotted time—to make the proper exit. Before Avedis could retire for the evening, he had one more mission to fulfill.

Avedis crawled up from under the covers, meeting face to face with Khan Natalie Breen. She smiled as she ran a hand down the side of his face. "Well done, Star Captain." She chuckled.

He returned the smile. "I serve my Clan and my Khan." Avedis paused as he adjusted his body on top of hers. He glanced downward. "In whatever capacity is desired."

The pair laughed as Avedis rolled free of Breen's body and slid next to her. They shared a silent moment before Avedis broke it. "What is our next target, and may I bid early?"

Breen turned her head. "Star Captain, just because we couple and share this bed does not mean you are privy to what is next for my Steel Vipers."

Avedis felt defeated. "*Aff*, my Khan. I meant no disrespect."

Breen smiled again and rolled to face him. "And none was taken." She reached out to run her fingers along the lines of his tattoo. It covered his entire chest, the tips ending on his shoulders. It was the face of his original Clan's namesake, an Ice Hellion. "You are a *ristar* amongst the Vipers, make no mistake. But we are not *sibkin*, nor are we from the same Galaxy." She poked the nose of the tattooed Hellion. "By Kerensky's blood, you are not even a true Viper."

Avedis winced at the words. They struck like a dagger in his gut. Breen saw the hurt on his face. "I am Khan, and I may do as I please." She placed a finger under his chin, lifting his head. "But still I...*we* must be careful. Warriors should have no care for politics, but yet, they are here. An enemy without form that must be fought skillfully, not bluntly. Perhaps, when you are a Star Colonel, something I am sure will happen before we set foot on Terra, there will be no more need for such skullduggery."

Avedis nodded. "*Aff.*"

"You looked away when I said you were not a true Viper. Tell me, Avedis, do you miss your Ice Hellions?"

Words caught in his throat as he tried to answer. *I should not be hesitating. I am a Steel Viper. I was shown their superior ways to my own Clan. But yet...*

The pause was long enough for Khan Breen. "There is no shame in such feelings. It can be a difficult thing. We are each taught the superiority of our own Clan from birth. To become bondsman to another and forced to accept what is new as better is not easy."

Avedis could not believe his ears. Reflexively, he moved back.

"But," Breen continued. "To do the things you have done—and so quickly—that is admirable. Very few have. You are almost mythical. Much like this Phelan Wolf we have heard of. To me, this speaks to the superiority of the Clan way. I do not think any of these Inner Sphere warriors, if they were captured by another House, would switch sides not only with ease like you have, but with the fire of the converted. Like you have."

Avedis let the words sink in. Perhaps Khan Breen was right. Perhaps it was not a matter of which Clan was superior. The Clans themselves were superior to all. Perhaps he was on a journey to make himself everything he could be for not just the Clans, but whatever lay ahead. He smiled at the prospect and his Khan's counsel.

Breen poked Avedis' chest, hitting the teeth of the Hellion. "Star Captain Avedis, are we done discussing Clan philosophy?"

"*Aff*, my Khan."

"Good." She grinned, pulling him closer, reaching down deep into the blankets. "We have one more mission to undertake."

NIGHTLORD-CLASS BATTLESHIP *DARK ASP*
JABUKA
STEEL VIPER OCCUPATION ZONE
17 APRIL 3052

Avedis paced nervously in the rally room aboard the *Dark Asp*. Anticipation churned in his gut as he waited with all the other warriors. Each glanced nervously at the massive screen set into the wall. All it displayed was the proud Steel Viper logo, surrounded in orbit by all the individual clusters from each galaxy in the *touman*. Most had been here for hours, waiting, waiting. And then waiting some more.

Elsewhere, Khans Breen and Zalman, along with ilKhan Ulric Kerensky and the rest of the invading Clans, were bidding which units would be utilized for the upcoming invasion of Tukayyid. This would be the proxy battle to decide their fate. Should they win, Terra would be theirs. Should the Clans fall, the invasion would be halted for a time. Avedis pushed those thoughts out of his head. That was an objective that could not happen. He would not let it happen.

The screen flickered, the Viper logo replaced by the face of Khan Breen. Her expression was serious, but Avedis could see a devilish glimmer behind her eyes. He knew she had done something unexpected. Something shrewd. The two had only seen each other a handful of times since Jabuka. It had been a long four and a half months, and Avedis found himself missing his Khan.

"Proud Viper warriors, I and saKhan Zalman salute you!" she said. "You are worthy and fierce warriors. An example to all the Clans as to what it means to truly follow our ways. We have chosen those of you that will participate in our battle for Holy Terra. Alpha, Gamma—" Breen paused as murmurs in the assembled warriors started. "—and Zeta Galaxies will be in the assault force. All warriors must immediately prepare, and all officers Star Captain and above will meet in one week's time to consult on the assault. *Seyla!*" The image faded as quickly as it appeared.

Avedis felt elation and confusion as the other warriors around him erupted in cheers or shouts of frustration. He understood Alpha and Gamma Galaxies being chosen, but Zeta was a confusing option. They were proud warriors, but clearly second line. He realized this is what he saw in Breen's eyes. *She has a reason for this. We will see it soon.*

Avedis dismissed the worrying thoughts from his mind, looking for the members of his Trinary. Now was a time of celebration.

DEVIL'S BATH
TUKAYYID
FREE RASALHAGUE REPUBLIC
6 MAY 3052

Now was a time of worry.

Star Captain Avedis plodded carefully forward in his *Battle Cobra*. The ground beneath his 'Mech's feet was barely ground at all. Thick, viscous mud bubbled and popped around his Trinary as they moved along. Compounding matters were dozens of granite rock formations everywhere. Pillars, mounds, and jagged pieces thrust up from the muck as if trying to escape. The icing on this most unwanted cake was the steam geysers. Some had clear exit points. Others seemed to appear out of nowhere. Regardless, they all erupted with scalding hot, sulfurous steam, which only made the area around them even hotter, the stench seeping into the cockpits and into the neurohelmets.

And among all this hid their enemy, the Com Guard. Their 'Mechs needed to be found, and quickly. But the steam and sweltering, bubbling mud were doing everything in their power to prevent this. The excess heat was playing havoc with the infrared sensors on the Viper 'Mechs, making visual sensors the only viable option to locate the enemy.

Alpha and Gamma Galaxies had entered the Devil's Bath as two separate forces, but it didn't take long for the two units to merge into a confused and scattered mess. The Com Guards were taking full advantage of their knowledge of the territory, the constant sniping and ambushes taking their toll. Not only in damage to the Viper force, but to the tempers of the Clan fighters. To a warrior, they hated the cat-and-mouse game the Com Guards played in the mud and steam.

Their anger turned to simmering rage when several OmniMechs fell prey to the deadly mud, stepping into sections that proved too weak to support their weight. The mighty machines were laid low in minutes, sinking into the bubbling hot sludge. Some of the 'Mechs and MechWarriors were swallowed whole, never to be seen again. Those quick enough to eject faced nearly as brutal a death from the heat and choking fumes. Trueborn warriors, consumed and soon to be dead before even scoring a kill in this, the most critical battle in the history of the Clans.

His Trinary now scouted for Khan Breen's assault Cluster—her own scouts having already been damaged or scattered—to find another route through the morass. Avedis was at the tip of the Viper fang they desperately wanted to sink into the skin of the ComStar forces.

Avedis' blood boiled like the mud they found themselves in.

A jet of steam burst forth ahead and left of his position, right next to a granite pillar in the current stone formation they were navigating around. The burst spooked a hiding Com Guard 'Mech, which lumbered toward new cover. Avedis' tactical computer identified it as a *Warhammer*, an aged but reliable design. The high temps in the Bath made full weapons strikes difficult, but Avedis wasn't about to let this gift go.

"There!" he shouted to the rest of his lead Star as he lined up his targeting reticule. "Do not let this one reach that next rock!" Avedis pressed the firing stud hard as it pulsed green. Hot air bathed his body, forcing another round of sweat to pour out. His natural body odor mixed with the rotten eggs from the Bath, challenging the contents of his stomach to stay down.

Avedis ignored it as both beams from his ER large lasers cut deep lines across the right side of the fleeing 'Mech. Those beams were joined by autocannon rounds and missiles from the other 'Mechs of his Star.

The *Warhammer* staggered under the assault, knocked off its path. To Avedis' surprise, it remained standing, though the right arm, which held a deadly PPC, appeared to be damaged beyond use.

Avedis despised throwing out the rules of *zellbrigen*, but it was immediately apparent that ComStar would have none of it, and both Viper Khans had dismissed the rules far too swiftly for Avedis' taste. It was just another item added to the list of things angering and frustrating the warrior about the battle and the opponent they faced.

The *Warhammer* regained its footing and trudged forward. Or attempted to. Mud rose quickly around the cloven-footed 'Mech's ankles. Avedis knew what was happening. If the pilot didn't do something immediately, the 'Mech would continue to sink, likely fully consumed. The *Warhammer* fought briefly against the pull of the mud, then stopped. Avedis contemplated briefly trying to save the warrior, but his anger overrode that mercy, choosing to let him die the way his Viper brethren had, consumed by this place. But the sinking MechWarrior had other ideas.

The mud around the *Warhammer*'s feet smoked and bubbled. With a loud splorching sound, it ripped free of the earthen shackles and rose on twin columns of heated plasma. *Jump jets.* The 'Mech rode the flame up, over and then behind the massive pillar of rock it sought for cover.

Avedis' comm crackled. "Star Captain, my readout on this 'Mech shows no jump jets."

Avedis grimaced at the fortune that favored his enemy. "Clearly, it is modified. ComStar trickery, yet again. Much like leading us into this hell hole."

He swung his *Battle Cobra* around, moving cautiously to flank the *Warhammer*. Taking a moment to look at the position the Com Guard 'Mech fled from, he studied the dozens of black-and-gray granite obelisks, all shrouded in a noxious haze, like a gothic architecture nightmare run amok.

Something didn't sit right. *That 'Mech was too heavy and slow to be alone.* Avedis knew there had to be more. He studied the stone shaft and the near countless ones now behind them, where Khan Breen and the rest of her unit were slowly pushing through. That's when he realized it.

"Ambush! An ambush is upon us!" Avedis shouted to the general comm.

It was as if the Com Guards also heard his cry. Avedis' taccom lit up as 'Mech after 'Mech appeared from behind cover on both sides. Designations pinged one after another. Many designs recognized, some not. But it didn't matter. They had walked right into a trap.

"Rudella, are you still with us?" Avedis shouted to the swaying *Shadow Cat* that had taken a laser strike across its upper chest and into the head of the 'Mech.

A muted and haggard reply. "*Aff,* Star Captain. I am here. It was a good hit, but these *surats* will not take me down so easily."

"As I expected. This *Lancelot* is using its cover to too good an advantage. You need to flush it out. Jump to that pillar 120 meters east. I shall cut off his escape from the west."

"*Aff,*" was Rudella's only reply as her *Shadow Cat* rocketed off on towers of flame toward the target.

Avedis kicked his *Battle Cobra* into high gear and darted in and around other granite formations, hoping to hide his movement from the *Lancelot.*

The battle after the ambush was fierce and deadly. The initial Com Guard assault hurt, but the Vipers recovered quickly, and were now giving better than they were getting. ComStar tempered the counterattack by continuing to be a wily opponent. Just when the Vipers thought the enemy's line was broken, more Com Guard 'Mechs appeared from hiding to fill the gap and push the Clan warriors back. It was a slow back and forth that grated on Avedis. He felt his Ice Hellion heritage screaming on the inside.

His *Cobra* slowed, rounding the side of a half-sphere shaped piece of granite. Mud and steam lathered the 'Mech as he crouched and crept forward. His taccom registered multiple warhead explosions; weapons fire from Rudella's *Shadow Cat.*

Right on cue, the *Lancelot* backed away, exposing itself to the *Battle Cobra.* Avedis braced for the heat that was about to sting his flesh as he swiveled into position, lined up his shot, and let the Com Guard 'Mech face his full fury.

The quartet of lasers speared out and struck true, searing a massive gash in the 'Mech's right side and traveling straight down its leg. Like the mud it stood in, the armor bubbled off, dripping and plopping to the ground. The beams lanced deeper, severing myomers and the structure beneath.

The now superheated bones of the *Lancelot* became weak and malleable. They gave under the 'Mech's weight, forcing the machine to tilt to the right. The pilot struggled to stay upright, but it wasn't enough. *The Lancelot* tipped and splashed into the mud around it. The viscous and dirty sludge clung to the Com Guard 'Mech. Avedis watched the pilot fight to upright his 'Mech, but it only made things worse. The mud seemed to be alive as it crawled up the sides of the *Lancelot*, slowly consuming it and making it appear like the 'Mech never existed in the first place. Avedis gritted his teeth in satisfaction at the kill.

"Score another one for the Vip—" Rudella's words were cut off by a heavy assault to her rear. Missile explosions and autocannon fire railed against the *Shadow Cat*, hammering it hard.

Like the *Lancelot* before her, Avedis watched as the woman he had beaten to become a Star Captain, the MechWarrior he had insisted be in his Trinary so they could grow as friendly rivals together, struggled to keep her 'Mech upright on the now unstable platform. And just like in their Trial, she failed. The *Shadow Cat* toppled, disappearing from sight.

Avedis' kept his teeth gritted, but the satisfaction was gone. As the *Battle Cobra*'s heat sinks shunted the last of the hot, thick air from his cockpit, he moved to get an angle on the new attackers.

Blood mixed with sweat to form a muted, red rivulet on the side of Avedis' face as he squinted, lining up his reticule on the Com Guard *Flashman* lumbering toward Khan Natalie Breen's *Crossbow*. The instant it pulsed, the extended range large laser burst forth. The beam seared a direct hit on the viewport of the cockpit, boring a hole clean through. The 'Mech jerked briefly but continued its run for a few more steps before lack of signal from a living pilot and momentum toppled the massive machine. It crashed ingloriously in the mud, forty meters from the feet of the battered but still standing 'Mech of the leader of the Steel Vipers.

The past several hours had been brutal. Viper casualties were low, but nearly every 'Mech was damaged to some degree. The death of the *Flashman* signaled the end of the initial Com Guard ambush. Avedis still raged at the game the Com Guards were playing, but his Elemental scouts reported an exploitable breach in the Guard lines deeper in the Bath. He knew the Vipers could easily regroup and punch through.

His *Battle Cobra* stopped just shy of Breen's *Crossbow*. He keyed his comm to the full unit channel. "My Khan, I have good news. My scouts have found a weak point in their line."

A private channel to his 'Mech dinged. It was Kahn Breen. "Yes, my Khan?"

"We will not be proceeding further, Star Captain."

Avedis heard defeat and exhaustion in her voice. "What? Why? I know we have sustained some damage, and lost a few 'Mechs, but I—"

Breen cut him off. "We have lost an entire Trinary, and we have not even pushed a third of the way through. This is not a battle we can win."

Avedis' anger returned with a vengeance. "Not a battle we can win? Who am I talking to? We are the Steel Vipers, and you are our Khan! You have fought to lead us to this point. We have bled to be at the vanguard in our quest to Holy Terra! You are abandoning us now, when we need you the most!" Avedis knew he was pushing the matter, so he softened his tone. "Natalie, do not do this to us."

The venom that flowed through the comm when Khan Breen replied made Avedis realize that he had indeed overstepped. "I am Khan Natalie Breen of the Steel Vipers! I have earned my position through Trial after Trial. I have taken and shed blood to reach the pinnacle of our Clan. I have earned my Bloodname in a Trial that left other warriors dead. I am the commander of this invasion! I decide where we go and when we go and who goes! And I will not take words from a Star Captain that is not even in my own Galaxy, and certainly not from one who is not even a Trueborn warrior from our own Viper *sibkos*!"

Before Avedis could even grasp the sting of the words thrown at him, the comm went dead and Breen's voice crackled out to the entire Viper assault force. "All units, we are pulling back. There is no discussion. This Devil's Bath will become the Viper's Graveyard if we press forward. These Com Guards have chosen their terrain well. We will regroup on the edges of this hellscape and formulate a new plan. Do not fret, my warriors. Soon, our fangs will stab deep into them, and they shall feel the Viper's venom."

Avedis let out a sigh. It was over. There was nothing he could say. Nothing he should. That bridge was burned. It was one thing to question his Khan in the privacy of her bedroom or over a private channel. But another matter entirely over a unit comm.

The anger stayed, now mixed with Breen's insult to his Ice Hellion heritage. Yes, they were in a dangerous area, and yes, the Com Guards had a terrain advantage, but superior Clan fighting and their technological edge should be enough to overcome those advantages.

Doing his best to place that rage in a separate compartment, he dialed his Trinary. "You heard our Khan. Move out."

The fallback was measured and orderly. The Com Guards kept their distance, paying the price when they didn't. Avedis' real challenge was keeping his Trinary under control. All of his warriors vented their anger on the private channel. Some spoke of Trials of Grievance. Others of outright defiance.

Avedis couldn't blame them. He felt the same. This was not the outcome they saw. The Vipers were going to end up like the Smoke Jaguars before them—defeated and beaten. Avedis already felt beaten by the dressing down Breen gave him earlier.

We just need a spark. We can turn this around.

Avedis' comm beeped, but the transmission was a broadband broadcast, not one of his command channels. He flipped it on. It was a voice he did not recognize, but knew immediately it belonged to the Com Guards.

"Attention Steel Vipers. Attention. This is Precentor Beeshor Yekel of the Sixth Division. I see that you are retreating. And so early in your assault. You still haven't pulled up your reserve units yet. We expected more. A lot more from you, for sure. On Terra, there are two kinds of snakes: the kind with fangs, and the kind that slink away to hide. I guess in Clan space, there's only one kind. Slither back to the Periphery, *Tin* Vipers. You'll never see Mother Terra, but don't worry, we *freebirths* will keep it safe from any dirty little snakes. Bye, now! Have a safe cower home!" Then static.

Avedis felt a spark in his gut, which transformed the embers of his anger into a raging inferno.

DEVIL'S BATH
TUKAYYID
FREE RASALHAGUE REPUBLIC
8 MAY 3052

"Are you certain?" Star Captain Avedis radioed back to Star Commander Donatis. The Elemental scouts were a half-kilometer ahead, desperately searching for a gap in the Com Guard line, and like before, they may have found it.

The most brutal fighting Avedis had ever experienced had filled the last two days. After the scathing taunt by Precentor Yekel, all restraint was cast to the wind. Breen's attitude and demeanor spun a complete one-eighty. With a roar, both Galaxies turned and charged back into the Devil's Bath.

Pillar by granite pillar and geyser by geyser, they pushed back against the Com Guards. Ammo supplies were nearing exhaustion and not a 'Mech was undamaged, yet the Vipers fought on. Some even engaged in dishonorable physical combat with mud-stained white 'Mechs of the Com Guards.

"*Aff*, Star Captain. Only a trio of 'Mechs here, medium weight, and no rock formations for hiding. The closest points for an ambush are a half-click to either side."

Avedis nodded. "It could still be a trap. Check those points, but we shall not wait." He keyed the comm to what was left of his Trinary. "My Viper brothers and sisters. Rally to me. We have found our path forward. Let them now feel the Viper's venom!"

Avedis kicked his *Battle Cobra* into a run, charging forward

Donatis' words were true. Only three Com Guard 'Mechs were here, surrounded by a kilometer-wide open plain of craggy, dried, and broken earth. A welcome, mud-free patch.

The granite boulders, pillars, and more were too few and far between to hide any 'Mechs.

The Guards retreated immediately as Avedis and what remained of his Trinary, a mere eight 'Mechs, came into view. The Star Captain looked to his long-range sensors. The combined Alpha and Gamma Galaxies were a little over a kilometer behind his force. *Good.*

The Khan was pleased with the news, but curt in her replies to Avedis. He expected that, the sting of her rebuke still lingering. *This shall erase all doubt from her mind, and mine as well. This Viper victory will cement it.*

A trio of lasers from different Viper 'Mechs, along with a PPC blast from another, bathed the Com Guard *Crab* from top to bottom, tearing away the last of the protection from its chest. Colored explosions and thin jets of superheated plasma shot from the 'Mech's insides, indicating heavy damage to the fusion reactor. It stumbled back and then to the side before collapsing in a heap to the hard ground.

The other two 'Mechs hesitated, returning fire ineffectually. Avedis pressed forward, gambling with his heat management. Lining up all four of his lasers, once again he unleashed an attack, this time on the *Wyvern*. The beams converged directly in the lower center of the 'Mech. The concentrated heat tore through the armor, snapping the structure of its pelvis. The 'Mech wobbled slightly on its now dissected mid-section before the upper half fell backward, while the legs and hips fell forward.

A final *Crab* remained. Avedis licked his lips and prepared to order the killing blow to the remaining eight 'Mechs in his trinary, then felt the earth rumble. He gasped as the ground surrounding his force exploded in a shower of dirt, rocks and smoke.

At first, the Star Captain thought it was an earthquake or numerous geyser eruptions. That faded quickly as the dust cleared and his taccom lit up target after target. Dirty and stained from hiding under the piles of rock and rubble, the white of the Com Guards was unmistakable.

In an instant, they were surrounded. Another trap.

"Khan Breen, this is Star Captain Avedis. Another ambush. This Viper Trinary will not survive. It has been a pleasure and an honor."

Avedis pulled his *Battle Cobra* into the tightening circle with the rest of what remained of his Trinary. Missile, laser, and autocannon fire erupted around them as the trapped Vipers desperately stuck back.

As Avedis' 'Mech started to buckle under the punishing assault, he barely heard the words of Khan Breen over their private channel.

"Star Captain Avedis. Give no quarter. Fight till the bitter end. You honor both your Ice Hellions and our Steel Vipers. *Seyla.*"

WE DO THE IMPOSSIBLE

JOEL STEVERSON

OVERLORD-C-CLASS DROPSHIP *SNARL*
ORBITAL INSERTION, TUKAYYID
FREE RASALHAGUE REPUBLIC
0600 HOURS, 05 MAY 3052

Death was coming for the Com Guard's Ninth and Tenth Armies. Bright white exhaust plumes winked out as more than one hundred DropShips finished their deceleration burns and maneuvered for orbital insertion. Nearly three hundred aerospace fighters screened the Clan Wolf armada like a swarm of angry hornets hunting for prey.

In the lead DropShip, Clan Wolf Khan Natasha Kerensky initiated the startup sequence of her *Dire Wolf*. The 'Mech came to life slowly, like the waking giant it was. First was the pleasant smell of warming electronics, and then a cascade of flashing lights as screens illuminated. Next air rushed in from numerous vents, chilling her cockpit to ten degrees. The tingling, crawling sensation of coolant flowing through her combat suit grabbed Natasha like a dozen cold hands fondling her body. Despite the adventures of her youth, she hated it.

Youth. Natasha chuckled softly.

As a MechWarrior, she'd never expected to live to see fifty, much less eighty. Yet, less than a year from her eightieth birthday, she was about to drop into the largest campaign of her career.

Despite the stakes, Natasha was calm and steady. *Somewhere there's a bullet with my name on it, and one day it will find me. But until then, a girl might as well have some fun.*

Something about an impending battle often led Natasha's thoughts to her *après*-fight celebration. Her options were limited to anyone other than Conal Ward. When the Galaxy Commanders gathered to plan the campaign, he had called her an ancient witch, but only behind her back. He lacked the courage to insult her openly. Even among her band of misfits, most just saw her age. Clan warriors thought life was over at forty. Most would scarcely believe someone her age could have the same needs and desires.

"Primary systems online," her computer purred. *"Initiate sequence for weapon activation."*

"Latrodectism," she said.

"All systems online."

Natasha burned through her final systems check. It was all automatic, muscle memory.

"Comm, Alpha Galaxy," she told her computer. It beeped twice when the channel was open. "Dire Wolves, we drop in twenty. We're the advance party on this mission. Our job is to clear the LZ and establish a perimeter. Winds are zero-nine-zero at one-six. Vis one-point-eight with moderate haze. Area of Operations is a ten-klick radius from sector zero-zero-one. Multiple hills and depressions have been tagged as Areas of Interest, along with twenty plus structures and three wooded zones. If anything seems suspicious, light it up first and then investigate in pairs.

"Ops reports no ground targets within thirty klicks of the LZ. Our threat level is low, just like three months ago on Altenmarkt, but stay frosty and watch your six. ComStar knows all the dirty tricks since the fall of Troy, and they will use them. Anticipate combined arms formations including infantry, aerospace, and artillery. Call out your unknowns and tangos. Engage them if practical, but do not get drawn out of the AO. *Zellbrigen* is suspended. The enemy will concentrate fire, and you had best do the same. Weapons free once you're out the door.

"ComStar thinks treachery will make them our equal, but it just proves they lack skill and courage."

Shortly after she signed off, her private channel pinged. IlKhan Ulric Kerensky looked haggard.

"Hello, sir," she said.

"Good briefing, Khan Kerensky."

"I hate making speeches."

"Regardless, you do them well." Ulric stroked his goatee. "I have an additional mission for you."

"Go ahead."

He outlined his plan.

"That won't be easy," she said.

"I thought difficult was your specialty?"

"It is." She changed subjects. "What's the sitrep?"

"Natasha, I want you focused on the campaign."

She cocked an eyebrow. "Is it that bad?"

Ulric knew that look. If he didn't tell her, she would just find out another way.

After a few moments, he conceded. "The Nova Cats made a good push in the Losiije Lake theater, but they expended much of their ammo approaching Joje. Without resupply, they may not prevail."

"You've sent them ammo, *quiaff*?"

"*Neg.*"

Natasha looked askance, but Ulric ignored her unasked question and pressed on. "The Smoke Jaguars were mauled in the Dinju Mountains. After both of their Khans were reported KIA, I ordered them to retreat."

"How many refused?"

"Only the Sixth Jaguar Dragoons and Jaguar Grenadiers."

"Not surprising." *They are fanatical idiots.*

"They are still fighting, but at best they will only disrupt the Com Guards a few days."

"And the rest?" *It must be bad. I usually don't have to draw it out of him.*

"The Vipers are locked in a static battle at Devil's Bath. It does not look good. The Falcons have somehow combined excessive caution with reckless abandon. Facing light resistance, they spent days crawling across the Prezno Plains.

When they reached the Prezno River, the Com Guards were dug in around two bridges. The Falcons dislodged them and then started crossing without an EOD sweep. The Com Guards had wired both, and the Falcons suffered many casualties when they went up."

"Costly and stupid," Natasha said with an eyeroll. She usually enjoyed a healthy dose of *schadenfreude* when it came to their rivals, but even the headstrong Falcons should have known when something was too easy. "Is anyone winning?"

"The Ghost Bears broke through the First Army's defenses near Luk, but reinforcements are inbound, and the Bears will be hard pressed." Ulric's voice tightened." The Sharks are still bogged down in the Kozice Valley."

Now that he had laid it all out, she understood his earlier reticence. The Tukayyid Campaign had fourteen objective cities. Victory went to the force that controlled seven. Seven Clans had been assigned two each. Surely they would each take a city. One Clan might fail, but it was equally likely that another would take both their objectives and make up the difference. If the unthinkable happened, four Clans could still win. For that matter, nothing technically prevented any Clan from taking more than two cities. The Jaguars had failed, and neither the Cats nor Bears were looking good. The campaign could go either way. It was exactly the kind of thrill Natasha craved, but Ulric preferred less daunting odds. If the Clans lost, it would be beyond devastating—it was unthinkable.

After she had finished absorbing the stakes, Ulric said, "Good hunting, Natasha."

"You'll help me celebrate after we win?" she asked with a Cheshire smile.

"Winning may be difficult."

"Ulric, we are Wolves," Natasha said. "We do the impossible."

Natasha's stomach tripled in weight and slammed into her feet as *Snarl*'s main drive flared to life in a breaking burn. Moments later, her *Dire Wolf* lurched sideways and into space.

The rest of her Command Star dropped simultaneously from their own doors.

The brief acceleration fooled Natasha's inner ear into thinking she'd gone down a short embankment. They called it sliding down the hill. The sensation quickly faded; replaced by a sense of floating, though she was actually a hundred klicks AGL—above ground level—and falling at more than seven klicks per second.

A half-forgotten memory flashed Natasha back to her days with Wolf's Dragoons training MechWarriors on Outreach. Upon hearing the starting altitude and velocity, a cadet had insisted the drop should be over in seconds. She gave him the explanation: descending into denser air increased atmospheric drag and steadily decreased velocity. *That's why a drop takes fifteen minutes instead of fifteen seconds.* Then she nicknamed him Digits as punishment for questioning her.

Reentry heating would incinerate an unprotected 'Mech in seconds. To prevent this, 25th-century engineers had invented an ablative cocoon known as a drop pod. Many MechWarriors called them coffins, because it was pitch black inside and if you didn't get out, you died. Gallows humor and the military were old friends.

Although *Snarl* could drop up to nine 'Mechs per minute, the last Star of 'Mechs wouldn't drop until the first Star was halfway down. 'Mechs exited their coffins roughly ten minutes after drop, but when combat was over in seconds, ten minutes blind and in the dark was an eternity. Also, defending aerospace fighters loved drop pods. They had a fixed trajectory and couldn't maneuver, so they made easy targets. It was one thing to fall in combat, but who could stomach the thought of being gunned down without the opportunity to shoot back?

As Natasha plummeted toward eighty klicks AGL, atmospheric friction ionized the gas around her coffin, creating a plasma cloud that blocked radio signals and sensors. This started the second-most dangerous part of the drop—the peak heating period. In two minutes, the drop pod heated to more than one thousand degrees. Gallows humor said that if the heat shield failed, MechWarriors should count their fingers and toes so they had something to do for the rest of their lives. Those who experienced such a fate never counted past their first hand. *Digits passed out after hearing that joke. That feels like it happened in another lifetime.* The memories faded, and her focus returned to the mission and killing Com Guards. *I hate those sanctimonious zealots. It's about time they got their due.*

Alone in the dark, Natasha fell past fifty klicks AGL. Velocity slowed to five klicks per second. Despite the ablative shield, her cockpit was an oppressive forty-five-degree sauna. Natasha's life support system cycled the air in her cockpit though a cooling unit. The gear heads claimed it dropped the temperature by twenty degrees and created a cooling breeze, but reentry overwhelmed it, just like firing most the *Dire Wolf*'s weapons, and instead all she got was a hot wind. Even with coolant flowing through her suit, she was drenched in sweat.

After nine point five agonizing minutes watching the clock, explosive charges fired and the ablative shroud ripped away. She was out of the coffin! Natasha blinked as light pierced her cockpit; altitude thirty-six klicks AGL; velocity three klicks per second and slowing; five minutes to touchdown; all nominal. She could see the curvature of the horizon. Puffy white clouds dappled above a bright blue sea. Multiple browns and greens sketched the tapestry of Boreal, the northernmost continent. Tukayyid was a pretty world.

Red-orange flashes of light should have been marking the fiery deaths of dogfighting aerospace fighters, but she couldn't see a single blossom. They were impossible to separate from ground clutter, but on level they could be seen for quite a distance. It took a few seconds for sensors and comms to come back online after a 'Mech left its coffin. *Where are the fighters? Did something force* Snarl *to drop us early?*

This was the largest engagement for the Wolves since absorbing the Widowmakers two centuries ago. The Wolf Spiders could fight their way out of any LZ, but on this drop they were the vanguard for the entire invasion. Hundreds of warriors were depending upon them to establish a beachhead. No defending fighters meant they had to be off-target.

Twenty-eight klicks AGL. Velocity dropped below two point eight klicks per second. Three point eight minutes to touchdown.

A chime marked the end of reentry blackout and Natasha's 'Mech started receiving telemetry. Her Command Star was at roughly the same altitude as she was. The rest of *Snarl*'s payload, six Stars of 'Mechs, stretched out in a column overhead. Additional columns of 'Mechs marked the cardinal points around Natasha. Her entire Wolf Spiders Cluster was in freefall and on target. The rest of Alpha Galaxy was in freefall a short distance away. The Lion-Hearted would secure the western side of the LZ. Cyclops Cluster was bound for the north and Golden Horde the south. Multiple Stars of aerospace fighters formed a defensive cordon around them. Everything was right where it should be—except the Com Guards.

Natasha keyed Command and said, "Wolf Actual, this is Black Widow."

"Go ahead, Black Widow."

"Alpha Galaxy is through the burn. Three mikes to touchdown."

"Roger."

"I show zero Com Guard fighters. This is a sensor error, *quiaff*?"

"*Neg*, Black Widow. Aero Boss reports no joy."

"Roger." Natasha signed off with a frown.

Fifteen klicks AGL. Touchdown in two minutes.

Her cockpit had cooled to a comfortable seventeen degrees. Unopposed landings were a common thing among the Clans, where armed and armored DropShips were viewed with the same disdain as civilian transports, but it was unheard of in the Inner Sphere. *The Com Guards must be planning an ambush.* Ulric thought force concentration would keep the Com Guards defensive counter-air at bay, but she had still expected *some* resistance. She shook her head. *He was right, and now I owe him a beer.*

Four klicks AGL. Touchdown in thirty seconds.

Landing was the most dangerous part of an orbital drop. Instead of jump jets, Natasha's *Dire Wolf* was fitted with a disposable jump pack. Every drop a handful of incredibly unlucky MechWarriors survived reentry, ran the gauntlet of defending aerospace fighters, exited their coffin, and then bounced because their jump pack failed or fired at the wrong altitude. It was simple really. Either it worked or she died.

Three.

Two.

One.

Thirty minutes later, Natasha was watching DropShips ground and keeping a wary eye on the perimeter. Sensors showed no targets, but she still expected the ground to spew forth Com Guards like a swarm of Clan Goliath Scorpion's eponymous totem animal emerging to defend their nest.

"Ax One to Black Widow," a familiar voice said over the comm.

"Go ahead, Phelan," she replied.

"We just cleared sector one-zero-two-one, still negative contact. I don't know where the party is, but it's definitely not here."

"Understood."

"Request permission to extend to sector two-zero-two-one."

Phelan was ten klicks out from the LZ. At its current pace, Ax Star would reach Objective Alpha by 1300 hours. The data provided by ComStar labeled it as Forest's End, a small agricultural processing center with dozens of large grain silos, warehouses, and housing for a population of several hundred. It was the best place to make a defensive stand. Civilians had been evacuated off-world prior to the campaign. That left a lot of empty buildings and a defender with no reservations about collateral damage. They would have plenty of cover and long, unobstructed sight lines. Any competent commander would have stationed skirmishers there at a minimum.

Open Prairie had just grounded at the LZ. Looming over the open field like a giant silver egg, the *Overlord*-Class DropShip was popping doors and extending ramps.

"*Neg*, Phelan," she said. "The Red Keshik will be disembarking in ten minutes. We are ahead of schedule, but it will still be at least another hour before we are ready to move. Hold your position."

"Roger, Black Widow. Tell Conal Ward I said hi."

Natasha could hear the snicker in his voice. Phelan knew how much she detested the Red Wolves' Galaxy Commander.

SKUPO
TUKAYYID
FREE RASALHAGUE REPUBLIC
2200 HOURS, 06 MAY 3052

It had been a solid day of fighting, and Phelan's Ax Star had performed admirably. The Wolf Spiders were screening the right flank as the Wolf force approached Forest's End. The Com Guard's 283rd Division had been holed up in a series of camouflaged trenches running perpendicular to the main road a half klick outside town. They had drawn first blood against the Fourth Wolf Guards, but took heavy losses in return. The 166th Division sprang from hiding near the Wolf Spiders, but were diverted north to relieve the 283rd, opening a hole in the Com Guard line the Wolves were happy to exploit.

Precentor Koivu sent the 282nd Division to blunt the Wolf Spiders. Their rapid response prevented the Wolves from enfilading the 166th, and pitted veteran warriors against the elite Wolf Spiders instead of the inexperienced 166th. After several hours of heavy fighting, the Wolves were forced to pull back to rearm and make field repairs while Star Colonel Kederk's Lion-Hearted kept pressure on the 282nd.

Phelan and Mahisha Trinary's other officers, Star Captain Samis and Star Commander Marco Hall had gathered at the feet of Natasha's *Dire Wolf* to chew the fat while downing rations.

"I had one kill today," Hall said, "a *Crab.*"

"Well done," Samis said. "I was victorious over a two opponents, a *Black Knight*, and a *Champion*; a curious name for such a dismal opponent. And you, Galaxy Commander?"

Natasha poured boiling water into a meal pouch, then said, "I bagged a *Thug* and a *Guillotine*, and had an assist on a *Flashman*."

"Bravo zulu," Samis said. "How did you fare, Phelan?"

"I almost had one," Phelan admitted, "but he got away."

"What happened?" Natasha asked.

"We had just cleared the hilltop when the Com Guards opened fire," Phelan said. "Ax Star was up against two *Wyvern*s, a *Kintaro*, a *Champion*, and a pair of *Sentinel*s. It's all gently rolling hills over there, not much cover. We didn't know where the Com Guards were hidden. Our closest contact was just over a klick away, and then suddenly these six are right in front of us. Apparently they hadn't heard that we weren't following *zellbrigen*, because this voice comes over the wideband, 'This is Adept Epsilon Brian Burke in the *Champion*, and I challenge your Star Commander to honorable combat.'

"Ace, Lee, and I lit him up. Ace's ER PPC sent a blue lightning bolt coursing up his left leg and melted most of the armor from its knee to its hip. Lee's LRMs went wide, but he connected with his LB 5-X, and I tagged its center mass with my ER Large Laser.

"He dodged right and put an autocannon slug into Lee's left leg. Must have been a bad armor plate, because that's when Lee reported his *Nova*'s hip was out, and I ordered him to start dropping back."

"A sensible order," Hall said.

"Thanks," Phelan said. "Thea and Dimitria were keeping the *Wyvern*s and *Sentinel*s at bay, so Ace and I hit the *Champion* again. Ace's ER PPC sheared off its right arm, not that it hurt the *Champion* much. I circled around to the left and raked its left torso with my ER Large Laser—"

"I would have closed range," Samis said.

"Of course you would," Phelan said askance. "Your *Gargoyle* more than doubles my mass."

"Do not blame me for your inability to pilot an assault 'Mech."

Unsure whether Samis was joking, Phelan frowned.

Natasha broke the tension. "Go ahead, Phelan."

"When Lee pulled back, both the *Kintaro* and *Champion* charged forward. They fired volley after volley of missiles. Ace had been tagged with a Narc beacon, and most the missiles homed in on him. His *Viper* took a pounding, but nothing punched through. I caught an autocannon burst in the left torso."

"And promptly fell over backward?" Samis asked.

Phelan ignored him and continued, "I couldn't get around to the *Champion*'s back, so I let him have all my lasers. Somehow, he kept it on its feet. Lee took another volley of missiles, which threw off his aim. I could tell we weren't going to win this one with acceptable losses, so I ordered a withdrawal. We traded shots with them for another three minutes before they disengaged. By then, we'd dropped one of the *Sentinel*s and crippled one of the *Wyvern*s. Somehow that *Champion* just kept coming. His engine will probably go critical if the wind blows, but last I saw, he was still up."

"All that and you still cannot finish your opponent?" Samis said, trying for deadpan, but his broad grin betrayed his intentions. "Perhaps you need softer targets?"

Phelan lobbed a ration bar at him in reply.

POZORISTU MOUNTAINS
TUKAYYID
FREE RASALHAGUE REPUBLIC
1234 HOURS, 13 MAY 3052

"How much longer are we going to play wolf and hare?" Phelan asked in a tone somewhere between frustration and boredom.

"As long as we must, *quiaff*?" Natasha replied, deadpan. *It's been a long week of difficult fighting. What the Com Guards lack in experience, they more than make up in enthusiasm and treachery. Somehow, we have to find our way to victory.*

When the skirmish at Forest's End had turned against the Com Guards, Precentor Koivu used massed artillery and close ground support fighters to cover their withdrawal and make a new line five klicks closer to Skupo.

The Wolves smashed into that with the bulk of Alpha and Beta Galaxies. Fighting ran through the night. By dawn, they were closing the noose around Skupo. The Tenth Army was still in fighting shape, though the Wolves had broken the 138th Division and bloodied the 282nd. The Com Guards still had four divisions in good shape, however, and held well-fortified positions around Skupo.

Delta Galaxy had started making headway against the 278th Division by midday on the seventh of May. The 278th was holding a position north of Skupo between it and Brzo. Delta took a pounding, but they broke the Com Guard's line. South of Skupo, the Wolf Spiders tap danced with the 166th.

At 1430 hours, Wolf orbital recon reported that the Ninth Army was mobilizing. It appeared they were abandoning their defense of Brzo and coming to relieve the Tenth.

The Wolves couldn't allow that. Natasha opened a channel to Ulric and sketched out her plan. Alpha Galaxy would assault from the south, rolling up along the Peak to Plains Highway, but leaving it open so the Com Guards would have a way out. She needed someone from up north to drive south and make it look like the Wolves were trying to encircle Skupo. She wanted Mikel Furey, but Gamma Galaxy was too far to the west and too close to the main force. If he advanced, the Com Guards might have suspected a frontal assault on Skupo.

Natasha needed them to think the Wolves were setting up a siege for her plan to work. Although she hated to admit it, she had told Ulric that Conal Ward and Delta Galaxy needed to make the northern attack. Ward had a reputation for following orders poorly. He would need to break contact with what was left of the 278th and leave a token rearguard while the rest of Delta Galaxy advanced south.

When the majority of two Galaxies moved to close the loop around Skupo, the Tenth Army would either dig in and fight street to street—and hope they could hold out long enough for the Ninth to break the siege—or they'd bug out and try to retake Skupo later.

The Wolves had launched the offensive at 1515 hours on the seventh of May. The Wolf Spiders massed as if to charge the 166th, then wheeled and hit the 138th instead. After ten minutes of heavy fighting, the 138th was all but obliterated. The survivors broke and ran using the Peak to Plains Highway.

Delta Galaxy smashed into the Com Guards' flank while the rest of the Wolves applied pressure from the east. The Com Guards held for two hours and then fell back. Conal Ward kept pressure on the retreating Com Guards, preventing them from regrouping and mounting a counterattack. By 1800 hours, the Wolves had captured nearly two hundred Com Guards, along with their first objective city.

That was almost a week ago.

Since then, the Com Guards had been strangely quiet. The Wolves expected they would try and retake Skupo on the eighth of May, but it didn't happen then; or on the ninth or the tenth. By the eleventh, it seemed the Com Guards were content to let the Wolves hold the city.

There had been several small skirmishes, and the Com Guards had made a few attempts on Wolf supply convoys, but they quickly realized that unlike the other Clans, the Wolf supplies were not easy prey. Ulric had dedicated all of Epsilon Galaxy to rear echelon security. He had urged the other Clans to plan for long campaigns and protect their supplies, but they mostly ignored his advice. The Smoke Jaguars had been particularly foolish, leaving only *solahma* to defend their rear echelon. Com Guard raids had taken out most of their supplies during the first two days of fighting.

"My fun meter is pegged," Phelan complained.

"Mine too, Ax One."

"I thought this was going to be a stand-up fight."

"So did the Jaguars, and you see what it got them, *quiaff*?"

Phelan shifted gears. "Does Brzo still appear undefended?"

"It does, but I suspect the Com Guards have multiple artillery batteries hidden in these mountains."

"Someone should do something about that," he said with a chuckle.

"Is that your way of reporting you have cleared sector four-two-oh-seven?"

"*Aff*, Black Widow."

"Roger. You are clear to scout Objective Theta."

POZORISTU MOUNTAINS
TUKAYYID
FREE RASALHAGUE REPUBLIC
1530 HOURS, 16 MAY 3052

The Wolves were advancing through the Pozoristu Mountains toward their final objective, Brzo. Dark clouds choked off the light, making it seem closer to sunset than mid-afternoon. Gale force winds whipped heavy rain into nearly sideways waves, and fouled the accuracy of everything but energy weapons. Fortunately for the Wolves, Ulric had ordered them to outfit predominately with energy weapons for the entire campaign. Lightning strikes came with such frequency that the thunder echoing off the mountainside formed a continuous rumble.

Natasha's Command Star—her *Dire Wolf*, two *Timber Wolves*, a *Mist Lynx*, and an *Ice Ferret*—was slogging through the mud a half-click behind the other Wolf Khan, Garth Radick, and his Command Star.

"This is Ax One. I have forty, four-zero, 'Mechs inbound to Sector four-one-three-four." Phelan's words came in staccato bursts.

Natasha reassured him that reinforcements were on the way and ordered him to attack. He wasn't happy with his orders, but would do his duty.

Her computer chirped, indicating she'd received a data file. Phelan had sent her some grainy images and his IFF scan data. The Com Guard unit appeared to be fresh reserves. In addition to the 'Mechs, there were twenty plus armored vehicles and dozens of motorized infantry platoons. Their insignia was a faceless specter clad in a black cloak with the ComStar sigil as its clasp. Her computer tagged them as the Com Guard's Thirteenth Army.

But ComStar only has twelve *armies...*

Afterward, Natasha would learn that the Com Guards had detached multiple Level IIIs from their command structure to create an ad-hoc Thirteenth Army. It was another in a series of deceitful tricks.

She was still preoccupied by the mystery when an anxious voice came on the radio.

"Beta Actual is down!"

The words were a gut punch. Khan Garth Radick was dead.

Natasha waited for the reticle to pulse gold, and then squeezed her trigger. A low thrumming sound, audible over the cacophony of battle, accompanied the capacitors' discharge as her Gauss rifle sent a nickel-ferrous slug downrange at supersonic speeds. It shattered the elbow joint of a Com Guard *Highlander*, leaving twisted wreckage and exposed wiring.

As the lower arm fell to the ground, its SRM-6 launcher completed its firing sequence, sending the missiles corkscrewing into the mountainside. The explosion sent shrapnel, mud, and rocks into an unfortunate infantry platoon that had been sheltering behind the shattered remnants of a pine tree. One soldier screamed and staggered a few steps into the open. The rest never had a chance to move.

Megajoules of coherent light sublimated armor plate into vapor on the *Highlander*'s left breast. One of Natasha's large pulse lasers pierced the *Highlander*'s LRM-20. Thick black smoke poured from the wound. The missile launcher was out of commission.

The *Highlander* pivoted on its right foot, and then 95 tons of charred metal leaped skyward on powerful jump jets. The flames silenced the screaming soldier. Seconds later, the Com Guard 'Mech reduced a copse of evergreen saplings to splinters as it settled atop the ridge line. Its return Gauss shot slammed into the mud a meter from Natasha's *Dire Wolf*. She slammed her throttle forward and started up the hillside, her Command Star close on her heels. According to Phelan's data, the *Highlander* she was hunting was piloted by Adept Epsilon Robert Beech. He was responsible for the skillfully placed headshot that had taken Khan Radick from the Wolves, and Natasha was going to kill him.

Ruby beams of light connected with her *Dire Wolf*'s torso as the *Highlander* fired its secondary weapons in an effort to slow her advance. Her Gauss rifle was still cycling, so Natasha returned fire with her Streak SRMs. Two flights of six missiles rocketed from above her cockpit and somehow found their target. The *Highlander* was peppered with rewarding explosions, but suffered no real damage. Despite the torrential rain and cold wind, her cockpit pushed thirty-nine degrees. Sweat ran down the back of Natasha's neck, where it met the coolant flowing through the collar of her combat suit and chilled her shoulders.

The *Highlander* dropped behind the hillside as the *Dire Wolf*'s Gauss rifle flashed ready. Natasha raced toward the top of the hill. The ground behind her erupted in geysers of mud and shrapnel as another Com Guard artillery barrage struck. She jinked left as she crested the rise, but her 'Mech still took a Gauss slug in its left arm. Warning klaxons blared and her armor display showed yellow, indicating her left arm's armor was nearly compromised.

The *Highlander* was already five hundred meters away, racing for the safety of friendly lines. A Com Guard *Thug* and *Bombardier* stepped up to provide covering fire. A high-pitched klaxon warned of incoming missiles as a cloud of smoke engulfed the *Bombardier*'s torso.

Forty LRMs arced toward Natasha's *Dire Wolf*. Her anti-missile system filled the sky between them with a lethal hail of munitions. Wind swept more than half of the salvo wide. They smashed into the rocky hillside, detonating against boulders and pine trees and showered her back with debris. Only a half-dozen of the on-target missiles got past her anti-missile system. Natasha's armor diagram blinked yellow, indicating moderate damage to her right leg.

The gangly *Thug* raised its arms and manmade lightning leaped from stubby barrels at its wrists. One struck Natasha's left leg, but failed to pierce its thick armor. The other missed wide right.

Her targeting reticle glowed, and she squeezed her primary trigger. Her Gauss rifle thrummed and triple large pulse lasers all spat their lethal energies. A heartbeat later, the *Highlander*'s torso was engulfed in flames as its LRM ammo exploded. The dying 'Mech's head burst open as its automatic ejection system rocketed the pilot skyward.

Star Commander Pelano and MechWarrior Aaron Carmichael opened up on the *Bombardier*. The Com Guard 'Mech staggered three steps and fell to the ground, down but not out. Both Wolf warriors piloted specially configured *Timber Wolf*-TCs that exchanged their ER large lasers for large pulse lasers. The close confines of mountains around Brzo gave few opportunities for the *Timber Wolf*'s legendary long-range firepower. Most of Natasha's Command Star had opted for pulse lasers over their extended range counterparts.

The *Thug* fired one PPC, then turned and ran. The lightning bolt streaked between Carmichael and Natasha. It briefly flooded comm channels with static, but had no other effect. Sensors showed the remaining Com Guards in the vicinity were in full retreat.

"Comm, ClusterTac," Natasha said. A double beep announced the open channel.

"Black Widow to Wolf Spiders. The Com Guards are in full retreat. Form up on me and forward to Brzo."

OVERLORD-C-CLASS DROPSHIP SNARL
BRZO DROPPORT
TUKAYYID
FREE RASALHAGUE REPUBLIC
2130 HOURS, 21 MAY 3052

The ilKhan looked up from his terminal. Blood stained the length of his right arm, its flow stemmed by a rag tied around his bicep. Numerous, untended gashes stippling his broad torso confirmed rumors that his *Gargoyle* had taken a head shot during the assault on Brzo. The lines on his face hinted that his worst injuries were the kind that didn't leave scars. Twenty-one days on Tukayyid seemed to have aged Ulric Kerensky ten years.

Natasha smiled and held up two beers. He gestured to an adjacent seat.

Clan Wolf had captured Brzo. The Com Guards fought for every meter of ground, reforming and rallying multiple times as the Wolves drove into the mountain valley. No matter what dirty trick or diversion the Com Guards tried, they eventually fell before the Wolf onslaught. The Wolves were whirlwinds of death, averaging a kill ratio of 1.5 to 1 in the final assault.

They had won both objectives, and could take great pride in being the only Clan to achieve this feat.

But the unthinkable had happened. The Clans had lost. It was sobering.

Natasha handed Ulric a bottle and eased into her seat.

"It's done, *quiaff*?" she asked.

"*Aff*, I formally acknowledged ComStar's victory twenty minutes ago. The Precentor Martial has graciously extended an offer of *hegira*."

"That was generous of him."

"Anastasius Focht is an honorable man. It was what I would have done in his place." Ulric opened his beer.

"You passed along Phelan's request?" Natasha asked.

"I did. Focht granted permission for the *Bloodright* to fill Cyrilla Ward's vacancy here on Tukayyid, but he will be unable to attend."

Natasha arched an eyebrow.

"The Primus has recalled him to Terra. He says he is to receive a reward, but he was being unusually evasive. I believe he fears something unsavory awaits him."

"The Inners are corrupt and foolish. They reward failure and punish success," Natasha said with a sneer. She had a passing thought of her long-dead lover, Joshua. *He had seen the inherent treachery of the Inner Sphere long before I did. If only I'd listened. Why do I always find him in my thoughts after a loss?* "This is why we will ultimately prevail."

"Perhaps," Ulric said. He paused, perhaps considering whether to say something more, but then changed subjects. "How did Alpha Galaxy fare?"

"Preliminary casualty reports put KIAs at twenty percent, with at least as many wounded. The Lion-Hearted were particularly hard hit during the final assault. They were involved in building-to-building combat prior to the Com Guards' surrender. Most of the casualties are Elementals, but they lost several promising MechWarriors as well."

"That matches our projections."

"*Aff*, it is unfortunate that we lost Khan Radick."

"Focht was watching the assault on Brzo closely. He said you made short work of the Level II responsible for Radick's death."

"I should have had that *Thug*, too."

"Six kills in just the assault on Brzo, and twelve total for the campaign. I think your reputation is safe."

"Speaking of reputations?"

"To the matter at hand then," Ulric agreed. "Assuming Phelan wins his Bloodname, he will be well-positioned to succeed Radick."

"You have found a sponsor?" Natasha asked, and then took a swig of beer.

"I was thinking you might ask Conal Ward."

She laughed so hard she nearly sucked beer in through her nose. Natasha set down her empty bottle, wiped her mouth and glared at Ulric. "Don't joke about that."

Ulric said nothing.

"You're serious?"

"I know what kind of person he is. I suspect if you put your mind to it, you can find a reason to convince him to support Phelan's nomination."

Natasha did the math. The Clans were split almost evenly into two factions, Wardens and Crusaders. Wardens believed in protecting the Inner Sphere, while Crusaders felt it was theirs to conquer, and cared little for the people they would subjugate. The Crusaders would take the loss at Tukayyid the hardest. Their most likely play would be to try and repudiate the truce and continue the invasion.

As Wardens, Ulric and Natasha both believed that was a mistake. With Garth Radick, the Wolves had been a unified front, and had the political capital to eventually continue the invasion in a humane way. Wardens had been largely responsible for keeping the invasion a limited—and not strategic—war.

Conal Ward, however, was a staunch Crusader. If he succeeded Garth Radick, he would split the Wolf vote. That one vote was not enough to give the Crusaders control in the Council, but the Wolves had allies with Crusader leanings. If the Wolves split their votes, others might follow suit, and that could hand the Council back to the Crusaders.

Ulric nursed his beer while Natasha thought through various scenarios. His logic was inescapable: Conal Ward couldn't succeed Radick.

"I'll have a chat with Conal," Natasha said. "I'm sure he will ultimately see things my way."

Ulric nodded his approval.

"And if Phelan fails to win his Bloodname?"

"Then you will have to speak in favor of the truce."

"You recall I hate making speeches?"

Ulric chuckled. "I do."

"Three weeks ago, when you asked me to try and keep Phelan from getting killed during this campaign, I had no idea you intended to elevate him to Khan so soon."

"I only hoped that he would survive, eventually earn his Bloodname, and someday become an object lesson for the Grand Council. I never thought it might happen so soon."

"That's good, Ulric. Because, I would have told you it was impossible."

"Natasha, we are Wolves," Ulric said with a wink. "We do the impossible."

BROKEN PROMISES

JASON SCHMETZER

OUTSIDE BRZO
TUKAYYID
FREE RASALHAGUE REPUBLIC
14 MAY 3052

"Skupo has fallen," someone said from behind Minka Woloczak in the crowded mess tent. She ignored the comment and the susurrus of whispered gossip it engendered. Instead, she concentrated on finishing her breakfast, meager as it was. The 222nd Division mess section had done the best it could, but there was only so much one could do with rehydrated rations. She pushed the morass of gluey, reconstituted eggs back on her tray and stood.

"So what?" someone called. "Two cities? Even the Clans have to get lucky now and then! We'll stop 'em here!"

"Let's go," she said to the MechWarrior with epsilon-branch tabs on his combat suit sitting next to her. The young man ignored her, continuing to shovel eggs onto a piece of dry toast and chew mechanically. She waited, then tapped him on the shoulder. "Schmitz."

With a final giant bite, the boy stood up. His face was dark with stubble and the same red-tinged, sleep-deprived eyes she saw in the small mirror every time she looked in it. He didn't speak, but preceded her out of the tent into the cool morning air.

The sky looked to Minka like a storm was brewing, all dark clouds and foreboding. She shivered—*from the cold,* she told herself—and led Schmitz back toward the area set aside for her troops.

"Her" troops. Minka shook her head. She'd landed on Tukayyid a couple months ago in command of a Level II in the 50th Division, callsign Kappa; now she commanded all that anyone knew of from the 50th that was still combat capable. People like Minka and her troops, and MechWarriors like Janus Schmitz.

Schmitz was a *Highlander* pilot who had fallen in with Minka's band in the retreat from Dinju and stuck with her. He'd proven himself a skilled, if taciturn, companion.

"Adept Woloczak," a gruff voice greeted her as she came around a corner in the tent camp. She found her senior acolyte, Enrique Miranda, waiting for her, with two infantrymen behind him as an ersatz camp guard.

"Acolyte," she replied, formally.

"Have you heard the skinny, ma'am?" Miranda asked. He nodded to Schmitz and fell into step beside her. The two infantrymen braced briefly, but didn't stop looking past her, laser rifles at the ready. Paranoia had kept them alive across half of Tukayyid. She wasn't about to try and dissuade them from glaring at their fellow Com Guards as if they could become threats.

"You mean about Skupo?"

"You've heard then."

"I heard someone say it," Minka said. "That doesn't mean it's confirmed."

"Yes, ma'am. But I think we can trust it. I caught a Mu brancher cutting through our section of the camp; he confirmed it to me. If anyone in this clusterf—sorry, ma'am, this *camp*—knows what's going on, it's intel, right?"

"You'd think," Minka said. She stopped, which made the other two stop. "If it's true, then it's Spanac all over again."

Across the prior days of the Tukayyid campaign, the Com Guards had fought each of the invading Clans. The Smoke Jaguars, the violent warriors who'd crushed the Fiftieth Division, had landed first, but the Com Guards had beaten them back. They'd repeated that across the planet, with each successive Clan. The Jade Falcons, the Diamond Sharks, the Nova Cats, and the Steel Vipers had all been stopped short of their objective cities.

The Ghost Bears has been stopped short of Luk, but had taken Spanac. Before now, it had been the only defeat the Com Guards had suffered.

Minka snorted, not caring about the interested look Miranda gave her. The organization called the Com Guard may have only suffered one defeat, but many of its individual pieces had been defeated. Her own 50th Division, like so many others, was shattered.

That was a defeat.

Her mind flashed on the order from the army commander she'd received after Dinju. It had come to her as the senior officer unwounded in the division; no one had seen or heard from Ncuthu in hours. *If you are unable to continue to fight, reconsolidate with Fifth Army logistics.*

"If you are unable." Orders did not routinely ask junior officers to make decisions. They delivered the decisions of their superiors. Minka had stared at the message, blinked, then deleted it and led her ad hoc force toward the sound of guns.

As long as her *Exterminator* could fight, she would fight.

Blake's will demanded nothing less.

That determination had led them across the planet, begging suborbital flights on DropShips as they could, to the 222nd Division and Clan Wolf. Along the way they'd met Com Guards that were scared and Com Guards that were haughty; most of the 222nd officers fell into the latter category, especially Adept Keynes.

"If Skupo has fallen, they'll be coming this way next," she said.

"Should we ask for orders?"

"Yes," Minka said, "but not here. Marshal the troops at the laager. I'll get Adept Keynes to assign us somewhere there."

Miranda grinned at her. "Harder to tell us we can't fight when we're standing in front of the guns, right ma'am?" He didn't wait for an answer. He grabbed Schmitz by the shoulder and turned, already bellowing the rally orders.

Minka took the moment of silence.

Skupo had fallen fast. Almost as fast as the Smoke Jaguars had crushed her division.

Clan Wolf wasn't messing around.

OUTSIDE BRZO
TUKAYYID
FREE RASALHAGUE REPUBLIC
18 MAY 3052

"So, we just wait here?" Acolyte Phuc asked.

"Until we get new orders, yes," Enrique Miranda said.

"But this is counter to doctrine," Phuc insisted.

Miranda closed his eyes and counted to four. He didn't say "You didn't know what the word 'doctrine' meant until I taught you a couple months ago." He didn't ask "You know this from your twenty years of artillery duty?"

Instead, he opened his eyes and forced himself to remember how Phuc had taken over assistant fire direction duties after Flores bought it.

"Do you think I don't know that?" he finally asked.

"No, Acolyte. Sorry, Acolyte."

Behind the diminutive Phuc, Rashid ibn Ibrami grinned and shook his head.

The hell of it was, the kid was right.

The scratch pair of Twos from the 50th had been assigned to guard a 222nd Division forward supply depot site a couple days ago. But it was just a patch of land. The damn loggies hadn't shown up until the middle of last night. As if cued, a metal saw screamed to life behind Miranda, where a technician crew was assembling field repair scaffolding for the 'Mechs and tanks sure to come back from the front.

To her credit, Adept Woloczak had, with due respect, screamed bloody murder at the 222nd adept who'd placed them here. In the end, she'd had to bow before the weight of chain of command. Which was how an artillery-heavy mechanized force of two 'Mechs, four Long Tom artillery pieces, six heavy armored personnel carriers, and a quartet of

Demon wheeled tanks had come to "secure" this depot. Four or five squads of foot infantry had joined them over the last couple days, but they were all survivors of decimated platoons.

"This sucks," Phuc finally said.

"The will of Blake is mysterious," Miranda said in his best proctor's voice. Then he smiled. "Now, you want to get back to plotting fire missions, or should I send you off with the Adept's scouts?"

"Yes, Acolyte," Phuc said. He stepped down into the shallow foxhole dug next to Two Gun and picked up the fire direction noteputer.

Miranda stared at him for a moment, wishing he could tell the boy he was right and that he, Miranda, agreed with him, but he couldn't. That would be prejudicial to good discipline, as the book described it. And since the sainted Blake had as yet declined to descend from the heavens and smite the Clans to defend his blessed Com Guards, the book was all they had.

Across the short open space near where the 'Mechs stood, Adept Woloczak spoke to the unlucky infantry detailed as forward observers.

"You understand your mission?" Minka asked.

The six Com Guard infantry troopers all nodded. The senior of them, an acolyte II named Gomez who looked like she might be going to prom in a few years, cleared her throat. "We've been over this, Adept, and we're trained for it." She glanced at her fellows. "We go out. Put in observation posts on all the likely approaches. We man the OPs in case the doggies come this way. Then we call for fire."

"Right." Minka didn't like to think of the Wolves as "doggies," but didn't correct her.

Gomez pushed dust around with the tip of her boot. "You trust the cannon-cockers to do their jobs, ma'am?"

Minka grinned, thankful Enrique Miranda wasn't close enough to hear the question. "I watched that battery take out a Point of Toads in direct-fire mode with flechettes, Acolyte. Some of the darts are still stuck in my *Exterminator*'s armor.

You can go look, but trust me—Blake himself couldn't keep that crew from putting fire down."

The young acolyte shrugged. "Fair enough, Adept."

Minka touched her shoulder. "We need you out there, but make sure you come back, okay?"

Gomez ignored the touch. "Let's go," she told her people, and they all lumbered toward the waiting heavy hover APC detailed to take them out beyond the wire.

Minka watched them go, then began the long climb back up to her *Exterminator*'s cockpit. She paused near the 'Mech's hip, looking over her shoulder at the repair gantry just beginning to take shape, and cursed that it wasn't finished already. A nice aluminum ladder would be a lot easier than the chain one she was struggling with.

She sneezed. Especially with whatever grew around here that bothered her sinuses so much. Minka thought it might be whatever laid the undertone of cinnamon in the air, but she didn't know. It hadn't been back at Dinju, that's for sure.

The infantry would do the best job they could. It was all she could ask of anyone.

And, if she was being honest, securing this repair point was a critical task. She faulted Keynes, the 222nd adept put in authority over them, for a lot, but him wanting to free one of his own units up for front-line duty wasn't one of them. From the reports, a number of the victories over the other Clans earlier in the campaign had come from the Com Guard's ability to seize their supply points. If the Wolves tried to turn the tables, it would be up to her unit to stop them.

So far, the Clans had been all for head-on attacks.

But Skupo had fallen quickly.

The Wolves were not playing by the rules.

Safely inside her cockpit, Minka checked the local security sensor first. Schmitz, buttoned up in his *Highlander*, would have sounded the alarm, but she hadn't survived this long without a healthy dose of paranoia herself. The screen was clear, so she moved to a most recent strategic download.

It was a day old.

"Great," she muttered. For centuries ComStar had used the faith of Blake to shepherd the communications of all humanity, but they couldn't get recent strategic data out into the field across a single planet.

Light caught her eye; the tech teams were continuing to weld the scaffolds together. Beneath them, Miranda and his red legs were continuing to dig their Long Toms in. Minka couldn't quite tell which of the moving forms was the venerable acolyte, but she was sure it was one of the ones *moving*. The past weeks had proven Enrique Miranda didn't have an ounce of quit in him. If they made it off this rock, she'd make sure he got moved to adept as soon as possible. He should be the senior artillery officer of a *division*.

If they made it off this rock.

That was the question, wasn't it?

"Iota Six, Iota Four-two," Miranda heard. "Fire mission."

"Four-two, Six," he replied. "Send grids." He muted his helmet and stood up to put his head above the lip of the fire direction pit. "Fire mission!" he bellowed. Then he pressed the control on his noteputer that brought Adept Woloczak into the conversation. She'd want to know why the guns suddenly started booming.

As he sat down, Acolyte Phuc dropped down into the pit beside him, pulling out the backup FD noteputer and mirroring Miranda's display. As the infantry squad leader read off the coordinates, Miranda confirmed they were accurate and in range; they were.

"One Star, moving slow," the squad leader finished. "Looks like a recon."

"Confirmed," Miranda said. He thought about the map, thought about the time of day, and made up his mind. He looked at Phuc. "Plot a fire mission for Five Gun, alone, for right here. Five rounds, FASCAM."

He waited until Phuc nodded. Then he keyed his helmet. "All guns except Four Gun, fire mission. Five rounds, HE, reload with HE." He waited a minute for Four Gun to reload, then triggered the sequence. The four remaining guns boomed, one round every nine seconds.

"Four-two, Six," he sent to the infantry squad. "Shot, over."

"Shot, out," the infantry replied.

Miranda watched the time-of-flight indicator, waiting. At five seconds he called, "Splash, over."

A few seconds. "Splash, over. Good effects. Up 900 and repeat, over."

Miranda keyed the targeting change. "Shot!" he called as the guns boomed again.

"Head's up, Schmitz," Minka said. "The guns are about to cut loose." She toggled frequencies to the repair depot channel. "Gamma, be aware, the artillery is about to cut loose," she sent, about four seconds before the guns first spoke.

"Thanks for the warning," came the laconic reply from the repair people, after the first stonk was away.

Minka rolled her eyes and toggled back to her unit's frequencies. She heard the squad leader call for more fire, but a blinking light warned her another incoming call.

"Kappa Six," she answered.

"Six, Iota Three-Six," came Gomez's voice, the senior infantry leader. "Be advised, you have a short Star headed your position, three 'Mechs with ticks, over." There was a pause. "I think they're tracking the guns, ma'am."

"Roger," she said, slapping an alert to Miranda, Schmitz and the tanks. "ETA?"

A red light pulsed on her tactical map as the infantry fed her information. The Wolves were just a few minutes away. "Hold your position," she told Gomez. "If we go quiet, report into the 222nd net."

"Blake protects, ma'am," Gomez said, and cut the channel.

"Blake protects," Minka murmured, but she was starting to have her doubts.

The repair depot was snuggled into a low valley with high, forested sides. There was only one likely way in, and the track was clear from the vehicles who'd dropped the field base materials here. Unless the Wolves were blind, that Star would come right in.

She set a nav point on her display and sent it to all her combat units. "They'll be coming through here."

"We're fully engaged at range, Adept," Acolyte Miranda sent. "I can put one gun on local defense, but no more."

"Repositioning," said Hikami, senior acolyte in the Demon crews. The four tanks oriented on the nav point Minka had set. Their Gauss rifles were powerful weapons, but none of them had full loads and one of the tanks' turret was locked forward. They could make gross aiming adjustments only by turning the entire tank.

"Just hold what you've got," she told them. Then she made the call she didn't want to make. "Woloczak for Keynes."

"I'm a bit busy, Adept," came the reply.

"We'll be in contact in two minutes," she said. "Any support?"

"You'll be in contact...what?"

"We have a short Star headed this way. I put out infantry scouts to keep an eye out."

"Are they sure? Division has the Wolves concentrated well away from you."

Minka breathed in, deeply, and out before she responded. "Any support, Adept?"

"Negative..." Keynes' voice trailed off. "But they're not supposed to be there..."

Minka cut the channel. "We're on our own," she told her unit.

"Like usual," Miranda added, right before she cut her mike.

She took a minute. She had to. It was all too much, too fast, after too many days of too much stress. Not even Jerome Blake himself could have kept up with this many moving pieces. The precentor martial might be able to, but he had a staff of people to help him. Minka had herself. Everyone else already had a job.

All she could do now was control her piece of the war.

"Demons," she said. "You're on Toad patrol, got it? Iota said they're coming in with ticks, so that means maybe fifteen Elementals. I need your SRMs to keep them back."

"That's affirm," Hikami said. "We'll do our best."

"Schmitz, that leaves the 'Mechs for you and me."

Schmitz double-clicked his microphone in the affirmative. He'd barely spoken since they'd gathered him up, but he listened, and he was a hell of a MechWarrior. His *Highlander* had moved a little off to the side, where it was partially screened from where she expected the Wolf 'Mechs to appear. It was a good perch; with tanks firing in front of them, Schmitz might get off one or two unanswered flank shots before they engaged him.

"On sensors," Hikami said.

Minka checked her board, checked her maps, and then gripped her controls. The *Exterminator* was a little battered, but it was fully armed and functional. The Wolves would get this little base over her dead body.

Blake's will be done.

The hypersonic *crack* of one of the Demon's Gauss rifles cutting loose was enough to break through the cacophony of the Long Toms' firing.

Enrique Miranda half-stood, hunched over, and looked where the tank had fired. A Clan *Dragonfly* was kicking its left leg like a man whose foot had gone to sleep. The Gauss slug had taken the machine in the knee. Two more Clan OmniMechs pushed past though, weapons firing.

One of the Demons took a PPC to the nose and exploded.

Miranda sat back down and took up his noteputer. "Fire mission!" he barked.

He had his own war to fight.

Losing a Demon in the first exchange of fire hurt, but Minka put it aside. She adjusted her aim and triggered her LRMs, sending ten warheads into the *Dragonfly* the tanks had already pegged. The medium 'Mech staggered and went down, overbalanced by damage, but it was scurrying back its feet almost immediately. The other two 'Mechs kept coming.

The nearer machine, the *Pouncer* that had killed the Demon, stalked forward regardless of the Com Guards' fire. Behind it, the third 'Mech, a 45-ton *Fenris* like the one she had tangled with the first day, hung back. If it was the most common model, it had a PPC that would mean a bad day for anyone it touched. Minka ignored it, concentrating on the *Pouncer.*

A blur slammed the *Pouncer's* right side, where the armpit would be in a human, knocking it a few steps to the left. Schmitz followed up his Gauss shot with a full barrage of twenty long-range missiles. More than half the warheads hit, further staggering the medium 'Mech. The *Pouncer* straightened and turned toward Schmitz, and even Minka could see the smaller machine hesitate when faced with 90 tons of Star League-era assault BattleMech.

"Nice shot, Schmitz," Minka said. She pushed her throttle forward and set an oblique course that would close on the trio of Clan 'Mechs so she could get her lasers into play. *Exterminators* had been built as hunter 'Mechs, but when the prey just walked right into sight...

She grinned, but in the back of her sleep-deprived brain, Minka knew she was forgetting something.

The last round in the current stonk left the tube. An instant later Enrique Miranda was on his feet, glancing around the battery pits and then over toward the 'Mech battle. The board was clear for a moment. He glanced from the 'Mechs to the guns and back, rubbing his chin.

"Phuc—" he started to say, but a roaring sound made him look up.

Clan Wolf Elementals were falling out of the sky on jump jets. They were already inside the perimeter. One landed in a crouch, extended its arm, and cut Jovanger and Torres in half with an underarm minigun. Rounds sparked and whanged off the trunnion, ricocheting into the air. The toad straightened up and marched forward. A pulse from its laser-gauntlet missed Five Gun by a hair and burst a patch of ground into a steaming mess.

"*TOADS!*" Miranda screamed. The loudness of his voice couldn't compare with the bellows of despair he heard in his mind. This had been his nightmare scenario since their first day on Tukayyid. These monsters loose, in close, with *his kids*...

He dropped down, clapping a hand over his helmet speaker. "Toads!" he repeated, making sure he was broadcasting.

Above the lip of the pit, fresh screams came from familiar throats.

"Oh, Blake's black *balls*," Minka swore. She triggered all four of her medium lasers at the *Pouncer*, but her eyes were already scanning her 360-degree vision strip for the artillery pit.

Miranda's warning had come at the worst possible time, just as she was getting stuck in with the Clan 'Mechs. None of the rest of the mobile units were well-equipped to go back and support the artillery crews. Schmitz was too slow, his *Highlander* too big, and the Demons had the wrong guns. A Gauss rifle was overkill for a battle armored infantryman, and their SRMs would do as much damage to the unarmored artillery crews as the Toads would.

Two of her lasers had hit, cutting into the crushed armor from Schmitz' first shot. If the shots did any additional damage it wasn't apparent; the *Pouncer* twisted at the waist and put two PPCs into the *Highlander*'s gut. Schmitz staggered back, armor crushed and smoking.

"Adept, get clear!" Hikami shouted. Minka stamped her feet down on her steering pedals, both at once, triggering the *Exterminator*'s jump jets. The 'Mech lifted up and out of the way, clearing the line of fire for the trio of remaining Demon tanks.

Three Gauss rifles fired as one. The *Pouncer* came apart into at least four pieces as the hypersonic slugs absolutely crushed it.

"Nice shooting," Minka said. She angled her burn so the *Exterminator* flew back toward the artillery park. "Keep it up. Schmitz, hold them here. I'm going to help the red legs!"

Schmitz double-clicked and the Demons rolled forward, turrets swinging. Minka gave them one last glance and then had to watch where she was landing.

Miranda put his hand on Phuc's shoulder where they both crouched in the FD pit. "Son," he said, "when I stand up, I want you to run for the APC—"

"Acolyte—" Phuc started, but stopped when Miranda squeezed.

"I want you to run for the APC," Miranda repeated, "and get the guns up, all right?"

The armored personnel carrier had a pair of machine guns in a small cupola turret above the personnel compartment. Against Toads they'd be little more than the popguns the artillery crews' sidearms would be, but in this case a little more was better than nothing.

Phuc nodded. His eyes were glassy, his face flushed, but he looked determined. Miranda stared at him for a couple seconds more, squeezed his shoulder again, and then let go. His hand dropped to grip the stock of the automatic shotgun he'd picked up along the way. He snugged the butt into his shoulder, closed his eyes long enough to whisper a quick prayer, then drew in a deep breath. He was straightening up before he began to exhale.

Beside him, Phuc burst out of the hole like a rabbit being chased.

Which he was.

As soon as Miranda's eyes cleared the rim of the pit he saw one of the Elementals, off to his right. The mouth of the shotgun came up, swinging right. His finger began taking up slack on the trigger.

The Elemental fired its anti-'Mech laser.

Ozone pricked his nose and eyes. The air smelled burnt.

Phuc's head exploded. His noteputer, still clutched in his hand, few away from spasming fingers.

Miranda saw this out of the corner of his eye as the shotgun bucked, slamming into his shoulder. He rocked with the recoil as the shotgun emptied its eighteen-round drum magazine.

All eighteen shots hit the Elemental.

None of them slowed it down a tick.

By the time the *Exterminator* landed, the Toads had spread throughout the artillery park. She watched one trigger its small laser at the barrel of one of the Long Toms; the shot burned a divot out of the tube, destroying its integrity. If anyone was dumb enough to try and fire it again, it would explode.

Minka tracked the battlesuit with her medium lasers, waited for the gold of target lock, and fired. One of her lasers missed; the other three combined to blast the Elemental to pieces.

One down.

"Miranda," she sent, looking for more targets. Two more Elementals were blasting down into a foxhole, killing both red legs hiding there. She prayed one of them wasn't Enrique Miranda. She angled the *Exterminator* that way, praying the lasers would recharge faster. "Miranda, come in."

One of the Elementals leaned back and triggered its paired short-range missiles. The fat warheads spiraled at her, but her Buzzsaw anti-missile system clawed them out of the air with a ripping-canvas buzz. There was no stopping the small laser beam that poked at her leg armor, but she ignored it.

Her return fire obliterated another Elemental.

"Skipper's down!" one of the tank crews called from behind her, but she ignored it. There was a *chance* Hikami and the crew of his Demon tank would survive the destruction of his vehicle; there was *no* chance the artillery crews would survive against the Toads.

Two of the Elementals lit their jump jets, coming toward her. She let go of her gunnery controls while the spent lasers recharged and grabbed the arm control waldos. She reached out with both arms, heavy fingers open, but one of the Elementals evaded her grasp.

She caught the other by the leg, squeezing. The light armor crumpled, and she flung the Toad down.

The other one clanged against her chest armor.

She jerked the waldo.

The *Exterminator*'s arm came back with a *clang*, slamming against its chest. The Toad popped like a bug.

Enrique Miranda saw death sweep past him as the Elemental's small laser twisted away to face the adept's BattleMech. He let himself breathe out, then set himself to reloading the shotgun. The damn drum wouldn't seat...*there*.

He swept it up again as Woloczak's 'Mech killed two of the toads. He swung away from it, bent down, desperate for something to shoot at. He didn't care that his shots didn't mean anything. His sight picture swept across the pile that used to be Phuc.

He didn't care.

He just had to do *something*.

Another Toad turned away from Five Gun, where it'd been burning at the trunnion with its laser. Miranda sighted and held the trigger down. The effect was the same as before; he didn't care.

Miranda dropped into a crouch, wrestling the empty drum free.

Three more Elementals were in the air, headed toward her, when a PPC took her low in the back of the leg. Minka stumbled forward, clutching at her controls as the gyro howled to keep the *Exterminator* upright. Two of the Toads missed their landing and rocketed over her shoulder; another grabbed a scrabbling handhold on her shoulder. She twisted the *Exterminator* around, looking for whoever had hit her. The motion threw the scrabbling Elemental off.

The *Fenris* was staggering, smoke pouring from its left hip. Schmitz's *Highlander* was missing an arm, but he slammed a flight of missiles into the medium OmniMech's side. A Demon tank, smoke billowing from a near-shattered turret, burped out a half-dozen SRMs at the same target.

It was being dealt with. She turned back to the Elementals.

More SRMs came at her. Her anti-missile system screamed, but ran its ammunition dry. Impacts cratered her armor. She pushed her throttle forward, hoping her speed would give her some protection. Alarms bleeped as the Elemental on her shoulder began to burn at her 'Mech's armor. She ignored it.

Men and women were still dying on the ground.

Luck placed her path near where one of the Elementals was firing at hidden artillery crews. She stutter-stepped, and then brought the *Exterminator*'s foot down, crushing the Toad. Her lasers chimed ready, and she fired again at a clutch of Elementals, killing one and winging two of them. They lit their jump jets and angled away, back toward the hill and the cover of the tree line.

They were breaking off.

Minka turned to look at the Toad on her shoulder, who was turning to flee. She brought her other hand up and grabbed for the armor suit. The huge fingers clenched around the Elemental, and she squeezed with all her might. Metal shrieked and ceramplast shattered in her inexorable grip. She pulled the 'Mech's hand away and opened it, dropping the pulverized remains to the muddy, churned-up ground.

She swung her 'Mech around in time to see Schmitz put a Gauss round through the *Fenris*' chest; the medium 'Mech collapsed. Behind it, a pyre marked where two Demons had spent themselves against the *Dragonfly*.

It was over.

Miranda found ibn Ibrami sitting on the ground near Phuc's corpse, holding the FD noteputer and staring at the boy's body. He approached cautiously; ibn Ibrami was still wearing his loader's exoskeleton. Blows enhanced by that pseudo-musculature would break bones, say, if the boy lashed out at a sound because his mind was still back at the fight.

"Rashid?" he asked softly.

"I thought he was going to make it..." ibn Ibrami said. "We'd been praying nonstop, both of us." He twisted around to look up at his acolyte. Tears had washed tracks down the grime and blood on his cheeks. "Why did the Blessed Blake protect me and not him?"

"Oh, hell, son..." Miranda sat down. "We can't know Blake's mind."

"I didn't ask for anything except that he protect Phuc," ibn Rashid insisted.

"Sometimes..." Miranda started, but he didn't know where to go. The pair sat there in a companionable silence for several long heartbeats.

"These ones didn't fight fair," ibn Ibrami said. His voice was different. Detached. Miranda's heart swelled to hear that detachment; he'd heard it in veterans any number of times in his career. "Clan Wolf. They didn't fight like the others."

"No, they didn't," Miranda said. He looked around, at the bodies being tended to by mates, at the distant trees on the canyon walls. The bastards could be up there right now, watching and laughing. He was too tired to care.

"They promised," ibn Ibrami said. "*Promised*. Hold your faith in Blake, and do your duty, and we'll all get through this."

Miranda recognized the intent of the words, if not the exact words. One of Precentor Ncuthu's speeches, before the Clans started dropping. Just three weeks ago.

A lifetime ago.

"Faith got us this, Acolyte," ibn Ibrami said. "It got Tranh killed." The exoskeleton's claw, faithfully repeating the young man's actions, patted the dirt near him.

"I know, son," was all Enrique Miranda could say.

MOUNT KLINE
TUKAYYID
FREE RASALHAGUE REPUBLIC
20 MAY 3052

Minka never thought she'd be back inside the precentor martial's Tamo Mountain bunker, but here she was. Standing in the same place, this time in a filthy, sweat-grimed combat suit she knew had to smell like six days down a chemical toilet, even if she could no longer smell it. The noteputer folio she tapped against her leg had dried blood on it; Phuc's blood, Minka knew, from when the Toad had decapitated him.

A precentor walked by, nose down in a noteputer. "Sir," Minka said, but the officer just walked past. She glared after him, until movement in the master holotank caught her attention. When last she'd been here, the tank had shown a system view. At the moment, it showed a tabular column of data. Minka squinted, trying to read the row headings...they were division names.

She was looking at a readout of the Com Guard army.

It was mostly red.

Uncaring about the technicians and acolytes in the room, Minka stepped through a door until she could read and confirm what she saw. It was a list of divisions, and their damage after the fighting. She looked down the list... there. The 50th Division, her old division.

It was red with a line through it.

"Well, that's pretty final," she muttered.

"Can I help you, Adept?" a voice asked. Minka turned and found a precentor with epsilon tabs—a MechWarrior—standing just outside the door. He had a bandage glued to the left side of his head. Where his divisional insignia would be, his uniform was torn. He regarded her with a frown, arms crossed.

"Adept Woloczak, sir," she said. "Fiftieth Division."

"There is no Fiftieth Division anymore," the precentor said. "Hasn't been one since day three or so. As I'm sure you just saw. Where have you been hiding yourself?"

"More fights than I can name," Minka said, ignoring the spike of red rage triggered by the word "hiding." She hadn't spent the war in this air-conditioned bunker. She stepped forward and held out the noteputer. "My report, sir."

The precentor made no move to take it. He opened his mouth, but before he could, an alarm beeped. He stiffened and looked behind him.

Minka looked with him, confused. The fighting was over. Were the Clans trying to make one more last-ditch assault?

Commandos—familiar commandos—appeared in the hallway, and a hatch opened in the far wall. A man stepped out, haggard, dirty with sweat. His face was deeply lined with exhaustion. His eyepatch looked loose, as if he'd lost a lot of weight in a short amount of time.

Minka realized, even over the stench of herself, she could *smell* him.

"Attention," a quiet voice whispered.

Minka braced automatically. The precentor martial must have heard the command, because he glanced up, gray eye flashing, then straightened himself. Some of the exhaustion disappeared from his face. "Stand e-easy," he said. His voice half-cracked on the last word. His one eye flicked around the room, onto Minka and then back off. She felt electrified. She felt more so when the steel gray eye flicked back.

"Adept..." the precentor martial prompted.

"Woloczak, sir," Minka barked, just like they'd taught her at Sandhurst. "Fiftieth Division."

"Fiftieth..." Anastasius Focht repeated. "Hard days in the Dinjus."

"Yes, sir." She closed her mouth, hesitated, then blurted it out anyway. "Lots of hard days since, too, sir."

"You've been fighting?"

"Just came off the field with Banished Thought," she said. "Against Clan Wolf."

"Well..." Focht glanced around, but none of the precentors or other officers deigned to claim her. "Come with me, Adept Woloczak. I'd like to hear the perspective on the ground."

"It was hell, sir," she said, not moving. Her mind saw several of the nearby precentors stiffen, but she didn't care. Minka Woloczak had seen too many men and women die under her command to care. "Blake looked away from us, sir."

"We won, Adept," the bandaged precentor growled. "Through his grace."

Minka didn't look away from the precentor martial. "There was nothing graceful about this, Precentor," she said with the certainty of a veteran. "They promised us victory if our faith held." She stopped, lip trembling.

"Well, we got our victory," she ground out. "But that promise was bullshit."

The bandaged precentor started forward, but Focht held up his hand. When the precentor stopped, the precentor martial turned his hand into a beckon. "Come here, Adept," he ordered. "Walk with me, and we'll talk of promises."

Minka went, still clutching the noteputer, past the hard eyes and judgment of the senior most officers of the Com Guard. She'd faced harder things.

BATTLETECH GLOSSARY

Clan military unit designations are used throughout this book:
Point: 1 'Mech or 5 infantry
Star: 5 'Mechs or 25 infantry
Binary: 2 Stars
Trinary: 3 Stars
Cluster: 4—5 Binaries/Trinaries
Galaxy: 3-5 Clusters
Nova: 1 'Mech Star and 1 infantry Star
Supernova: 1 'Mech Binary and 2 infantry Stars

ABTAKHA

An *abtakha* is a captured warrior who is adopted into his new Clan as a warrior.

AUTOCANNON

This is a rapid-fire, auto-loading weapon. Light autocannons range from 30 to 90 millimeter (mm), and heavy autocannons may be from 80 to 120mm or more. They fire high-speed streams of high-explosive, armor-piercing shells.

BATCHALL

The *batchall* is the ritual by which Clan warriors issue combat challenges. Though the type of challenge varies, most begin with the challenger identifying themself, stating the prize of the contest, and requesting that the defender identify the forces at their disposal. The defender also has the right to name the location of the trial. The two sides then bid for what forces will participate in the contest. The subcommander who bids to fight with the number of forces wins the right and responsibility to make the attack. The defender may increase the stakes by demanding a prize of equal or lesser value if they wish.

BATTLEMECH

BattleMechs are the most powerful war machines ever built. First developed by Terran scientists and engineers, these huge vehicles are faster, more mobile, better-armored and more heavily armed than any twentieth-century tank. Ten to twelve meters tall and equipped with particle projection cannons, lasers, rapid-fire autocannon and missiles, they pack enough firepower to flatten anything but another BattleMech. A small fusion reactor provides virtually unlimited power, and BattleMechs can be adapted to fight in environments ranging from sun-baked deserts to subzero arctic icefields.

BLOODNAME

A Bloodname is the surname associated with a Bloodright, descended from one of the 800 warriors who stood with Nicholas Kerensky to form the Clans. A warrior must win the use of a Bloodname in a Trial of Bloodright. Only Bloodnamed warriors may sit on Clan Councils or hold the post of Loremaster, Khan, or ilKhan, and only the genetic material from the Bloodnamed is used in the warrior caste eugenics program.

BONDCORD

A woven bracelet worn by bondsmen who has been captured and claimed by a Clan member. Warrior-caste bondsmen wear a three-strand bondcord on their right wrists, with the color and patterning of the cords signifying the Clan and unit responsible for the warrior's capture. The cords represent integrity, fidelity, and prowess. The bondholder may cut each strand as he or she feels the bondsman demonstrates the associated quality. According to tradition, when the final cord is severed, the bondsman is considered a free member of his or her new

Clan and adopted into the Warrior caste. Each Clan follows this tradition to varying degrees. For example, Clan Wolf accepts nearly all worthy individuals regardless of their past, while Clan Smoke Jaguar generally chose to adopt only trueborn warriors.

BONDSMAN

A bondsman is a prisoner held in a form of indentured servitude until released or accepted into the Clan. Most often, bondsmen are captured warriors who fulfill roles in the laborer or technician castes. Their status is represented by a woven bondcord, and they are obliged by honor and tradition to work for their captors to the best of their abilities.

CASTE

The Clans are divided into five castes: warrior, scientist, merchant, technician, and laborer, in descending order of influence. Each has many subcastes based on specialized skills. The warrior caste is largely the product of the artificial breeding program; those candidates who fail their Trial of Position are assigned to the scientist or technician caste, giving those castes a significant concentration of trueborn members. Most of the civilian castes are made up of the results of scientist-decreed arranged marriages within the castes.

The children of all castes undergo intensive scrutiny during their schooling to determine the caste for which they are best suited, though most end up in the same caste as their parents. This process allows children born to members of civilian castes to enter training to become warriors, though they belong to the less-prestigious ranks of the freeborn.

CIRCLE OF EQUALS

The area in which a trial takes place is known as the Circle of Equals. It ranges in size from a few dozen feet for personal combat to tens of miles for large-scale trials. Though traditionally a circle, the area can be any shape.

CRUSADER

A Crusader is a Clansman who espouses the invasion of the Inner Sphere and the re-establishment of the Star League by military force. Most Crusaders are contemptuous of the people of the Inner Sphere, whom they view as barbarians, and of freeborns within their own Clans.

DEZGRA

Any disgraced individual or unit is known as *dezgra*. Disgrace may come through refusing orders, failing in an assigned task, acting dishonorably, or demonstrating cowardice.

DROPSHIPS

Because interstellar JumpShips must avoid entering the heart of a solar system, they must "dock" in space at a considerable distance from a system's inhabited worlds. DropShips were developed for interplanetary travel. As the name implies, a DropShip is attached to hardpoints on the JumpShip's drive core, later to be dropped from the parent vessel after in-system entry. Though incapable of FTL travel, DropShips are highly maneuverable, well-armed and sufficiently aerodynamic to take off from and land on a planetary surface. The journey from the jump point to the inhabited worlds of a system usually requires a normal-space journey of several days or weeks, depending on the type of star.

FREEBIRTH

Freebirth is a Clan epithet used by trueborn members of the warrior caste to express disgust or frustration. For one trueborn to use this curse to refer to another trueborn is considered a mortal insult.

FREEBORN

An individual conceived and born by natural means is referred to as freeborn. Its emphasis on the artificial breeding program allows Clan society to view such individuals as second-class citizens.

HEGIRA

Hegira is the rite by which a defeated foe may withdraw from the field of battle without further combat and with no further loss of honor.

ISORLA

The spoils of battle, including bondsmen, claimed by the victorious warriors is called *isorla*.

JUMPSHIPS

Interstellar travel is accomplished via JumpShips, first developed in the twenty-second century. These somewhat ungainly vessels consist of a long, thin drive core and a sail resembling an enormous parasol, which can extend up to a kilometer in width. The ship is named for its ability to "jump" instantaneously across vast distances of space. After making its jump, the ship cannot travel until it has recharged by gathering up more solar energy.

The JumpShip's enormous sail is constructed from a special metal that absorbs vast quantities of electromagnetic energy from the nearest star. When it has soaked up enough energy, the sail transfers it to the drive core, which converts it into a space-twisting field. An instant later, the ship arrives at the next jump point, a distance of up to thirty light-years. This field is known as hyperspace, and its discovery opened to mankind the gateway to the stars.

JumpShips never land on planets. Interplanetary travel is carried out by DropShips, vessels that are attached to the JumpShip until arrival at the jump point.

KHAN (kaKhan, saKhan)

Each Clan Council elects two of its number as Khans, who serve as rulers of the Clan and its representatives on the Grand Council. Traditionally, these individuals are the best warriors in the Clan, but in practice many Clans instead elect their most skilled politicians. The senior Khan, sometimes referred to as the kaKhan, acts as the head of the Clan, overseeing relationships between castes and Clans. The junior Khan, known as the saKhan, acts as the Clan's warlord. The senior Khan decides the exact distribution of tasks, and may assign the saKhan additional or different duties.

The term "kaKhan" is considered archaic, and is rarely used.

LASER

An acronym for "Light Amplification through Stimulated Emission of Radiation." When used as a weapon, the laser damages the target by concentrating extreme heat onto a small area. BattleMech lasers are designated as small, medium or large. Lasers are also available as shoulder-fired weapons operating from a portable backpack power unit. Certain range-finders and targeting equipment also employ low-level lasers.

LRM

This is an abbreviation for "Long-Range Missile," an indirect-fire missile with a high-explosive warhead.

POSSESSION, TRIAL OF

A Trial of Possession resolves disputes between two parties over ownership or control. This can include equipment, territory, or even genetic material. The traditional *batchall* forms the core of the trial in order to encourage the participants to resolve the dispute with minimal use of force.

REMEMBRANCE, THE

The Remembrance is an ongoing heroic saga that describes Clan history from the time of the Exodus to the present day. Each Clan maintains its own version, reflecting its opinions and perceptions of events. Inclusion in The Remembrance is one of the highest honors possible for a member of the Clans. All Clan warriors can recite passages from The Remembrance from memory, and written copies of the book are among the few nontechnical books allowed in Clan society. These books are usually lavishly illustrated in a fashion similar to the illuminated manuscripts and Bibles of the medieval period. Warriors frequently paint passages of The Remembrance on the sides of their OmniMechs, fighters, and battle armor.

SEYLA

Seyla is a ritual response in Clan ceremonies. The origin of this phrase is unknown, though it may come from the Biblical notation "selah," thought to be a musical notation or a reference to contemplation.

SRM

This is the abbreviation for "Short-Range Missile," a direct-trajectory missile with high-explosive or armor-piercing explosive warheads. They have a range of less than one kilometer and are only reliably accurate at ranges of less than 300 meters. They are more powerful, however, than LRMs.

SUCCESSOR LORDS

After the fall of the first Star League, the remaining members of the High Council each asserted his or her right to become First Lord. Their star empires became known as the Successor States and the rulers as Successor Lords. The Clan Invasion temporarily interrupted centuries of warfare known as the Succession Wars, which first began in 2786.

SURAT

A Clan epithet, alluding to the rodent of the same name, which disparages an individual's genetic heritage. As such, it is one of the most vulgar and offensive epithets among the Clans.

TOUMAN

The fighting arm of a Clan is known as the touman.

TROTHKIN

Used formally, *trothkin* refers to members of an extended sibko. It is more commonly used to denote members of a gathering, and warriors also frequently use it when addressing someone they consider a peer.

TRUEBORN/TRUEBIRTH

A warrior born of the Clan's artificial breeding program is known as a trueborn. In less formal situations, the Clans use the term truebirth.

WARDEN

A Warden is a Clansman who believes that the Clans were established to guard the Inner Sphere from outside threats rather than to conquer it and re-establish the Star League by force. Most Wardens were opposed to the recent invasion of the Inner Sphere.

ZELLBRIGEN

Zellbrigen is the body of rules governing duels. These rules dictate that such actions are one-on-one engagements, and that any warriors not immediately challenged should stay out of the battle until an opponent is free.

Once a Clan warrior engages a foe, no other warriors on his or her side may target that foe, even if it means allowing the death of the Clan warrior. Interfering in a duel by attacking a foe that is already engaged constitutes a major breach of honor, and usually results in loss of rank. Such action also opens the battle to a melee.

CLAN INVASION TIMELINE
3048–3051

(For more information about these events in the BattleTech *universe,*
see **Era Report: 3052***)*

3048 -

27 September: The *Outbound Light*—belonging to ComStar's Explorer Corps—jumps into the Huntress system. The crew is captured by Clan Smoke Jaguar and interrogated by Khan Leo Showers. He uses this incident to reopen the Great Debate of whether Clans should invade the Inner Sphere.

21 November: All Clans except Wolf vote in favor of Inner Sphere invasion. Clan Wolf demands a Trial of Refusal and loses. In the Trial, both Ghost Bear Khans are killed.

12 December: Leo Showers is elected ilKhan by the Council. He is given command of Operation Revival, the invasion of the Inner Sphere.

3049 -

21 February: The first Clan advance units leave Clan space and head for the coreward Periphery.

12-28 June: Over Strana Mechty, the forces of the four invading Clans—Smoke Jaguar, Ghost Bear, Wolf, and Jade Falcon—gather to start their journey toward the Inner Sphere.

August-September: The first Clan forces appear in the Periphery and make short work of any defending forces.

13 August: Phelan Kell—son of Morgan Kell and member of the Kell Hounds mercenary unit—is captured by Clan Wolf on The Rock. The Kell Hounds are the first Inner Sphere unit to encounter the Clans, and retreat with vital information about the new attacker.

2 November: After a couple of less fortunate attempts resulting in the destruction of two vessels, the Explorer Corps is able to make contact with the invading Clans.

3050 -

January: Precentor Martial Anastasius Focht, sent by Primus Myndo Waterly, is appointed ComStar ambassador to the Clans. The Clans, except for Clan Wolf, who were done by September of the last year, finish their first Periphery actions, and now prepare for a first wave into the Inner Sphere.

15 January: While on board the *Dire Wolf*, Anastasius Focht and Phelan Kell—now bondsman of the Wolves—meet.

18 February: IlKhan Showers convenes a Grand *Kurultai*—a war council of the Clan Khans—on the *Dire Wolf*, orbiting Paulus Prime.

23 February: The *kurultai* on the *Dire Wolf* adjourns. Last changes to the strategy are discussed and the Clans are ready to launch their invasion.

7 March: The Clans launch the first wave of Operation Revival, the invasion of the Inner Sphere.

20 March: The Jade Falcons launch their first invasion wave.

30 March: Clan Smoke Jaguars invade Turtle Bay. They—unknowingly—capture Hohiro Kurita, son of *Gunji-no-Kanrei* Theodore Kurita. He is locked away in the Kurushiiyama prison.

13 April: The Jade Falcons attack Trell I (Trellwan). They almost capture Victor Steiner-Davion, heir to the throne of the Federated Commonwealth, in the process.

Late April: The First Wave ends. Upon learning about the invasion, Jaime Wolf recalls Wolf's Dragoons to Outreach.

May: The Clans begin the Second Wave, kicked off by the Wolves.

7 May: The *Ryugawa-gumi*, a group of yakuza on Turtle Bay, stages a jailbreak from the Kurushiiyama prison. Hohiro Kurita is rescued in the process. The Smoke Jaguars, upon learning of this, decide to withdraw all their troops and stage an example. The WarShip *Sabre Cat* razes the city of Edo. Hundreds of thousands are killed.
All the other Clans condemn this attack as cowardice or—worse—criminally stupid. Clan Wolf declares it will never again bid naval support during the invasion. All the other Clans follow this example in order not to lose honor. Meanwhile, Clan Wolf releases its revised invasion plan to the other Clans.

17 May: Clan Ghost Bear's Beta Galaxy's WarShip is struck by an asteroid in the Damian system, resulting in the destruction of one Cluster.

Late May: The Second Wave ends, although the Jade Falcons continue the wave until late June.

12 June: As a result of the disaster in the Damian system, Clan Ghost Bear votes on the invasion. By a narrow margin, it is decided to continue.

5 June: Clan Wolf Third Wave begins. Clan Wolf JumpShips deposit supply caches in orbit around uninhabited worlds deep in enemy space. All the other Clans by now have to fight with logistic problems, and the long supply lines to the Homeworlds hinder their operations. The Smoke Jaguars and Ghost Bears begin the Third Wave shortly after the Wolves.

23 June: With the final conquest of Twycross, the Jade Falcons end their Second Wave. The Third Wave is by now underway.

4 July: Clan Ghost Bear Khans Jorgensson and Kabrinski—elected on 24 June—arrive on the *Dire Wolf* to begin bidding for Rasalhague. After Clan Wolf has won the right to invade, the attack starts 12 July; the next day Elected Prince Magnusson flees the planet and within five days, the capital of the Free Rasalhague Republic is conquered.

Mid-July: The Clans Wolf and Jade Falcon launch their Fourth Wave.

August: The Smoke Jaguars and Ghost Bears begin their Fourth Wave.

Late August: IlKhan Showers allows the use of Provisional Garrison Clusters (PGCs) on Inner Sphere worlds to free up more frontline units for the invasion.

10 September: Twycross is counterattacked by Federated Commonwealth forces, consisting of the Tenth Lyran Guards RCT, the Ninth F-C RCT, and two Kell Hound regiments. The world is retaken, and the destruction of nearly all the Falcon Guards Cluster creates a political backlash that leads to Timur Malthus retiring from saKhanship.

2 October: Clan Smoke Jaguar is defeated on Wolcott, and as a result swear never to invade the world again.

31 October: A suicide attack by Rasalhagian pilot Tyra Miraborg on the *Dire Wolf* kills ilKhan Showers.

1 November: A Grand *Kurultai* convenes on the *Dire Wolf* and it is decided to return to Clan space and vote for another ilKhan. This starts what is later called the "Year of Peace"—an event that allows the Inner Sphere to close the technological gap on the Clans and prepare for their eventual return. All Bloodnamed warriors are invited to return—including Natasha Kerensky, who returned to Clan Wolf from Wolf's Dragoons.

8

5 November: Adam Steiner—who was on Tharkad training cadets when his homeworld was invaded by Clan Jade Falcon—retakes Somerset.

1 December: The Bloodnamed warriors of the invasion force rendezvous at Paulus Prime to begin their journey back to the Clan homeworlds. Here, Natasha Kerensky rejoins Clan Wolf.

3051 -

January: Clan Jade Falcon begins to stage raids on Somerset, whittling away Adam Steiner's strength.

12 January: Called by Wolf's Dragoons, a council of war is held on Outreach. Jaime Wolf releases massive amounts of information about the Clans to the Inner Sphere. The leaders of the Inner Sphere decide to work together to fight this external foe.

5 February: Theodore Kurita and Hanse Davion conclude a non-aggression pact on Outreach.

19 June: Khan Ulric Kerensky is tried before the Grand Council for his actions during the invasion. He is acquitted and elected ilKhan. Natasha Kerensky replaces him as Khan of Clan Wolf. The ilKhan activates Clan Steel Viper (to help Clan Jade Falcon), Clan Nova Cat (to help the Smoke Jaguars), and Clan Diamond Shark (reserve) to help with the invasion.

15 October: Anastasius Focht returns to the Clans at Engadine upon learning of ilKhan Kerensky's return.

29 October: The Clan invasion resume with the Fifth Wave.

7 November: Clan Wolf resumes its offensive one week after the other Clans.

20 November: Ulric Kerensky asks ComStar for information on Luthien in preparation for attacking it.

3052 -

4 January: The Battle for Luthien begins as the Smoke Jaguars and the Nova Cats attack. Having been tipped off early, *Kanrei* Theodore Kurita has the world well-prepared, and receives assistance from Hanse Davion in the form of the Kell Hounds and Wolf's Dragoons mercenary units. A total of twelve front line and three militia regiments defend the world against five Galaxies. After two days, the Inner Sphere forces throw the Clan invaders off the planet.

5 January: On Satalice, Ragnar Magnusson, the heir apparent to the throne of the FRR, is captured by Clan Wolf.

7 January: Primus Myndo Waterly meets with ilKhan Kerensky on Satalice, and learns that the objective of the Clan invasion is Terra.

BATTLETECH ERAS

The *BattleTech* universe is a living, vibrant entity that grows each year as more sourcebooks and fiction are published. A dynamic universe, its setting and characters evolve over time within a highly detailed continuity framework, bringing everything to life in a way a static game universe cannot match.

To help quickly and easily convey the timeline of the universe—and to allow a player to easily "plug in" a given novel or sourcebook—we've divided *BattleTech* into six major eras.

STAR LEAGUE
(Present–2780)

Ian Cameron, ruler of the Terran Hegemony, concludes decades of tireless effort with the creation of the Star League, a political and military alliance between all Great Houses and the Hegemony. Star League armed forces immediately launch the Reunification War, forcing the Periphery realms to join. For the next two centuries, humanity experiences a golden age across the thousand light-years of human-occupied space known as the Inner Sphere. It also sees the creation of the most powerful military in human history.

(This era also covers the centuries before the founding of the Star League in 2571, most notably the Age of War.)

SUCCESSION WARS
(2781–3049)

Every last member of First Lord Richard Cameron's family is killed during a coup launched by Stefan Amaris. Following the thirteen-year war to unseat him, the rulers of each of the five Great Houses disband the Star League. General Aleksandr Kerensky departs with eighty percent of the Star League Defense Force beyond known space and the Inner Sphere collapses into centuries of warfare known as the Succession Wars that will eventually result in a massive loss of technology across most worlds.

CLAN INVASION
(3050–3061)

A mysterious invading force strikes the coreward region of the Inner Sphere. The invaders, called the Clans, are descendants of Kerensky's SLDF troops, forged into a society dedicated to becoming the greatest fighting force in history. With vastly superior technology and warriors, the Clans conquer world after world. Eventually this outside threat will forge a new Star League, something hundreds of years of warfare failed to accomplish. In addition, the Clans will act as a catalyst for a technological renaissance.

CIVIL WAR
(3062–3067)

The Clan threat is eventually lessened with the complete destruction of a Clan. With that massive external threat apparently neutralized, internal conflicts explode around the Inner Sphere. House Liao conquers its former Commonality, the St. Ives Compact; a rebellion of military units belonging to House Kurita sparks a war with their powerful border enemy, Clan Ghost Bear; the fabulously powerful Federated Commonwealth of House Steiner and House Davion collapses into five long years of bitter civil war.

JIHAD
(3067–3080)

Following the Federated Commonwealth Civil War, the leaders of the Great Houses meet and disband the new Star League, declaring it a sham. The pseudo-religious Word of Blake—a splinter group of ComStar, the protectors and controllers of interstellar communication—launch the Jihad: an interstellar war that pits every faction against each other and even against themselves, as weapons of mass destruction are used for the first time in centuries while new and frightening technologies are also unleashed.

DARK AGE
(3081-3150)

Under the guidance of Devlin Stone, the Republic of the Sphere is born at the heart of the Inner Sphere following the Jihad. One of the more extensive periods of peace begins to break out as the 32nd century dawns. The factions, to one degree or another, embrace disarmament, and the massive armies of the Succession Wars begin to fade. However, in 3132 eighty percent of interstellar communications collapses, throwing the universe into chaos. Wars erupt almost immediately, and the factions begin rebuilding their armies.

ILCLAN
(3151-present)

The once-invulnerable Republic of the Sphere lies in ruins, torn apart by the Great Houses and the Clans as they wage war against each other on a scale not seen in nearly a century. Mercenaries flourish once more, selling their might to the highest bidder. As Fortress Republic collapses, the Clans race toward Terra to claim their long-denied birthright and create a supreme authority that will fulfill the dream of Aleksandr Kerensky and rule the Inner Sphere by any means necessary: The ilClan.

LOOKING FOR MORE HARD HITTING BATTLETECH FICTION?

WE'LL GET YOU RIGHT BACK INTO THE BATTLE!

Catalyst Game Labs brings you the very best in *BattleTech* fiction, available at most ebook retailers, including Amazon, Apple Books, Kobo, Barnes & Noble, and more!

NOVELS

1. *Decision at Thunder Rift* by William H. Keith Jr.
2. *Mercenary's Star* by William H. Keith Jr.
3. *The Price of Glory* by William H. Keith, Jr.
4. *Warrior: En Garde* by Michael A. Stackpole
5. *Warrior: Riposte* by Michael A. Stackpole
6. *Warrior: Coupé* by Michael A. Stackpole
7. Wolves on the Border by Robert N. Charrette
8. *Heir to the Dragon* by Robert N. Charrette
9. *Lethal Heritage* (The Blood of Kerensky, Volume 1) by Michael A. Stackpole
10. *Blood Legacy* (The Blood of Kerensky, Volume 2) by Michael A. Stackpole
11. *Lost Destiny* (The Blood of Kerensky, Volume 3) by Michael A. Stackpole
12. *Way of the Clans* (Legend of the Jade Phoenix, Volume 1) by Robert Thurston
13. *Bloodname* (Legend of the Jade Phoenix, Volume 2) by Robert Thurston
14. *Falcon Guard* (Legend of the Jade Phoenix, Volume 3) by Robert Thurston
15. *Wolf Pack* by Robert N. Charrette
16. *Main Event* by James D. Long
17. *Natural Selection* by Michael A. Stackpole
18. *Assumption of Risk* by Michael A. Stackpole
19. *Blood of Heroes* by Andrew Keith
20. *Close Quarters* by Victor Milán
21. *Far Country* by Peter L. Rice
22. *D.R.T.* by James D. Long
23. *Tactics of Duty* by William H. Keith
24. *Bred for War* by Michael A. Stackpole
25. *I Am Jade Falcon* by Robert Thurston
26. *Highlander Gambit* by Blaine Lee Pardoe
27. *Hearts of Chaos* by Victor Milán
28. *Operation Excalibur* by William H. Keith
29. *Malicious Intent* by Michael A. Stackpole
30. *Black Dragon* by Victor Milán
31. *Impetus of War* by Blaine Lee Pardoe
32. *Double-Blind* by Loren L. Coleman
33. *Binding Force* by Loren L. Coleman
34. *Exodus Road* (Twilight of the Clans, Volume 1) by Blaine Lee Pardoe
35. *Grave Covenant* ((Twilight of the Clans, Volume 2) by Michael A. Stackpole

36. *The Hunters* (Twilight of the Clans, Volume 3) by Thomas S. Gressman
37. *Freebirth* (Twilight of the Clans, Volume 4) by Robert Thurston
38. *Sword and Fire* (Twilight of the Clans, Volume 5) by Thomas S. Gressman
39. *Shadows of War* (Twilight of the Clans, Volume 6) by Thomas S. Gressman
40. *Prince of Havoc* (Twilight of the Clans, Volume 7) by Michael A. Stackpole
41. *Falcon Rising* (Twilight of the Clans, Volume 8) by Robert Thurston
42. *Threads of Ambition* (The Capellan Solution, Book 1) by Loren L. Coleman
43. *The Killing Fields* (The Capellan Solution, Book 2) by Loren L. Coleman
44. *Dagger Point* by Thomas S. Gressman
45. *Ghost of Winter* by Stephen Kenson
46. *Roar of Honor* by Blaine Lee Pardoe
47. *By Blood Betrayed* by Blaine Lee Pardoe and Mel Odom
48. *Illusions of Victory* by Loren L. Coleman
49. *Flashpoint* by Loren L. Coleman
50. *Measure of a Hero* by Blaine Lee Pardoe
51. *Path of Glory* by Randall N. Bills
52. *Test of Vengeance* by Bryan Nystul
53. *Patriots and Tyrants* by Loren L. Coleman
54. *Call of Duty* by Blaine Lee Pardoe
55. *Initiation to War* by Robert N. Charrette
56. *The Dying Time* by Thomas S. Gressman
57. *Storms of Fate* by Loren L. Coleman
58. *Imminent Crisis* by Randall N. Bills
59. *Operation Audacity* by Blaine Lee Pardoe
60. *Endgame* by Loren L. Coleman
61. *A Bonfire of Worlds* by Steven Mohan, Jr.
62. *Isle of the Blessed* by Steven Mohan, Jr.
63. *Embers of War* by Jason Schmetzer
64. *Betrayal of Ideals* by Blaine Lee Pardoe
65. *Forever Faithful* by Blaine Lee Pardoe
66. *Kell Hounds Ascendant* by Michael A. Stackpole
67. *Redemption Rift* by Jason Schmetzer
68. *Grey Watch Protocol* (Book One of the Highlander Covenant) by Michael J. Ciaravella
69. *Honor's Gauntlet* by Bryan Young
70. *Icons of War* by Craig A. Reed, Jr.
71. *Children of Kerensky* by Blaine Lee Pardoe
72. *Hour of the Wolf* by Blaine Lee Pardoe

YOUNG ADULT NOVELS
1. *The Nellus Academy Incident* by Jennifer Brozek
2. *Iron Dawn* (Rogue Academy, Book 1) by Jennifer Brozek
3. *Ghost Hour* (Rogue Academy, Book 2) by Jennifer Brozek

OMNIBUSES
1. *The Gray Death Legion Trilogy* by William H. Keith, Jr.

NOVELLAS/SHORT STORIES

1. *Lion's Roar* by Steven Mohan, Jr.
2. *Sniper* by Jason Schmetzer
3. *Eclipse* by Jason Schmetzer
4. *Hector* by Jason Schmetzer
5. *The Frost Advances (Operation Ice Storm, Part 1)* by Jason Schmetzer
6. *The Winds of Spring (Operation Ice Storm, Part 2)* by Jason Schmetzer
7. *Instrument of Destruction (Ghost Bear's Lament, Part 1)* by Steven Mohan, Jr.
8. *The Fading Call of Glory (Ghost Bear's Lament, Part 2)* by Steven Mohan, Jr.
9. *Vengeance* by Jason Schmetzer
10. *A Splinter of Hope* by Philip A. Lee
11. *The Anvil* by Blaine Lee Pardoe
12. *A Splinter of Hope/The Anvil* (omnibus)
13. *Not the Way the Smart Money Bets (Kell Hounds Ascendant #1)* by Michael A. Stackpole
14. *A Tiny Spot of Rebellion (Kell Hounds Ascendant #2)* by Michael A. Stackpole
15. *A Clever Bit of Fiction (Kell Hounds Ascendant #3)* by Michael A. Stackpole
16. *Break-Away (Proliferation Cycle #1)* by Ilsa J. Bick
17. *Prometheus Unbound (Proliferation Cycle #2)* by Herbert A. Beas II
18. *Nothing Ventured (Proliferation Cycle #3)* by Christoffer Trossen
19. *Fall Down Seven Times, Get Up Eight (Proliferation Cycle #4)* by Randall N. Bills
20. *A Dish Served Cold (Proliferation Cycle #5)* by Chris Hartford and Jason M. Hardy
21. *The Spider Dances (Proliferation Cycle #6)* by Jason Schmetzer
22. *Shell Games* by Jason Schmetzer
23. *Divided We Fall* by Blaine Lee Pardoe
24. *The Hunt for Jardine (Forgotten Worlds, Part One)* by Herbert A. Beas II
25. *Rock of the Republic* by Blaine Lee Pardoe
26. *Finding Jardine (Forgotten Worlds, Part Two)* by Herbert A. Beas II

ANTHOLOGIES

1. *The Corps (BattleCorps Anthology, Volume 1)* edited by Loren. L. Coleman
2. *First Strike (BattleCorps Anthology, Volume 2)* edited by Loren L. Coleman
3. *Weapons Free (BattleCorps Anthology, Volume 3)* edited by Jason Schmetzer
4. *Onslaught: Tales from the Clan Invasion* edited by Jason Schmetzer
5. *Edge of the Storm* by Jason Schmetzer
6. *Fire for Effect (BattleCorps Anthology, Volume 4)* edited by Jason Schmetzer
7. *Chaos Born (Chaos Irregulars, Book 1)* by Kevin Killiany
8. *Chaos Formed (Chaos Irregulars, Book 2)* by Kevin Killiany
9. *Counterattack (BattleCorps Anthology, Volume 5)* edited by Jason Schmetzer
10. *Front Lines (BattleCorps Anthology Volume 6)* edited by Jason Schmetzer and Philip A. Lee
11. *Legacy* edited by John Helfers and Philip A. Lee
12. *Kill Zone (BattleCorps Anthology Volume 7)* edited by Philip A. Lee
13. *Gray Markets (A BattleCorps Anthology)*, edited by Jason Schmetzer and Philip A. Lee
14. *Slack Tide (A BattleCorps Anthology)*, edited by Jason Schmetzer and Philip A. Lee

MAGAZINES

1. *Shrapnel Issue #1*
2. *Shrapnel Issue #2*
3. *Shrapnel Issue #3*

The march of technology across BattleTech's eras is relentless...

Some BattleMech designs never die. Each installment of *Recognition Guide: IIClan*, currently a PDF-only series, not only includes a brand new BattleMech or OmniMech, but also details Classic 'Mech designs from both the Inner Sphere and the Clans, now fully rebuilt with Dark Age technology (3085 and beyond).

RECOGNITION GUIDE: ILCLAN VOL. 01

RECOGNITION GUIDE: ILCLAN VOL. 02

RECOGNITION GUIDE: ILCLAN VOL. 03

RECOGNITION GUIDE: ILCLAN VOL. 04

RECOGNITION GUIDE: ILCLAN VOL. 05

RECOGNITION GUIDE: ILCLAN VOL. 06

BATTLETECH TLETECH TLETECH TLETECH TLETECH

STORE.CATALYSTGAMELABS.COM

Printed in Great Britain
by Amazon

19381449R00120